A Perilous Bargain

A Perilous Bargain

Jane Peart

Fleming H. Revell
A Division of Baker Book House Co
Grand Rapids, Michigan 49516

Published by Fleming H. Revell
a division of Baker Book House Company
P.O. Box 6287, Grand Rapids, MI 49516-6287

Second printing, October 1998

Printed in the United States of America

Library of Congress Cataloging-in-Publication Data

Peart, Jane.
    A perilous bargain / Jane Peart.
      p. cm.
    ISBN 0-8007-5626-6 (paper)
    I. Title.
    PS3566.E238P47   1997
    813'.54—dc21   96-29629

For current information about all releases from Baker Book House, visit our web site:
                  http://www.bakerbooks.com

The Ocean Liner Mesalina, en route from New York to England

March 1895

Oriel had been standing alone at the ship's rail, deep in her own troubling thoughts, when through gauzy shreds of fog, the tall figure of a man emerged.

As he took a place beside her, the man nodded. "Looks like we might be in for a rough crossing. Temperamental, the Atlantic, this time of year."

His comment needed no response. The ocean, smooth as glass upon leaving New York harbor three days before, now churned in choppy waves. Strong wind rocked the large ship as if it were a small fishing boat, sending most of the passengers below to seek refuge in one of the many lounges or to huddle miserably in their stateroom bunks.

"We seem to be the only ones braving the storm."

Oriel glanced over her shoulder to confirm he was speaking to her. Indeed, they were the only two on deck.

"Perhaps I should introduce myself. I'm Morgan Drummond."

The introduction was unnecessary. Oriel had recognized him at once. He was the grandson of Brendan Drummond, millionaire industrialist and well-known philanthropist. Morgan Drummond had been the subject of shipboard gossip from the first day out, the target of romantic speculation among many hopeful women on board—that is, until they learned he was engaged to an English debutante, Edwina Parker.

Oriel took a discreet glance at the man standing beside her. He *was* impressively handsome—over six feet tall, wearing a tweed Norfolk jacket. His profile, outlined against the fog, was classically sculptured with a high-bridged nose and a strong chin.

"And you are . . . ?" he asked.

"Oriel Banning." She gave her name reluctantly.

"Not many of our fellow passengers seem to have sea legs. You must be a good sailor."

"I'm fortunate to come from a long line of New England seafarers." At once she regretted her reply. It seemed to invite further comment. She did not want to enter into an idle conversation with a stranger. She had too much on her mind. She moved slightly down the rail, distancing herself from him. Besides, what could they possibly have in common? Their paths would never have crossed if she had not been traveling with her wealthy employers. She would not have been among his affluent fellow passengers in the first-class section of this luxury liner.

Although her passport listed her occupation as social secretary and companion, it would be easy for Morgan Drummond to assume Oriel belonged on the A deck. Her appearance warranted that. But appearances can be deceiving. She had often been told she resembled the popular British royal, Princess Alexandra of Denmark, whose hairstyle and dress were widely copied in both Britain and the States. Tall, slender, with a graceful carriage and confident manner, Oriel had an understated elegance that seemed aristocratic. However, her situation and that of the princess could not have been more different. While the popular princess, married to Edward, Prince of Wales, heir to the British throne, lived a luxurious life, Oriel's had been a precarious existence.

Oriel gazed down into the pewter-colored sea, picking up the thread of her thoughts. Being hired by the McPhails was one of the many strange coincidences that had marked her life. After her father's financial ruin and death, Oriel had obtained a position at the fashionable boarding school she had once attended. When Berenice McPhail enrolled, Oriel had been assigned the thankless task of tutoring her to bring up her grades to passing. Neecy was an indolent student at best. Her mother, Mrs. Clarence McPhail, widow of a manufacturing tycoon, approached Oriel to take on an unusual job—to groom Berenice for her debut into society. The salary Mrs. McPhail offered far exceeded Oriel's pay as a teacher, so she had accepted.

Oriel felt she had earned every cent of the salary that had at first seemed so generous—was *still* earning it. The flighty, pampered girl was a handful. Looking after her had proved a round-the-clock chore.

Now, two years later, they were on their way to England, where Berenice was to be married to an English aristocrat, Valmont Thorndyke. Berenice was what the yellow journals of the day vulgarly called a "dollar princess," meaning an American girl from a rich family who made a mutually beneficial European marriage. The Americans gained titles, the British, fortunes to save ancestral estates.

The relief Oriel might have felt once the wedding took place was overshadowed by a problem—Oriel's job would be finished. What next? That need had prompted her to escape from the confines of her adjoining cabin to Neecy's. After a late night, her charge had chosen to spend the day in bed, eating chocolates and reading a romantic novel. Mrs. McPhail, feeling unwell, was also closeted in her stateroom. Oriel had jumped at the rare opportunity of being by herself.

It wasn't the first time Oriel had faced an unknown future. After her mother's death, when Oriel was only a child of eleven, she had become her indulgent father's companion. They had traveled the world, stayed in the finest hotels, visited the best European resorts. Then, when she was seventeen, a series of bad investments coupled with a national financial panic had swept away her father's fortune. Shortly afterward, her father had suffered a fatal heart attack. In a matter of weeks, Oriel's life had changed drastically. She had faced the unexpected challenge of making her own living with only her courage, energy, and intelligence to help her make her way in the world.

Her privileged background had been her only asset, and she used it. Thanks to her father, she had received an excellent education, a cultured background. These qualifications served her well but did not pay adequately. Penny-pinching had become a way of life.

The hardships Oriel had endured, however, had developed qualities she had not dreamed she would ever need. She had tasted poverty and it was bitter. The job with the McPhails had shown her the kind of life she herself might have enjoyed if things had been different.

She had made her own living for the last six years, and she would continue to do so. She needed to think, to plan. When they returned to the States, should she apply again at Miss Porter's Academy or seek some other kind of employment? At the moment, her future seemed as dense as the fog that surrounded the ship.

The muffled blast of the foghorn cut through the damp, clinging air, jolting her. There was an eerie loneliness in the sound. Darting a quick look around, she saw that the man who had stood beside her was gone—gone just as he had come, in a drift of fog.

Contrary to Oriel's assumption that meeting Morgan Drummond had been a single, random encounter, she had several other such chance meetings as their ship moved toward England. The weather continued to be bad. Oriel soon discovered that Morgan Drummond was among the few hardy passengers like herself who took an early morning stroll on the deck regardless of the weather. Neecy and Mrs. McPhail preferred to stay snug in their cabins and have their breakfast brought in by the stewards. A brisk walk in the misty morning air eased Oriel's anxiety and enabled her to better face the day. Whenever they passed each other, Mr. Drummond always nodded, saying, "Good morning, Miss Banning." Sometimes he even slowed his long stride to murmur some remark on the weather or make a casual comment.

One evening at the dinner table, Mrs. McPhail complained of an annoying draft on her shoulders and sent Oriel back to her stateroom to fetch her shawl. In the passageway, Oriel ran straight into Morgan Drummond, looking splendid in his evening clothes, on his way to a predinner party in the captain's quarters.

Oriel was wearing one of Neecy's castoffs that she had altered and remodeled, a claret-colored taffeta, more becoming to her olive complexion and mahogany brown hair than it had been to Neecy's bland coloring.

"How charming you look this evening, Miss Banning." Morgan bowed, adding with an amused smile, "I don't believe I've ever seen you except wrapped in scarves or muffled in a mackintosh."

Oriel felt foolishly pleased by his compliment. She had followed in Neecy's social shadow so long she realized she wasn't used to attention, especially from an attractive man.

The next time Oriel encountered Morgan it was an excruciatingly embarrassing moment. Constant friction existed between Mrs. McPhail and her daughter, with frequent eruptions over Neecy's behavior. Even though engaged, Berenice flirted openly with every male on board. Oriel often found herself acting as a buffer or, more often, as a silent bystander during fierce arguments. This particular one took place one evening at the entrance to the dining room. Forgetful that other passengers were within hearing, both voices were raised. Oriel was trying to think of some tactful way to intervene without infuriating the combatants further, when Morgan Drummond suddenly appeared. Oblivious of being observed, the McPhails continued their dispute. For a single second, Morgan's gaze met Oriel's. In that look was shared mutual disgust.

Realizing that her own thoughts were being read, Oriel lowered her eyes. It would never do to show, even by so much as a flicker of an eyelash, the contempt she felt for her employers' display of bad manners. Without a word, Morgan passed by, pretending not to have seen or heard anything.

Five days later, docking in Southampton, Oriel was sent up on deck to stand guard over the McPhails' mountains of luggage while they bid leisurely good-byes to shipboard acquaintances.

Oriel was glad to see the ocean voyage over. It had been, as Morgan Drummond predicted, a rough passage, but it was not just the stormy weather that had made the journey unpleasant. The relative confinement of the accommodations had subjected Oriel to the peevish demands of the mother and the irresponsible selfishness of the daughter. Her relief at the journey's end was short-lived, however, since there was still the wedding to get through. She would be expected to deal with its myriad details.

Trying to distract herself, Oriel glanced around at her fellow passengers. Eager now to start their travels on foreign soil, they crowded to the rails to wave at their welcomers. She saw Morgan Drummond come up on deck.

He nodded and walked over to her. "Good morning, Miss Banning. Ready to put your feet on solid ground?"

"Yes, it will be a nice change, although I've not minded the weather all that much."

"So you said. From a long line of seafarers, right?" He smiled. "Well, I wish you a pleasant stay in England." Then, as an apparent afterthought, he asked, "Where are you staying?"

"We have reservations at the Claridge Hotel."

"So do I. Perhaps our paths will cross again." With that, he tipped his hat and moved away to join others at the ship's rail.

Oriel watched him lean forward over the rail, as though searching into the sea of people waiting to meet passengers. Then she saw him wave.

At last, the giant ship was docked and the gangplank let down. Passengers began to throng ashore. Curious to see who Morgan Drummond had been so eager to find, Oriel moved over to the rail and followed his tall figure until she saw him greeted by an exquisite blonde. Her royal blue cape, lavishly furred in silver fox, flowed out behind her as she embraced him. She must be his fiancée, Edwina Parker.

Next Morgan turned to greet a well-dressed couple, who evidently had accompanied her. The older woman, a stout fading blonde, might be a forecast of Edwina twenty years hence. Did men notice such things? Oriel wondered ruefully.

The McPhails arrived just then, flurried and fussing. Oriel was caught up in the ensuing confusion of getting a porter to trundle their baggage down the gangplank and securing a coach to take them to the train station for their trip to London. By then, Morgan Drummond and his party had long since departed.

London, England

Two Weeks Later

he newlyweds had hardly left for their honeymoon when the mother of the bride disappeared into her hotel room. Oriel was left to settle all the bills, to pay the caterers, wine merchants, musicians, and others who had provided their services for the reception. It was her task to tie up all the loose ends after Neecy's windswept departure.

Soon after this was accomplished, Oriel was summoned to Mrs. McPhail's suite. Eunice McPhail, in a peach satin jacket, was still in bed, propped up on pillows, her breakfast tray on her lap. The morning papers were scattered over the quilted coverlet.

She listened with pursed lips and narrowed eyes to Oriel's accounting of the financial responsibilities she had completed. Then, flourishing one diamond-ringed hand, she said, "Well, that's the end of your duties, Miss Banning. Now that Neecy's settled, we will, of course, no longer need your services. You will need to find other lodgings."

At first, Oriel wasn't sure she'd heard correctly. Puzzled, she asked, "You mean until we return to the States?"

Mrs. McPhail's eyebrows arched, as if she was astonished at the question. "*We?* I thought you understood. I am not going back home right away—not until Neecy returns from her honeymoon. Naturally *you* are free to make any arrangements you choose."

For a moment Oriel was speechless. Slowly, the meaning of Mrs. McPhail's announcement began to sink in. Still she needed to clarify the statement. "Then my passage back to the States will not be paid?"

Mrs. McPhail looked outraged at such a suggestion. "Certainly not! We made no such guarantee. With Neecy's marriage, your employment ended."

Stunned, but too proud to plead or protest, Oriel managed to say, "I will need a letter of reference, Mrs. McPhail."

Mrs. McPhail seemed startled, maybe at the calm way Oriel seemed to be taking her announcement. Perhaps she had expected some kind of outburst. Shrugging her plump shoulders, Mrs. McPhail said impatiently, "Yes, of course. I'll leave it with your check for this month's wages. You can pick them up at the desk."

Not trusting herself to say more, Oriel turned to leave.

Mrs. McPhail's shrill voice followed. "It's not that you were unsatisfactory, Miss Banning. I'm sure Neecy benefited a great deal from her association with you. You're a clever girl—I'm sure you'll have no problem finding a new position."

Oriel felt her face flush. Her hand already on the doorknob, she did not turn around. Quick, hot anger rushed through her, but she refused to give Mrs. McPhail's throwaway compliment the dignity of a reply. She stepped into the hallway and closed the door behind her.

Mrs. McPhail's lame comment rang in her ears. Oriel recalled having to drum even the simplest formalities into Neecy's empty head. What she *could* have retorted to Mrs.

McPhail was, "Indeed your daughter *did* benefit from my training. I taught her how to conduct herself in society. Until I'd coached her, she didn't even know how to enter a room properly or which spoon or fork to use at a formal dinner! If it weren't for *me*, your daughter would not at this moment be honeymooning on the Riviera with the son of one of England's most prominent families!"

There was plenty Oriel could have said, but she knew it would have been useless. Mrs. McPhail was worse than her daughter, unaware of her shortcomings. She blundered her way with only her money making her acceptable. Any rational self-justification would have only been self-defeating. It would have fallen on deaf ears; more likely, it would have brought down Mrs. McPhail's wrath, possibly even vindictive retribution. Oriel needed her reference letter if she was to explain the two years spent with the McPhails to any prospective employer.

Outside Mrs. McPhail's hotel room, Oriel's knees nearly buckled. She steadied herself against the door frame. A waiter wheeling a cart rattling with a load of dishes gave her a curious glance as he went past. Oriel drew a long shaky breath, straightened her shoulders, and walked stiffly down the corridor to her own room.

Once there, she closed the door behind her. Feeling weak and dizzy, she sat down on the edge of the bed. She had, of course, expected it—but not this soon. Not like this.

I should have known better, she thought, *should have found out about my return ticket before leaving New York.* It had simply not occurred to her that she would receive such shabby treatment. *Dismissed!* She'd had no notice, and worse, no severance pay.

Gradually Oriel's righteous indignation subsided and her practical nature emerged. She had not been on her own since she was seventeen for nothing. It was useless to expect anything from Mrs. McPhail. The woman was not only without conscience but without gentility. Oriel should not have been surprised at her shoddy behavior.

Oriel's first thought was What shall I do? The second one came as naturally as breathing. Pray. At an early age, she had been taught to seek God's help in an emergency. This situation certainly qualified as that.

Next she drew a long breath. She knew she needed to take one thing at a time. Obviously she could no longer stay in this luxury hotel, where the daily rate would probably pay for a week's rent in more modest accommodations. How was she to go about finding one? She did not know London. Her time, so far, had been limited to the details of Neecy's wedding, dealing with tradesmen, shopkeepers, and the hotel staff.

She would not panic. She would be sensible, practical, use her brains. Her gaze fell on the morning paper, which had been delivered with her breakfast tray. It was still folded. She had not had time to read it before being called into Mrs. McPhail's suite. Turning to the ad section, she checked several smaller hotels. The rates still seemed too high for the small amount of money she had. Perhaps a rooming house would be better. She would probably only need a place for a few days. As soon as she received the check for her salary, she would buy passage back to the States. She marked three ads that specified "Gentlewomen Only." After all, Oriel *was* alone in a large city where everything was unfamiliar and she knew no one. It would be wise to be careful.

Oriel quickly packed her belongings, then tucked that section of the newspaper into her handbag. At the concierge's desk she left word that she would need her luggage brought out to her cab. Then, holding her head high, she walked across the lobby to the entrance.

The doorman, looking like a gold-braided general, tipped his hat and greeted Oriel courteously as she came out onto the steps. She had arrived here with the McPhails in all their ostentatiousness. They had been given the awed respect such obvious affluence brings. Now everything had changed.

She had been ignominiously dismissed, treated like a nobody. Oriel lifted her chin defiantly. If she was to be thrown out, she was going in style. She asked the doorman to whistle for a cab for her. In a short time, one arrived and Oriel's luggage was stowed inside.

After giving the cabbie the first address she had marked, Oriel took one last look at the entrance of the elegant hotel before entering the carriage and settling back against the worn leather seat. Her stomach tightened painfully, but she refused to indulge in self-pity. This was simply another challenge to be met.

The cabbie moved the hansom out of the line of splendid carriages arriving at the hotel and into the street. Peering out the window, Oriel began to notice a gradual change in the neighborhoods through which they passed. The farther they got from the Claridge, the dingier things got. The buildings on either side were drab and soot-stained, the sidewalks more crowded, the people's clothes shabbier. Ragged little boys swept horse droppings or sold newspapers. Vendors peddled meat pies and roasted chestnuts.

The first place Oriel stopped, the room advertised had already been taken. At the second, however, she had more success. This turned out to be a tall brick house with a tiny fenced front, scrubbed doorstep, and dark green painted door. A cardboard Vacancy sign was placed in front of starched lace curtains in one of the narrow downstairs windows.

Oriel asked the cabbie to wait, although she knew it would add to his fare. A small plaque under the doorbell read, "E. M. Pettigrew." Oriel twisted the metal bell and heard it echo inside. A thin, spectacled woman with graying hair opened the door.

"Mrs. Pettigrew?"

"The same," the woman replied, folding her arms and surveying Oriel critically.

"I'd like to see the room you have for rent if it is still available," Oriel said pleasantly.

The sharp eyes moved over Oriel, not missing an inch of her simple yet stylish blue suit and feathered bonnet. Evidently Oriel passed whatever criteria the woman had because she opened the door wider and said, "It is. Come in. I'll show it to you."

Oriel followed her into a dark hallway, up a long stairway, past one landing, and up another flight of stairs. At the top of the steps, the woman opened a door. "This is it. Step inside and have a look."

The room was high-ceilinged and sparse in furnishings—a far cry from the luxurious hotel room Oriel had just left. Still, it was neat and clean. There was an iron bed, a table, one straight chair, an armchair, a wardrobe, and a small stove.

"The bathroom is down the hall, shared with other tenants. Each roomer has a scheduled day of use for hot bathwater. I require a week's rent in advance and then paid weekly for as long as you stay."

The rental price she stated seemed reasonable. "I'll take it," Oriel said. "Since the room is available, I suppose it's all right if I move in today?"

"It is, and you may," the woman said briskly.

Oriel opened her purse and counted out the money.

"Come down to my parlor and I'll give you a receipt. What's your name?"

"Oriel Banning."

As they started down the steps, Mrs. Pettigrew asked, "How long do you plan to keep the room?"

"A week, possibly two. It depends on how soon I can book passage back to the States." That was as close to the truth as Oriel could manage.

"So you *are* American." The woman paused, turning to look back at her. "I thought I recognized the accent."

"Yes." Oriel was not able to discern interest or disapproval in Mrs. Pettigrew's voice.

Their transaction was quickly done. Oriel went out to the cab, paid the driver, and tipped him for his help in bringing in her two large suitcases. He dropped them just inside the door and left. *Better get used to fending for myself again,* Oriel thought as she struggled back up the steep staircase with her bags.

Once alone in the spartan room, the enormity of her situation struck with full force. She had been reacting on a practical level, doing what needed to be done. Now the emotional impact hit. Here she was in an unfamiliar place among strangers. There was no one to whom she could turn for advice or help, no one to depend on but herself.

She must keep her wits about her and not give way to despair. First, she must decide what to do. The small amount of money she had would not last long. Perhaps the best thing to do would be to buy the cheapest passage back to the States on one of the smaller ocean liners. Mrs. McPhail had handled the arrangements for their tickets to England. Oriel had no idea what even a second-class ticket back to the United States might cost. She might not be able to afford even *that!* She certainly hoped she wouldn't have to travel steerage.

Nonsense! She was imagining all sorts of horrible possibilities when the whole thing would be settled tomorrow after she went to the Claridge and picked up her check and letter of reference. Things would fall into proper perspective. There was no use in worrying needlessly.

She had the whole day ahead of her. At last rid of both the McPhails, she could do as she pleased and go where she wanted, with no one to answer to, no one to accommodate but herself. A wonderful feeling of freedom replaced the downward spiral her spirits had been taking. She would explore London on her own, something she had been longing to do.

Putting on her jacket and hat again, Oriel set out. If she had known what the next day would bring, her step would not have been quite so jaunty nor her spirits so high.

*O*riel awakened after a restless night. Although she had not slept all that well, she had made a decision, and having made it, felt positive. After she picked up her check from Mrs. McPhail she would go directly to a shipping office, find out how much a second-class ticket would cost, and book passage on a ship leaving for America as soon as possible. She would feel more secure once she was back in the States. She was almost certain she could get a teaching job again at Miss Porter's. If not there, some other school would take her.

Having a definite plan of action, Oriel set out for the Claridge Hotel. This time she chose a more economical mode of transportation, the horse-drawn omnibus, which carried up to sixteen passengers. Two blocks from the hotel, she got off and walked the rest of the way. Ahead of her the large structure rose majestically, overlooking the busy street. A continuous parade of shiny carriages drew up in front of the impressive entrance and discharged fashionably dressed people. Only the day before *she* had gone in and out, a part of it all. Now it seemed rather intimidating.

At the registration desk, the clerk looked at Oriel without recognition. She had spoken to him every day when she came to pick up or leave messages for Mrs. McPhail, yet he regarded her now as if he had never seen her before. His attitude lit sparks of indignation in Oriel. With elaborate politeness, she asked for her letter.

"A *letter?*" His brow wrinkled as if she had asked for a rare jewel of some sort.

"Yes, for Miss Oriel Banning. Mrs. McPhail was supposed to leave one for me." The man looked baffled, so Oriel was forced to explain. Checking her irritation, she said, "I was a guest here with the McPhail party."

"The McPhails?" His nose wrinkled slightly. Then, lifting his eyebrows, he said, "The Americans?"

"Yes, Mrs. Clarence McPhail and Miss Berenice McPhail. We had a suite." Oriel gritted her teeth, wanting to add that the suite had been one of the hotel's most expensive and lavish ones. She would not, however, give the clerk the satisfaction of seeing her lose her temper. "Will you please check? Miss Oriel Banning," she repeated evenly.

He turned, briefly surveyed the boxes on the wall behind him, then shook his head. "No, miss. There is nothing here under that name. The McPhail party checked out yesterday," he added coldly.

Startled, Oriel stared at him. "*Checked out?* But she couldn't have—I mean, Mrs. McPhail didn't say anything about leaving. Are you sure?"

Looking offended, the clerk said, "Quite sure, miss. Mrs. McPhail left to take the boat train. I assume she was going to France. Left no forwarding address."

"And *nothing* else—no letter? You're sure?"

"Nothing, miss. I'm *quite* sure." His tone was icy. "Now if you'll excuse me." He glanced past her, over her head. Oriel realized there were people standing behind her, hotel guests whom he obviously considered far more important than she.

Oriel stepped away from the counter in disbelief. Would Mrs. McPhail really have gone off without leaving her final check? And no letter of reference? Surely she couldn't have. There must be an explanation of some sort. Perhaps Mrs. McPhail intended to mail it from France. Oriel could not believe the woman would do anything so blatantly dishonest. Thoughtless, selfish, inconsiderate—Eunice McPhail was all those things, but *dishonest?*

Oriel moved a little distance from the reception desk. This was an entirely unexpected blow. No forwarding address had been left. How could she contact her former employer? What should she do now?

As she stood there trying to get hold of herself, she became aware of the activity around her. It was the luncheon hour and the lobby was full. Well-dressed men and women moved toward the dining room. All at once, Oriel's unfocused gaze picked out a familiar figure. It was Morgan Drummond, accompanied by the same exquisite creature who had met him the day the ship docked. Once again, the woman was dressed in the height of fashion. This time she wore a cinnamon velvet jacket with sable collar and cuffs. Her extravagant hat was of black velvet, lined with turquoise satin and trimmed with black ostrich tips, its curved brim framing her lovely face. That day at the docks in Southampton, she had looked excited and happy. Today she looked flushed, petulant. Morgan, too, looked upset. They hardly presented the picture of a blissful couple.

Shielded behind one of the marble pillars, Oriel was hidden from sight. However, Morgan and Edwina paused just on the other side of where she stood. Since Edwina made no effort to lower her voice, Oriel heard every word she spoke.

"I'm *not* going to change my mind, Morgan. It's out of the question. How could you possibly expect me to agree to such a thing?"

What had he asked that was so impossible? Oriel knew about the trivial concerns of people of wealth. She had heard the McPhails argue endlessly about the simplest matters. What could someone like Edwina Parker, with her beauty, her wealth, her future, have to complain about? Possibly Morgan's choice of play or musicale tickets.

Then Oriel heard Morgan's voice, edged with annoyance, say, "You're being completely unreasonable, Edwina. You haven't even seen—"

"I don't have to *see* to know I'd hate it!" she interrupted. "No, Morgan, you can't persuade me. *Never!*"

Oriel watched as they left the hotel, Edwina sweeping ahead of a grim-faced Morgan. It was a lover's quarrel, a silly tiff that would be over in a few hours. Oriel shrugged and walked back across the lobby, consumed by her own immediate problem.

Remembering her former employer's tendency to procrastinate, Oriel hoped the promised check and letter of reference would come soon—maybe even tomorrow. She would have to wait to buy her steamship ticket. She didn't want to use up her available cash should Mrs. McPhail delay sending the check.

Oriel pushed out through the front doors of the hotel just in time to see Morgan Drummond and Miss Parker get into a shiny black carriage and drive off.

It had begun to rain, and Oriel had no umbrella. Catching the doorman eyeing her suspiciously, Oriel drew on her gloves, went down the steps, and hurried to where she could catch the omnibus back to the rooming house.

As she waited under a store awning for the bus, the scene she had witnessed between Morgan Drummond and his fiancée played through her mind. How strange to see Morgan Drummond again and to overhear that snatch of argument. *So even the wealthy have problems,* she thought. Her own, however, were more urgent.

Maybe she should try to find work of some kind to supplement the wages due her. She would have to look in the employment ads in the newspaper. She hailed a paperboy and bought the evening *Times*. The omnibus appeared and she boarded, seated herself, and opened the paper to the employment columns. As her eyes tracked her finger down the list of available positions, her heart began to sink. Governess, companion, lady clerk, milliner's assistant—why would anyone hire an American for these positions when there were probably many qualified English ladies ready to fill them?

She stopped reading the list when she realized that the bus was nearing her stop. She warded off her creeping depression by assuring herself that her dilemma was only temporary. The promised check and reference would surely arrive tomorrow. Tomorrow she would return to the Claridge to pick them up. Tomorrow things would look different.

It was still raining when she got off the omnibus. To avoid getting drenched, she ran the few blocks to the rooming house, using the folded newspaper as a makeshift umbrella.

She reached the steps almost the same time as another young woman, who then stood on the stoop closing her umbrella before entering the house. With a glance at Oriel and a quick motion, she pushed open the door and together they both rushed into the entry hall.

Vigorously shaking the rain from her umbrella, she turned to Oriel, laughing. "That was close, I'd say! No umbrella, dearie? You ought to carry one always. Doesn't pay to take chances this time of year. Never know when you'll get caught in a downpour."

The woman had a round, friendly face, with a sprinkle of freckles across an upturned nose. Regarding Oriel with curious eyes, she said, "I'm Nola Cooper. I live upstairs in the third floor front flat. You must be the new roomer."

Oriel introduced herself.

"Pleased to meet you, I'm sure." Nola smiled. "Mrs. Pettigrew tells me you're an American. I have a cousin who lives in Boston. Do you know it?"

"Yes, as a matter of fact, I lived quite close when I was growing up—in Lynwood."

"Well, I'd say that was a coincidence, wouldn't you?"

"Yes, I suppose it is."

"Well, I'm off to get out of these wet duds. My intended is taking me out to the music hall tonight." She smiled. "Be seeing you, I'm sure. Ta-ta!"

With a wave of her hand, Nola ran up the stairs, leaving Oriel to follow more slowly. Suddenly her day seemed wasted—the long bus ride, the futile errand. As she plodded wearily up the stairs, she felt discouraged and lonely.

*O*riel awoke to another gray London day. A full week had passed since Mrs. McPhail had sailed for France. Oriel had gone every day to check if her money and reference had come. Although she did not always have to deal with the same clerk to make her inquiry, Oriel always received the same answer—no letter, no nothing.

Today was Friday. If the check and letter didn't come, Oriel faced a weekend of worry. Her money was dwindling fast. She tried to economize by eating only one meal a day at a restaurant near the rooming house. If there was nothing from Mrs. McPhail today, Oriel would have to find work, even if only temporary, to tide her over. Maybe she would stop by the employment agency she had seen advertised in the newspaper and fill out an application. With her education and qualifications, she should be able to get some type of teaching or tutoring job. Even better would be a position as a traveling companion, perhaps even back to the States.

Bolstered by a determination not to be defeated by her circumstances, Oriel got up and got dressed. Conscious of the importance of making a good impression, Oriel chose a walking suit of Prussian blue wool, its jacket edged with darker blue braid. Her bonnet was trimmed with matching ribbon. It was one of the outfits she had made for herself, not one that had once belonged to Neecy. Over the years, out of necessity, Oriel had become quite a skilled seamstress.

Satisfied with her appearance, Oriel set out with high hopes. She was just leaving her room as Nola came down the steps.

"G'morning. You're off, then? I take the omnibus at the corner. Want to walk together?"

Glad for Nola's cheerful company, Oriel agreed. Together they went the rest of the way downstairs, with Nola merrily recounting her evening out with Will. On the way to the bus stop, Nola kept up a running chatter, telling Oriel she was a tailor's apprentice, an orphan, that Will was her steady beau and they were saving their money so they could get married within the year. At the bus stop, Nola asked, "Where are you off to?"

Oriel hesitated for a moment before saying, "The Claridge Hotel."

Nola looked surprised. "You work there?"

"Well, not exactly. Actually, I'm looking for work."

Nola gave her a searching, sympathetic look. She seemed about to say something when they heard the sound of horses' hooves and the heavy wheels of the omnibus.

"Here comes mine," Nola said as the bus pulled to a stop. She hopped on board and waved her hand, calling back, "Well, good luck."

At the hotel, Oriel received the same negative answer to her inquiry. She turned away, shaken, discouraged. All her brave optimism disappeared. She had to face the truth. Mrs. McPhail was not going to come through. There was no point in hoping. She was stranded in London, with little money.

She didn't want to go back to the rooming house, to her curious landlady and cold room, where the small stove emitted meager heat. Besides, she had to take action. If she got a job, perhaps within a few weeks she could earn enough money to buy the cheapest steamship ticket back to the States. She had noticed while riding the omnibus that the employment office was only a few blocks away from the hotel. She walked toward it resolutely.

The small brass plate identified the severe-looking woman behind the desk as Miss Ellerbee. Frowning, she studied the questionnaire Oriel had filled out, put it aside, then gave Oriel the bad news. The world economy that winter was on a slow downturn; the employment picture, even for those most qualified, was bleak. She looked over her nose glasses at Oriel and sighed.

"I must be quite honest with you, Miss Banning. I don't know any place I could send you where you might be employed. To be truthful, you have two major disadvantages. First, you are an American seeking employment in England at a time when many native gentlewomen are also doing so. Second, you are young and quite attractive. I'm afraid any woman who might interview you as a social secretary or a governess would have some reservations—especially if she had a husband with a wandering eye, or an attractive son."

Oriel's astonishment must have shown. She started to protest, but Miss Ellerbee interrupted. "I hate to be so brutally frank, but there it is."

"Even as a domestic?" Oriel asked desperately.

Miss Ellerbee shook her head. "You have no such training, Miss Banning, nor any references, I might add. The servant system in England is a very regimented one. Girls go out into service at twelve or thirteen, work themselves up from scullery or cook's assistant to parlor or lady's maid. It is also a very closed system. I doubt you would ever be admitted."

That brought the interview to an end. In a bewildered frame of mind, Oriel left. Weary and downhearted beyond belief, she caught the omnibus. Preoccupied by her own disturbing thoughts, she missed her stop. She then had to walk three blocks back. Her head and her feet ached. Oriel was just rounding the corner in sight of the shabby rooming house when she saw Nola hurrying along just ahead of her.

At the doorway, Nola asked, "Any luck yet, dearie?"

"Not yet."

Something in Oriel's tone of voice caused Nola to give her a sharp glance. They went inside. "Why not come up to my room. We'll have a cup of tea."

"That's very kind of you."

"Not at all. I like a bit of company and a good chat. Come along up."

Nola's room was furnished much the same as Oriel's. However, Nola had made it distinctly her own with special touches. There were several ruffled throw pillows with satin-stitched quotations in swirling script, artificial flowers in painted vases, and large bows for curtain swags.

Nola got a fire going right away and set on the kettle. She kicked off her shoes and put on a pair of purple house slippers.

"There, that's better!" She sighed, then said to Oriel, "Take off your hat, dearie, and get comfy. You look tired. Job hunting's no fun. Not a nibble, eh?"

Oriel shook her head. "It seems I'm overqualified for some and underqualified for most."

Nola pursed her lips. "Don't American girls learn a trade?"

"Some do," Oriel began, wondering how much of her background she could share with this nice girl without alienating her. They had grown up not only in different countries but in different social worlds.

The hissing of the kettle halted any revelations. Nola busied herself making their tea. She handed Oriel a cup decorated with seashells.

"Well, don't worry, dearie. You're pretty and smart," Nola said comfortingly. "Something's bound to turn up sooner or later."

It better be sooner, Oriel thought, sipping her tea. It was the *later* that was depressing. She dreaded to think how long *later* could be.

Nola held her cup with both hands thoughtfully for a moment. Then she leaned forward and said, "Want a bit of advice, dearie?"

"Of course."

Nola hesitated a second or two. "If I were you, dearie, I wouldn't say nothin' to Mrs. Pettigrew about being unemployed. She's a nosy old biddy and, well—just a word to the wise." She gave Oriel a wink.

A word to the wise, indeed. The truth of Nola's statement confirmed Oriel's own intuition about their landlady. Although pleasant enough, Mrs. Pettigrew had shown a growing curiosity about her. What was Oriel actually doing in London? Where did Oriel go when she went out each day? Oriel had seen her peeking out the parlor window when she returned from her futile errands. Mrs. Pettigrew always seemed to have some reason to come to the door of her downstairs apartment or to the row of mailboxes in the hallway to engage Oriel in probing conversations. Her narrowed eyes asked the questions her nimble mind was thinking. Why was Oriel, an American, apparently without a job or friends, staying in London?

With a great deal of trepidation, Oriel paid another week's rent, then began a relentless job search.

She dredged up the courage to go into stores and shops of all kinds and ask if there was any available work. She had hoped her neat appearance and manner would overcome her lack of references. That had not been the case. She had been consistently turned down. For the most part, Oriel withstood the cold looks and the suspicious questions, but by the end of a week of tramping the bleak London streets, she was exhausted and discouraged.

She was almost at the end of her rope. Next week her rent would be due again—then what? Could she go to the American embassy as a last resort and plead destitution? She shuddered. Not yet. She wasn't giving up.

One gray morning, chilled and depressed, Oriel started to return to the rooming house after another failed job search. She halted at the thought of a possible grilling by Mrs. Pettigrew. She decided as long as she was already out, she would walk to the Claridge. By some chance, a very slim one, just maybe . . . Oriel whirled around and went in the other direction.

A few blocks from the hotel, it began to drizzle. Oriel hurried along, trying to stay close to the buildings to protect herself from a sharp wind that penetrated her light wool suit. She turned up her jacket collar, hoping she could get to the hotel before the leaden clouds opened up and poured down sheets of rain. Resentful thoughts of Mrs. McPhail spurred her to walk faster. Her former employer was probably basking in the sunshine at some European resort!

Stopping at the curb across the street from the Claridge, Oriel paused as a carriage clattered past. Its wheels hit a puddle, sending a spray of dirty water onto Oriel's skirt and soaking her shoes.

Oriel let out a gasp and looked helplessly after the offender. All she could do, really, was hurry on. She hoped the dampened edge of her hem wouldn't show as she entered the luxurious lobby. She didn't want to look as bedraggled and poverty-stricken as she felt.

At the top of the hotel steps, Oriel came under the appraisal of the uniformed doorman. She suspected he was considering whether he should run down with his large umbrella to escort her into the lobby. While he debated, Oriel lifted her head and started up the steps, trying to look as much as possible like a returning guest.

Concentrating on maintaining her poise, she was startled to hear a deep, masculine voice behind her say, "Miss Banning?"

5

*O*riel turned. *Morgan Drummond!* She stared at him, astonished that he remembered her name. Then he was towering over her, sheltering her with his large umbrella, looking as surprised as she felt.

"Miss Banning, what on earth are you doing here?" he asked. "I thought you'd left with Mrs. McPhail. I saw her leaving and I naturally assumed that since you were with her on board our ship—"

"I'm no longer in her employ," Oriel replied, cutting off any further speculation on his part.

"Ah, I see," he said, still puzzled. "But you are still staying here at the hotel?"

Uncomfortably aware of his scrutiny, Oriel said, "It's rather a long story." Just then, a strong gust of wind tugged her hat brim, blowing it up from where she had fastened it to her hair.

"Well, let's not stand out here in this wind. You can tell me about it inside. Let's get out of this storm." He smiled. "We always seem to be meeting in inclement weather, don't we?"

He took her arm and escorted her up the steps through the entrance. Inside the lobby, Oriel straightened her hat, tucked back a stray strand of hair, and smoothed down her jacket collar.

"To answer your question," she said, "I returned today to see if my letter of reference and my—" She stopped herself before blurting that she also awaited her badly needed funds. "Mrs. McPhail promised . . ." Her words trailed off, leaving her thought dangling. Did Morgan guess what she was hoping that letter contained?

If he did, he brushed it off easily. "No matter. Now that we have encountered each other again, might I suggest you join me for tea? I've been out all this miserable morning on a dreary round of business appointments. I'm badly in need of some cheerful company. Would you accommodate me?" A smile softened his face.

Oriel considered whether it would be proper to accept his invitation. Under ordinary circumstances, no. She hardly knew Morgan Drummond. However, the fact that they had been fellow passengers might bend protocol a little. More importantly, the emptiness in her stomach reminded her she had had only a scant cup of tea and single slice of bread for breakfast. She *was* very hungry. Practicality overtook propriety. With just the right amount of ladylike hesitation, Oriel accepted. "How very kind. Yes, thank you."

"Fine. Come along, then. You can check for your mail afterwards."

Oriel had had enough experience with the affluent to realize they could not imagine her urgent need for money or understand anything about being unemployed and impoverished. Morgan Drummond had no idea how desperate checking her mail was for her. Still, Oriel decided to put her anxieties aside and enjoy this unexpected meeting and the opportunity for a comforting tea. She had not the least premonition of the importance of this chance encounter.

At the door of the dining room, the head waiter greeted Morgan by name, bowed deferentially, and led them to a table near a window. A waiter appeared and Morgan ordered.

Soon a large pot of tea and a covered plate were placed before Oriel. When the waiter lifted the silver dome, a delicious aroma of grilled chops, bacon, and sausage rose tantalizingly. There were also tomatoes, mushrooms, and a mound of creamy scrambled eggs. A dish holding toasted crumpets dripping with butter and currant-studded buns was set between them, along with an assortment of jams, jellies, and marmalades. Oriel had not had such a meal for quite a while. With great effort, she tried to eat daintily and not appear too hungry.

With her second cup of tea, Oriel felt revived. Sitting across from him, Oriel realized again how good-looking Morgan Drummond was. He was kept from being entirely handsome by a nose that was slightly crooked. He had black wavy hair and a keen, intelligent face with defined features. Heavy dark brows met over penetrating eyes, which gave his face a discontented, brooding expression. It seemed strange that anyone with his wealth, power, and physical attributes should be unhappy, but Oriel knew everyone had secret problems. Morgan Drummond was probably no exception. Even as she considered this possibility, she became aware that Morgan Drummond was regarding *her* thoughtfully.

At first, their conversation had been polite small talk about the crossing, some of the events on board, the English climate. Nothing personal was discussed until he signaled the waiter for a fresh pot of tea. Then, leaning forward, he asked, "So, Miss Banning, now that you are no longer with the McPhails, do you intend to stay in London? Or do you have other plans?"

"I have no special plans at present. I've been waiting—" Oriel halted. Ordinarily a truthful person, she felt reluctant to tell him about her financial dilemma. Nor did she want to appear to be seeking sympathy. One didn't pour out one's heart to a stranger.

If he noticed her delay in answering, he did not show it. He simply waited, keeping her in his steady gaze.

Oriel improvised. "I'm considering several possibilities." That, at least, was true. "And you, Mr. Drummond, are you enjoying your stay in London?"

The frown between his brows deepened. "Actually, it's become more business than pleasure, and somewhat unpleasant, I'm afraid. I've been meeting with my grandfather's lawyers." His mouth straightened. "I have received some bad news." He paused. "It seems I've inherited a castle."

"A castle? That doesn't sound like bad news! It sounds very exciting."

He looked glum. "In *Ireland.*"

Oriel had to laugh. "Wherever! When I was a little girl, I used to pretend I had a fairy godmother who would one day appear and give me three wishes. One wish was always to live in a castle."

Morgan looked half-amused, half-doubtful. "Sounds like you've an active imagination, Miss Banning. Is it possible you're a bit Irish yourself?"

Oriel smiled. "My great-grandmother was, I think. At least partly." She mimicked a brogue. "Name of O'Meara."

Morgan laughed. "Ah, Miss Banning, I do think you have the famous Irish sense of humor. I wish I had more of that in my nature. I'm afraid along with the castle I've inherited the dark side of Irish character. Somehow the thought of the long, gloomy Irish winters always depresses me." He sighed and frowned again. "The castle comes with a requirement. I have to take possession within a month."

"Oh, so you'll be going to Ireland to see your inherited castle? That should be interesting."

"I shall have to," he said grimly. "Actually, Miss Banning, it isn't the great gift you seem to think. It is very complicated. I hadn't planned on *living* in Ireland."

"I see," Oriel said quietly.

Morgan shook his head. "No, you don't. You couldn't really see unless you knew the whole story."

His tone was dismissing and Oriel felt rebuffed. "I'm sorry."

"No, I'm the one who's sorry. I shouldn't have brought the matter up." He signaled the waiter for the check. "Other people's burdens are a bore. I don't intend to spoil this delightful interlude we've had by doing that."

He rose and came around to help Oriel from her chair. "I am taking the night boat to Dublin and then will journey to Kilmara to inspect my new property. My grandfather has paid a large sum of money to maintain a staff there all these years in the hope that he could return himself. The castle became his hobby, actually. He dispatched agents to buy furnishings, rugs, paintings, and other artifacts to further glorify his boyhood dream of one day living there at Drummond Castle."

Morgan gave a derisive laugh. "One man's folly, and I am supposed to appreciate all that has gone into it and live out Grandfather's dream. A family legacy, and I am the only one left to see to it. Do you have any such family legacy to uphold, Miss Banning, or are you more fortunate?"

"I don't know whether I would call myself *fortunate,* Mr. Drummond. Both my parents are dead, and I have no brothers or sisters—a fact I've often regretted."

"Forgive me, I spoke facetiously. I did not mean to offend you."

Oriel shook her head. "No offense taken."

They walked out to the lobby. Although Oriel felt uncomfortable, Morgan accompanied her up to the reception desk while she asked if there was any mail for her. It did not escape the haughty clerk's notice that this time Morgan Drummond was standing beside Oriel. He was a little less hasty in his negative reply that the hoped-for letter had not come. Disappointed, Oriel turned away, trying to hide her dismay as best she could.

"Why don't you leave an address where you can be reached?" Morgan suggested. "If your mail comes in the afternoon post, the hotel can send it to you and save you another trip."

Of course. It was the sensible thing to do. Oriel wondered why she had not thought of it herself before this. She was a little hesitant to give the address to the haughty clerk, sure he would recognize the neighborhood in which it was located, but there was nothing else to do. As coolly as she could, she gave the address, noting the slight rise of the clerk's eyebrows. However, with Morgan beside her, the clerk was politeness itself, and he assured Oriel that anything bearing her name would be forwarded.

"You can't go traipsing around in this dreadful weather. I insist on calling you a cab." Morgan gestured to the long, satin-draped windows through which they could see a steady downpour. He pulled a comic face. "Pity me. They say weather in Ireland is much worse!"

"Well, I wish you the best." Oriel smiled. "I've always heard Ireland is a fascinating country, full of beauty and mystery."

Morgan walked her to the hotel entrance. When Oriel thanked him for the tea, he shook his head slightly. "It is I who should thank you, Miss Banning, for the company. I was in a foul mood when we met. You gave me a most enjoyable distraction from what had been a bad day with depressing news. I'm grateful." He then handed Oriel over to the doorman, who took her carefully down to the waiting hansom.

As it drove off, Oriel peered through the rain-splattered window to wave at Morgan, who was still on the top step. It was quite a coincidence, their meeting again like this. It was then that Oriel realized he had not mentioned his wedding or Edwina Parker. In a way, it was like having read a few random chapters of a story, not knowing how it began or how it would end. Now she would never know. She certainly never expected to see Morgan Drummond again.

6

The London Law Offices of Tredwell, Loring, and Sommerville

April 1895

Durwin Tredwell regarded his client with narrowed eyes. Although he had known and liked the grandfather, his opinion of the grandson was—not to put too fine a point on it—suspect. He held the view that heirs to great fortunes were usually not worth the trust they were given by their benefactors. There was always the danger of them going rapidly through the hard-earned money they inherited, no matter what their lawyers did to prevent it. A favorite saying of his own grandfather, the eminent lawyer who had founded the prestigious law firm of Tredwell, Loring, and Sommerville had been, "From shirtsleeves to shirtsleeves in three generations."

The third generation of the Drummond fortune was sitting opposite him at the present moment, reading over a copy of his grandfather's lengthy will. Durwin was wary. In the first place, the man was an American. Durwin had had few dealings with Americans. Further, although the firm had carried on an extensive correspondence with Morgan Drummond, Durwin had never met him before he'd come to London a few weeks ago. When Durwin had been given the case to handle by his father, Morgan had been described by him as being "too good-looking, too rich, and too clever for his own good." Durwin studied him. In person, Morgan Drummond validated the description; he was tall, magnificently built, dark-haired—too handsome by far.

When Morgan finished turning the last page, he tossed the document back on Durwin's desk, saying grimly, "That's it, then. No loopholes, no escape clauses. This is unbreakable, right?"

"It has been legally signed, witnessed, and officially filed. The only reason it would not be upheld is if *you* decided you did not wish to fulfill the requirements of the inheritance. In that case, your grandfather signed a codicil, giving us the authority to assign the full amount of the estate to the various charities and institutions he listed."

Morgan muttered something under his breath, sprang up from his chair, and began to pace the room in long strides. "There must be another way."

Durwin placed his hands in an arch, fingertips touching, and slowly shook his head. "Not, I'm afraid, unless the young lady in question changes her mind."

"That won't happen." Morgan's jaw clenched.

For a moment, a tense silence hung in the high-ceilinged, wood-paneled room. From beyond the windows, draped heavily in green velvet, the muffled sound of London traffic could be heard.

After a long while, Morgan said slowly, "There might be a solution. That is—" He turned to the lawyer, pulled the chair closer to his desk, and leaned forward to outline his idea.

Durwin leaned back in his high-backed leather chair and listened. It was a bizarre plan, but it might work. There was nothing illegal about it, although some might find that it rather stretched the limits of the intention of the will. He would have to check to see if there were any unforeseen traps before drawing up such an agreement.

"So what do you think?" Morgan demanded.

Durwin surveyed his client curiously. "And you say this young woman is—"

"Yes, without financial resources—no parents, no family. It couldn't be better. An only child *and* an orphan!"

A sardonic smile lifted the corners of Morgan's mouth slightly, hardening the expression. For a moment, Durwin felt a chill at the cold-bloodedness of the scheme.

On the other side of London, late that afternoon, Oriel dragged herself up the steps of the rooming house, opened the door, and wearily mounted the stairs to her room. Without taking off her hat or coat, she sank down on the chair by the window. Outside it was getting dark, and rain was beading on the glass.

It had been a long, discouraging day. She had checked out two promising job ads, one at a stationery firm, where someone was wanted to copy legal documents and address envelopes, and the other at a bookstore, where a clerk was needed. Knowing she wrote a fine hand, she thought she could qualify for the first job. Since she was well-read, she could certainly suggest titles for browsers, which should make her a good choice for the second job. She had started out feeling fairly optimistic. However, after a tedious bus ride and an almost frantic search for the small, out-of-the-way bookstore, she found both positions had already been filled—by *men*.

Oriel took stock. Her situation was becoming desperate. After paying another week's rent, she would barely have enough to last two weeks—if she were extra careful. That meant making the allotment of coal for the stove stretch for two days and limiting her food to one full meal a day. If Mrs.

McPhail failed to pay her, there was only one week's rent left between Oriel and the poorhouse.

Oriel chided herself for being melodramatic. Maybe this was the worst crisis she had faced in her life, but she still wasn't ready to give up. On the bus, she had picked up a newspaper another rider had discarded. She unfolded it and began to scrutinize the employment section. She sat up late going over the Help Wanted ads in the newspaper. Maybe she had overlooked something, a job she had not considered possible before. Then she saw it: "WANTED IMMEDIATELY: Piecework women to do plain sewing. Fast workers needed. Earn good pay. Apply Mr. Jarman." An address followed.

Sewing! At least she knew she could do that. It didn't sound too difficult.

She left the rooming house early the next morning, not wanting to miss the opportunity for a job as she had the day before. She also did not want to run into either Mrs. Pettigrew or Nola. Nola had begun to look at her cautiously, as though not sure whether to ask how the job search was going. As for Mrs. Pettigrew—well, who knew what the landlady was thinking. As long as she could still pay the rent, Oriel did not want to have to deal with her.

After a long bus ride, Oriel found herself in a drab street with dark, soot-stained buildings rising on either side. It was an industrial section of London. Clutching the ad with the address of a possible workplace, Oriel hurried down the dirty sidewalk.

When she saw a line of shawled women hurrying toward a wide wooden door, she quickened her step. Touching the arm of one of them, she asked, "Are they hiring today?" The woman jerked a thumb. "Jarman's the one to see," she told Oriel in a hoarse voice, then hurried on.

Oriel joined the end of the line that was moving slowly toward the entrance, then followed the last woman through the door. The interior was so dim, she halted to let her eyes become accustomed to it. Just a few feet away stood a man slouched against the wall.

She advanced cautiously. "Mr. Jarman?"

"That's me." He had a blotched face with small, curious eyes, a bulbous nose, and slack mouth. "What do you want?"

"A job. I mean, I saw your advertisement and I—"

The man's eyes roved over her skeptically, boldly challenging. "Can you make buttonholes, take out basting stitches?" he asked.

"Yes, of course," Oriel answered.

"You get paid by the piece. Understand?" he demanded, moving a toothpick from one side of his mouth to the other. "The more you can do in a day, the more's your pay. Get it?"

"Yes."

"Well, come on, then. Meg's the supervisor in the workroom. You've got to see her. She'll find you a place and assign your work."

Oriel followed him down a narrow hall. He opened a door and barked, "Meg, come here!"

A large woman with a coarse complexion and a pinched expression walked over to him. He jerked his thumb toward Oriel. "New worker. Find her a place and get her started." Then, with one more evaluating look at Oriel, he sauntered off.

"Hang your coat and hat over there," Meg said sharply, "then come with me."

The workroom was narrow. Hazy light from grimy windows was augmented only slightly by smoky oil lamps hanging from the ceiling. Women were seated on either side of long tables bent over great piles of material, their shoulders hunched forward as they squinted over their work.

Oriel was directed to a table where there was an empty chair at one end. As she took her place, she nodded and smiled tentatively at her fellow workers, but received only blank stares in return.

A pile of material was dumped in front of her, and a tin container holding scissors, thread, a thimble, and a needle was put down beside it. "See you take care—if you lose or break a needle, another one is docked from your pay, understand?" Meg said harshly. It wasn't really a question.

The hours ticked by in endless monotony. No one spoke; everyone worked steadily, hardly glancing up at one another. Oriel's neck began to ache painfully and her shoulders stiffened. She tried to shift her position in the hard chair, but it was almost impossible. The chairs were placed so close together that if she tried to move, she bumped into her neighbor.

Her eyes began to water from strain. The light was so dim it was difficult to work on the dark material. By the time a shrill bell rang announcing the end of the day, Oriel could barely move. Every bone and muscle protested. Her fingers were sore; her back and arms ached.

As she gingerly stood up, she discovered one foot had gone to sleep and tingled painfully. When she glanced around at the other women, she had a horrible realization. Their pale faces, red-rimmed eyes, and rounded shoulders told a tragic story. Who knew what circumstances had forced them into this grinding, unrewarding work? How long had they worked here under these conditions? Again, no one spoke as they wearily reached for hats and jackets and filed out of the workroom into the crowded London street. It was nearly dark when Oriel emerged from the building. She was as close to despairing tears as she had been in all these anxious weeks.

That night, she was too tired even to stop and get something to eat. She could hardly undress before she fell across the bed, pulling the quilt over her and falling into a deep sleep. It was morning before she could believe it. The jangle of her alarm clock jolted her upright, and she stumbled out of bed. It was still dark as she hurried to the bus stop, wondering how she could possibly get through another day in the workroom. She had to earn at least enough to pay another week's rent; surely by then Mrs. McPhail's check would come. She dared not think what the alternative would be.

The days of that week ground by slowly. The work was not only mindlessly boring but wearying. The silence of the workroom was oppressive. No one seemed inclined to relieve the heavy atmosphere with any sort of conversation. The watchful presence of Meg and Jarman, who periodically stalked the aisles between the tables, was enough to discourage anyone inclined to converse. Every time Oriel raised her head from her work when Jarman was in the workroom, she met his speculative glance. She had to suppress the uneasy feeling it gave her. She told herself she would wait until the end of the week and see if working here was worth it. She *was* a quick worker and found the work simple. She never got to the end of it, though. The minute she finished her allotment, another pile was dumped before her.

She managed to get through the tedious hours by using her imagination. After her mother's death, Oriel had discovered she could live in another world peopled by imaginary characters. In the dreary workroom, she told herself stories and thought of her beloved father, who had given her everything to make her happy. What would he think of her present situation, the circumstances in which she now found herself?

On Friday morning, Oriel woke up with a sense of relief. She had survived the awful week. She was sure her fast work had added up to a good sum, at least enough to make next week's rent. On Saturday, she planned to go to the Claridge and check her mail just in case the clerk had not forwarded her letter as she had requested.

Taking the last stitch, Oriel knotted her thread and snipped it with the scissors. She replaced her needle into the pincushion, placed it with the scissors and thimble back into the small tin container, and folded her last piece just as the bell rang. Today was payday, and even among the quiet workers there was a sense of anticipation. They lined up to get the envelopes containing their wages, given to them by Jarman, who sat at a desk near the building entrance. As the last hired, Oriel was last in line. As she approached the table, Jarman looked up.

"So you made it, Miss Banning." His mouth twitched in his version of a smile, one that looked more like a sneer. "I had a wager you wouldn't. Made me lose my bet, didn't you?"

Oriel did not answer. She waited. He must have her check. Why didn't he just hand it to her? Finally, she said, "My pay, please?"

"Meg says you're a fast worker. Did more than your quota." Stubby fingers with dirt under the nails flipped over the file cards. "Did you expect a little bonus, Miss Banning?"

A queer sort of alert quivered through Oriel. She was the only one left in the workroom. She had heard the outer door slam after the last two workers had gotten their pay envelopes and gone. She felt a tingling along her scalp, a warning of danger. She felt her breath rise, become shallow. She wanted to get out of there. She held out her hand. "No bonus, just what's coming to me, Mr. Jarman."

He shoved back his chair. It made a grating noise on the cement floor. He stood, picked up a pay envelope, and came around the desk. His bulky height loomed over her. He pushed his face close to Oriel's, and she could smell liquor on his breath as he said, "Then how about a little bonus for *me*, Miss Banning? That is, *if* you want your pay."

She stepped away from him, but he reached out and grabbed her upper arm. She struggled, trying to shake loose, but his fingers tightened. "Ah, no you don't, Miss High and Mighty."

Panic swept through her, gave her strength. Oriel pulled away from him, and with her free arm, brought her handbag up and smashed it full in his face. The bag had an ornamental metal clasp that scraped his forehead. He groaned and dropped her arm. His hand went to his face and Oriel saw that the blow had drawn blood. Taking advantage of his momentary incapacity, she ran for the exit and pushed through the wide doors into the street.

She kept running, not looking back until ahead she saw her omnibus slowing at the corner. She picked up her skirts and ran faster. Breathless, she mounted the steps and sank into a seat, weak with relief. The vehicle moved forward. She felt faint from the hideous episode and her narrow escape.

It was only a few minutes later that she realized she had not received her pay. A sickening sensation washed over her. That terrible week and nothing to show for it. The thought of going back to claim her wages made her shudder. Jarman would probably deny everything. He might not even admit she had ever worked there.

Oriel felt drained. She slumped against the bus seat. Her futile attempt to survive had ended in a grotesque nightmare. She stared out the window, then wearily pulled the bell at her stop. She got off the bus and with great effort, doggedly headed toward the rooming house.

Oriel felt the rise of panic and fought it. She had known the soul-wrenching anxiety of poverty, always a step away from calamity, teetering on the yawning abyss of illness, accident. Trusting God was the only security. The job with the McPhails had proved that. As a child, Oriel had been taught to pray. However, she had also been told not to expect miracles. A good mind, imagination, and strength of character were given to a person to find her way out of difficulties. With God's help, she would get through this.

Letting herself into her room, Oriel shivered. It felt dank, chilly. There was no more coal in the bucket. She picked up her purse, emptied the contents, and counted out enough coins for a scuttle of coal. At least she could be warm while she figured a way out of her dilemma.

She marched downstairs and knocked at her landlady's door. Oriel had avoided Mrs. Pettigrew all week, but getting the coal was now a necessity.

"Oh, it's *you*, Miss Banning!" the landlady said as she opened the door. "I was just thinking about you. I must've missed you coming in. I kept an eye out, but then I went to fix my tea. You must've come in while I was in the kitchen. I have something for you—come this afternoon by special messenger."

Mrs. Pettigrew turned, bustled back into her cluttered parlor, then hurried back, holding out an envelope to Oriel.

Puzzled, Oriel took it, examining the fine quality of the paper. Then, seeing the gold-embossed lettering of the Claridge Hotel on the back flap, she felt a wave of relief. It must be the check and letter of reference from Mrs. McPhail.

Though Mrs. Pettigrew was quivering with curiosity, Oriel was not about to open it in front of her. "Thank you," Oriel said, tucking the letter into her sweater pocket. She handed the landlady her coins and said, "Could I have my ration of coal, please?"

Mrs. Pettigrew looked disgruntled as she accepted the coins and filled the scuttle for Oriel. Unable to contain her curiosity, she remarked pointedly, "I hope it's not bad news."

"Oh, I'm sure it isn't. Thank you, Mrs. Pettigrew." Oriel went back upstairs, trying not to appear to be hurrying.

7

*I*n her room, Oriel set down the coal scuttle and tore open the envelope. Inside were several pages written in a bold, slanted hand—but it wasn't from Mrs. McPhail, and there was no check enclosed. She quickly turned to the last page and read the signature. Oriel blinked with astonishment. It was from Morgan Drummond. It contained the most bizarre offer Oriel had ever received.

My dear Miss Banning,

Although our meeting the other day might have seemed the slightest of chance, in retrospect I believe it to have been one of those rare opportunities fate places in our paths.

If you have not made other plans that will take you back to the States and have no other commitments in England, I would like to present a suggestion for a year's employment of a rather unusual kind. It comes with generous financial compensation and future security.

If this interests you, would you please meet me Tuesday next at the offices of my lawyers—Tredwell, Loring, and Sommerville. I sincerely hope you will come. I believe when you learn the details of this plan, you will find that it not only solves your present uncertain position, but also appeals to your obvious sense of adventure.

With all good wishes and the sincere hope that you will agree to come to discuss the possibilities of mutual benefit in this arrangement.

Yours very truly,
Morgan Drummond

A business card was enclosed with the engraved name of the law firm and the address.

Oriel's first question was why? Something vaguely disturbing hovered in her mind. Why would Morgan Drummond contact her in such a mysterious way? Chance and casual gallantry might have explained the invitation to tea the other afternoon, but they did not begin to explain this. Her curiosity was piqued, however. Though Oriel did have some vague misgivings, she put them aside. What did she have to lose at this point? Could this possibly be the miracle she had been taught not to expect?

The Tuesday of Oriel's appointment to meet Morgan Drummond at his lawyer's office, she awoke early. Peering out the window, she saw the sky was leaden, the streets were once again wet. She chose her outfit carefully. Having no idea what type of position Morgan planned to suggest, she decided to wear her best—a persimmon wool dress under a gray fitted coat with a short shoulder cape. Her hat was a black velvet pancake shape with shiny black feathers curled over the small brim. Before she set out, she checked her well-worn map of London for the location of the lawyers' office.

As the bus rattled through the streets, the scene outside the window became more and more impressive. Oriel got off at the entrance to a tree-lined square. A parkway divided tall stone buildings on either side. All the buildings seemed identical, with dark shiny doors and discreet brass plates bearing the names of the firms doing business within.

At last Oriel found the one marked Tredwell, Loring, and Sommerville. The polished door outside opened into a thickly carpeted foyer. A clerk took her name and asked her to follow him down the hall to another office.

"I will let Mr. Tredwell know of your arrival." The clerk bowed slightly.

Oriel glanced around at the handsome furnishings. Leather chairs were placed in front of a marble fireplace, above which hung a gold-framed portrait of a gentleman in a judge's wig and robes.

A moment later, a tall, well-dressed middle-aged man walked toward her. "Good afternoon, Miss Banning. I'm Durwin Tredwell. Mr. Drummond is waiting in the inner office. Later, I will be available to answer any questions you may have—anything you would like clarified about the proposal we have drawn up at Mr. Drummond's request."

"Thank you," Oriel responded.

Mr. Tredwell led the way back to an equally well furnished room. Floor-to-ceiling bookcases lined the walls, filled with maroon leather-bound law books. The tall windows were curtained in green velvet.

Morgan Drummond rose from one of the leather armchairs. Seeing Oriel again in her simple, yet stylish outfit and becoming hat, he decided his judgment had been right. Oriel Banning had a definite air of understated refinement. She would fit in anywhere. Certainly she could not be called beautiful; however, the slight irregularity of features gave her face a distinctive individuality. Besides, hadn't he discovered, to his recent disillusionment, that flawless physical beauty did not guarantee other qualities he also considered important? Instinctively, he felt that Oriel Banning might possess other characteristics he would find admirable and valuable—certainly ones essential for carrying out the plan he was about to present to her.

"Good afternoon, Miss Banning. Thank you for coming." After greeting her, Morgan again sat down in the leather chair opposite the one Tredwell had indicated for her.

Once seated, Oriel studied Morgan Drummond. She was still puzzled as to the motive behind this meeting. His letter had indicated "mutual benefit." What could that possibly be?

Tredwell took his seat behind a massive desk, and a short silence followed. Oriel wondered which of the two men would broach the subject of this meeting. Tredwell seemed in no particular hurry; perhaps he was waiting for his client to begin. That seemed to be the case, because Morgan then came directly to the point.

"Miss Banning, I want you to know I appreciate your coming on such brief notice and under such ambiguous circumstances. However, I could not be more explicit in my letter. The plan I am about to unfold needed to be explained to you in person. You are obviously an intelligent young woman and must be puzzled at the method I have used. I am sure you have even questioned the propriety of coming here. After all, most shipboard acquaintances end at docking." He smiled slightly.

Oriel gave him her complete attention.

"You may remember I told you I had been meeting with my grandfather's lawyers about my inheritance. You may also recall I said it was quite complicated. Grandfather left some strange conditions to his will, conditions I found not only difficult, but nearly impossible to meet."

He broke off, his mouth tightening into a stern line. "Actually, I have been trying with the lawyers to work out some way to modify or alter the terms." He sighed and shook his head. "However, it has finally been concluded that I must comply with them or lose all of the inheritance. This would affect not only me personally, but also many of the institutions—charitable and altruistic foundations—that my grandfather expected me to continue to support. Out of loyalty to him, I feel I must do this.

He paused and then began again. "Let me explain. Grandfather came to America as a poverty-stricken boy from Ireland during the devastating potato famine in 1840. He was the only one of his family to leave Ireland. All the others had died when they were forced off their farms by absentee landlords. My grandfather had brains, courage, and luck; he prospered, married, raised a family, and gradually became very successful. Unfortunately, his three sons, one of whom was my father, all died young. I'm the only remaining Drummond, so I became my grandfather's heir."

Morgan glanced at Tredwell as if for confirmation. The lawyer nodded solemnly. Morgan continued, "Grandfather never forgot his humble beginnings, even though he had become a very rich man. He felt great nostalgia for the land he'd been forced to leave and for all things Irish. On a trip to Ireland, he went back to the village where he had often walked past the great manor house the villagers called the castle. As a barefoot lad, he'd peer through the gates. Now it had fallen into a bad state of disrepair, for the English aristocracy had departed once the land no longer provided them the wherewithal to live luxurious lives. On impulse, Grandfather bought the castle of his youth, intending to retire there and bring it back to its original splendor. Sadly, when he went back to the States, he became ill and was never able to return and carry out his plan."

Morgan's voice had a bitter edge as he said, "Strange, isn't it, that the dead are at peace and their survivors are left with the trials and tribulations of the world?" He shrugged. "So now the castle belongs to me—that is, *if* I decide to carry out Grandfather's plan and fulfill the conditions of his will. With that comes all his other wealth and the responsibilities that go with it. However, this is not my decision alone." He paused.

"I'll be quite blunt, Miss Banning. You may have heard I was engaged to Miss Edwina Parker. I believe it was common knowledge on board ship." He seemed to be quite used to the idea of being the subject of gossip. "Our plan was to be married here in London, where she has been staying. When I found out the conditions of my inheritance—that I must live with my bride for a full year in the castle in Ireland—and told Edwina . . ." He gave a harsh laugh. "Well, I can only leave it to your imagination when I say she did not go along with such an idea."

His expression changed. A shadow fell across it, hardening the line of his mouth, setting his jaw. "Maybe I could have handled it more diplomatically. Or maybe that wouldn't have mattered—maybe nothing would have mattered. You see, my fiancée absolutely refused to marry me under those conditions. Her exact words were, 'What? Stay in a drafty old castle in an isolated village through a wretched Irish winter? You must be out of your mind!'" Quoting Edwina, Morgan's voice shook with anger. He continued, "The result is our engagement has been broken."

Not knowing what else to say, Oriel murmured, "I'm sorry."

Morgan held up his hand. "I didn't tell you this to gain your sympathy, Miss Banning, but rather to explain why I am seeking your help."

"My help?" Oriel was still confused.

"I wouldn't have thought to involve you with my personal problems if I didn't suspect you have your own crisis at the moment—one that is far more crucial in some ways. That's why I want to make you an offer—a legal proposition, actually—that might solve both our dilemmas."

"And what is that, Mr. Drummond? How does this concern me?"

Morgan's gaze riveted on her. "This is what I propose. It must be clear to you by now that Mrs. McPhail is not going to live up to her promise to send you your pay. I am also assuming you have not been able to secure a job since I last saw you. I am suggesting an alternative for you to consider."

Oriel clasped her hands tightly in her lap as Morgan explained. She would enter into an "in name only" marriage with him and live at the castle in Kilmara for one year, legally fulfilling the requirements of his grandfather's will. At the end of the year, they could obtain a quiet annulment, claiming an unconsummated marriage. At that time, Oriel would collect the large amount of money placed in a trust fund for her in return for her agreement to stay the year.

"This has been discussed thoroughly with my lawyers, as Tredwell here can assure you," Morgan stated. "Everything will be spelled out legally, duly witnessed, and signed. The lawyers will make sure everything is done with utmost legality." Morgan's mouth twisted upward as he glanced at Tredwell. "This is a well-known firm of unquestioned integrity and propriety. The contract we sign will be valid and carried out to the letter. Even if you have doubts about me, you would be guaranteed complete protection by this document."

Speechless, Oriel looked from Morgan to Tredwell, then back to Morgan.

"Naturally, we expect you would want to think it over carefully, consult someone you trust, ask advice," Tredwell said.

"Naturally," concurred Morgan, not taking his gaze off Oriel, weighing her reaction. Oriel's candid eyes met his. She did not seem so much shocked as interested. This confirmed his impression of her intellectual curiosity. It was, however, impossible to tell what she would decide. He waited.

The silence seemed to lengthen interminably. Then, drawing a long breath, Oriel said, "You have been quite frank with me, Mr. Drummond. I shall be equally honest with you. I *am* in desperate financial straits. My plans have not worked out as I had hoped. Giving my former employer the benefit of the doubt, there is still a chance I may receive my salary check and reference. In that case, it would be best for me to return to America, where my chances of employment are better than they are here."

Oriel paused. "I have no immediate family, no one whose advice I could seek in regard to this matter. Although agreeing to your plan would help me over my present difficulties, whether in the long run it would be a good thing to do, I am not sure."

"At least you haven't completely rejected my idea, nor do you seem offended," Morgan said, a glint of amusement—and admiration—in his eyes.

"I have lived on the edge of poverty most of my adult life, Mr. Drummond, so the possibility of financial security is tempting, whatever the conditions. However, my position with the McPhails was supposed to have offered me that and it has turned out quite differently. Naturally, I am cautious. My situation has grown more urgent every day, so I am forced to make a decision quickly. That is why you might understand how your proposal—I should say offer of *employment*—seems less shocking than it otherwise might. Of course, I would need time to consider."

She met Morgan's intense gaze. To think of spending a year with this man under the oddest of circumstances seemed bizarre, indeed. And yet . . .

"As long as we are being frank with each other, Miss Banning, there is one more thing," Morgan said, squinting a little. "I must ask you a question that would seem intrusively personal if we were not discussing a *business* proposition. I must assume there is no *romantic* interest in your life at present who would object to your making such a contract, who might at some later date cause a problem?"

Taken aback, Oriel did not answer at once.

"You see, I wouldn't want any old attachments coming up. Someone from your past suddenly appearing on the scene would be very awkward. Although our association would be strictly a *business* arrangement, there *are* appearances to be kept up, especially in a small village like Kilmara, where all eyes will be upon the residents of the castle. You understand, I'm sure, the importance of the public image of a happily married couple, spending their first year together on the idyllic Irish seacoast, as was my grandfather's hope." Morgan's mouth moved into a wry smile; then he went on. "You can understand how awkward someone with a romantic interest suddenly showing up would be."

How ironic the question seemed to Oriel. When, in the poverty-driven past few years, would she have had time for a romantic relationship? But a man used to moving in high-society circles, where shallow flirtations and casual romances were commonplace, would not understand that. In other circumstances, she might have considered Morgan's probing inappropriate, but that was before she had come to such desperate straits.

Returning his calculating look, Oriel simply shook her head and replied coolly, "No, there is no one."

Morgan nodded as if satisfied and did not question her further. "I sincerely hope you will accept this proposal, Miss Banning. The castle *is* isolated, and I don't care much for entertaining. Still, there is much to enjoy for a person not given to social life. I believe someone with your education and background will find much to appreciate at Kilmara. My grandfather's estate has a hundred acres overlooking the ocean on the southern coast of Ireland. There is a well-stocked library, and you will certainly be free to go up to Dublin, a half-day's journey, to shop or attend the theater."

"How soon must I let you know?" Oriel inquired.

"The sooner the better as far as I'm concerned, so that my year at Kilmara can begin. But I certainly want to give you adequate time to think over the matter and consider your answer. A week? Perhaps ten days at the latest." His voice deepened as if to emphasize his next words, "I can promise you I will carry out my end of our bargain in every way. You will have no regrets if you agree."

"I will give it my fullest consideration. Now I think I must go."

Tredwell got to his feet at once. "Of course. Let me see you out."

Morgan rose also. "Good day, Miss Banning. I will be waiting for your answer."

Tredwell escorted her to the firm's carriage, which had been brought around to the front of the building to take her home. As he handed her in, the lawyer said courteously, "I am at your disposal, Miss Banning, for any assistance you might need to reach your decision. You need only send me a note."

"Thank you. You have been most kind," Oriel replied.

As the carriage moved off, Oriel let out a long sigh. What a curious turn of events. It was all rather overwhelming. She might indeed call upon Mr. Tredwell for answers to her myriad questions. First she had a great deal of soul-searching to do.

For the next few days, all Oriel could think about was Morgan Drummond's startling proposal. She paced around her small room and went for long walks, considering the advantages and disadvantages of accepting. She vacillated between disregarding the whole thing and wondering if it was some sort of miracle.

She had so many questions. For example, the startling information that Morgan's marriage to the beautiful Edwina had been called off—what was *she* thinking? Her engagement was broken, her plans in shambles. Oriel recalled all the planning Neecy's wedding had required. Edwina must have been planning the same kind of society affair. How upset and angry Edwina must have been to call all that off at the last minute. She must have been dead-set against spending a year in Ireland to break her engagement. Perhaps that was what the quarrel was about the day Oriel saw them in the lobby of the hotel. How would Edwina feel about their arrangement?

To live a year in an Irish castle sounded like a fantasy come true, especially considering her current situation. On the other hand, there must be pitfalls Oriel could not foresee.

She searched for hidden hazards, unknown perils. She hardly knew Morgan Drummond. Could she trust him? What kind of year would it be, spent with a man wounded by the woman he loved? What repercussions from his own unhappiness would fall upon her?

Yet deep within Oriel was the longing for a richer life, a life protected and safe. The horror of her experience with Jarman was still vivid. His was the kind of world in which most women fending for themselves were forced to live. She had struggled to support herself for so long that the idea of having her future so well secured was tempting. Still, Oriel wavered.

She knew her own nature, her faults as well as her strengths. She had survived the hardships of these past years determined that things would get better for her if she took advantage of the opportunities God sent her way. She was also a romantic, clinging to the hope that one day she would find a true love. If she accepted Morgan Drummond's offer, would she be forfeiting that kind of love for herself? Would entering into a loveless marriage ruin her own chances later on?

After two days of debate and heartfelt prayer, Oriel woke to gray skies, still unresolved, soon another week's rent due. She knew she would not be able to force herself to go back to the workshop and demand her rightful pay from that wretch, Jarman. Common sense and practicality began to win over all the arguments to the contrary. Perhaps this *was* God's way of providing for her. She decided to go to the offices of Tredwell, Loring, and Sommerville and see Morgan's lawyer once more. Only then could she make her final decision.

Seated again in Mr. Tredwell's office that afternoon, Oriel listened intently as Mr. Tredwell began to explain. It was a repetition of everything Morgan had already told her. Everything would be handled with extreme confidentiality, including the ultimate deed—the annulment at the end of the year. When Mr. Tredwell named the amount Morgan would place in the trust fund to be paid to Oriel at the end of the year in Ireland, she had to control a gasp. Her mind whirled.

With that much money, Oriel could buy what she desired most—freedom. She'd have freedom from constant anxiety, from the never-ending search for a position with adequate wages, from the fear of poverty in old age. If she were careful, the money could provide her with lifetime security. She could travel, maybe even buy a little house. For years Oriel had lived in a series of rented flats, teacher's quarters, and other people's houses. Now, something she had thought was forever beyond her means, a home of her own, was within the realm of possibility.

With a stroke of the pen, all this could be a reality. All that remained was her signature. Was the risk of signing this strange bargain worth the rewards?

Tredwell's discerning gaze rested upon Oriel Banning as she read over the document he had handed her. Morgan's judgment of her character seemed to be correct. If Morgan was determined to go through with the strange scheme, he may have chosen the best candidate for the bizarre arrangement. She was taking long enough to go over the agreement paper, reading the fine print. Tredwell silently congratulated her caution. Unobtrusively, he took out his watch and checked the time.

Just then, Oriel raised her head and looked at him. Her eyes—her best feature, large, hazel, and long-lashed—met his in a look both intelligent and candid. Would Oriel Banning sign or wouldn't she?

Oriel packed feverishly. Since she had signed the agreement, she had kept herself constantly busy. Having made up her mind, she dared not look back. Second thoughts were now out of the question. It was too late. As she rushed through the preparations, she kept reminding herself that it would be only for a year. Maybe it would be the greatest adventure of her life.

She was to meet Morgan Drummond at the Registry Office later that morning. The terms of the agreement were very clear and seemed reasonable. Oriel had stopped worrying about the right or wrong of it. Her own motives were simply survival. God had sent her an opportunity and she had grabbed it.

But Morgan? His reasons seemed far more complicated. Even without fulfilling the terms of his grandfather's will, he would still have been wealthy. Was it some kind of distorted revenge? Oriel wondered. There was no mistaking the strong emotions under that sophisticated surface. His broken engagement must have been a blow to his pride. Resentment, anger, and bitterness might seethe beneath his outer calm. Would those volatile feelings ever be turned against her? No, she decided. Emotion did not enter into their relationship. Theirs was strictly a business agreement, nothing more. She had to believe that. They were practically strangers; partners for the length of a year's contract—nothing more.

Oriel buttoned the jacket of her blue suit. As she anchored her bonnet with a pin and adjusted the polka-dot veil, she took a brief glance in the mirror. Hardly a bridal outfit, but then she was hardly a typical bride. She thought ruefully of her childhood dreams of weddings. This would not be like those fantasies—just an impersonal Registry Office ceremony, with Mr. Tredwell and one other court-appointed witness. After the signing of a legal document, it would be over. She would be married to Morgan Drummond, at least for a year.

Her suitcases opened, Oriel made a quick survey to be sure she had not forgotten to pack anything. The rented room where she had spent some of the most worried nights of her life was now empty, stripped of even the most basic personal belongings. Leaving here, she would leave not a trace of herself.

She shut her suitcases and fastened them, then glanced at her lapel watch. It was time to go, time to begin the next phase of her life. Morgan was sending a carriage for her and she wanted to be ready when it came.

Just as she stepped out into the hallway with her suitcases, Nola, leaving for work, came down the steps. "Oh, my, aren't you looking chipper this morning!" Her gaze went to the suitcases. "You're leaving? Did you find work, then?"

Oriel hesitated. What would Nola think of her strange bargain with Morgan Drummond? Quickly she juggled the facts. "Well, yes, in a way. I'm going to Ireland."

"*Ireland!* Oh, my! That's a long way off. I hope they're paying you well. What kind of work will you be doing?"

Realizing Nola assumed she'd secured a job, Oriel replied, "A sort of companion."

"Well, I do wish you luck, dearie. I was getting worried about you—looking so long and hard with nothing turning up."

"Thank you. That was very kind of you."

"Well, is there anything I can do for you? Here, let me take one of them bags." They started down the stairs together.

Nola's sincerity touched Oriel. She suddenly realized Nola was the only person in London that knew her or cared the slightest bit about what happened to her. When they came down into the entry hall, Nola put her finger to her lips, winking at Oriel as they slipped by their landlady's door. Once outside, she set down the suitcase and adjusted her hat, saying, "I've got to be on my way or I'll be late for work, and old Snyder, my boss, don't like that one bit. You sure there's nothing I can do? Maybe you could give me your address, just in case it don't work out or you get some mail?"

Oriel considered that. Even at this late date, Mrs. McPhail *might* come through with the check and letter of reference. Since she'd given the clerk at the Claridge this address, it would be sent here.

"Oh, would you? That would be very kind. I am rather expecting a letter—from my last employer. It would have my last month's wages in it as well." Nola, a working girl herself, would certainly understand the importance of such a letter.

Addresses exchanged, Nola started down the steps. Halfway she stopped, then ran back up and gave Oriel a hug. "Good luck, dearie, and the Lord bless!" she said. Then with a wave, she hurried back down the steps and along the street toward the bus stop.

Oriel, looking after her, felt quick tears. Why this impulsive gesture by someone she had known only a few weeks? Had Nola seen some vulnerability in her, some of the anxiety in her eyes? Whatever the reason, Nola's show of concern warmed her heart.

A few minutes later, the splendid carriage Morgan had hired to pick her up arrived. Oriel was glad Nola wasn't there to see it. She surely might have drawn the wrong conclusions about Oriel's job as a companion. With a mixture of apprehension and excitement, Oriel got into the carriage. It started off, carrying her inexorably to her destiny.

*The Steamer Donnegal, en route
from Liverpool to Dublin*

April 1895

*I*t was with an eerie sense of déjà vu that Oriel again
stood in swirling fog at the ship's rail. This time it
was on the steamer *Donnegal* departing for Ireland.
She nestled her chin into the mink collar of the short black
Persian lamb cape, relishing its warmth. Morgan had given
it to her after they left the Registry Office. As she opened the
box from the famous furrier, he had said offhandedly, "Irish
weather is miserable."

The wedding gift was as practical and unsentimental as
the civil ceremony itself had been. Oriel had not expected
to feel emotional about it, so she had not been prepared for
her own reaction. In the short time since she had signed the
agreement, she had been reassuring herself that it was simply a contract and *not* a real marriage. Yet, when the moment came to give her responses, she had felt dizzy. She had
always regarded marriage as a sacred step taken by two

deeply committed people. To regard it as a temporary contract suddenly seemed wrong.

As she hesitated, Oriel had looked at Morgan, wondering what he was feeling. Was he thinking of another ceremony, another bride? Conscious that both the magistrate and Morgan were staring at her, she had breathlessly responded, "Yes, I will."

Then it was over.

From the Registry Office, they had gone to collect Morgan's luggage at the Claridge. They had had a quiet lunch before catching the train to Liverpool. On the train, Morgan had read the *Times* while Oriel gazed out at the passing landscape, trying not to dwell on the strange circumstances.

In Liverpool, they had boarded the overnight boat to Dublin. Upon boarding, Oriel had been shown to her small but nicely appointed single cabin. She wondered if the steward thought it strange that the Drummonds had separate accommodations.

She had come back up on deck, where she now stood in the fog. Within a few minutes, Morgan joined her at the rail. The salt-scented air and thin mist brought back Oriel's vivid memory of their first encounter on board the ocean liner *Mesalina*. At that time, she could never have imagined the strange turn of events that had brought them to this moment.

Watching the lights of Liverpool recede as the boat slid into the sea, neither of them spoke. Eventually Morgan said, "Good night," and went below.

When the steamer docked the next morning, Morgan and Oriel were met by a coachman in a dark green uniform trimmed with gilt braid. He greeted Morgan respectfully and led the way to a handsome black carriage with bronze trim hitched to two coal-black horses. The interior was lined and cushioned with a velvety plush. This, Oriel thought, was the kind of comfort the rich took for granted. After her days of riding rickety trolleys, omnibuses, and other plebeian means of transportation, traveling in style might be very easy to get used to—maybe too easy.

After their luggage was loaded, they rolled through the city streets and out into the surrounding countryside. At first, Oriel was too busy looking out the window to note that Morgan had slipped into a moody silence. When he failed to respond to several of her comments, she observed that he was slumped in one corner, his chin resting on his doubled fist, elbow propped on the ledge, staring morosely out the window on his side of the carriage.

Was this his reaction to returning to Ireland? Was it *that* depressing to him? Of course, Oriel realized he was not with the companion of his choice. He had hoped to be bringing Edwina here as his bride. Oriel felt that tact was appropriate and after that was silent. Soon the rocking motion of the carriage made her drowsy and she drifted off to sleep.

She awoke with a jerk at a sudden jolting of the carriage wheels. Peering out the window, Oriel saw dark clouds overhead. Strong, gusty winds blew against the swaying carriage. They were no longer traveling on the main road but had turned off onto a rutted narrow one. Oriel turned toward Morgan, who evidently anticipated her question.

"We're almost there," he said. "Another twenty minutes or so and we'll be in the village of Kilmara. Then it's only a short distance to Drummond Castle." His voice held an edge. His expression was unreadable, and Oriel was left to interpret it on her own. Was Morgan already regretting their arrangement?

As for herself, Oriel had mixed feelings at their approach to Drummond Castle, the place where she would be spending the next year of her life. She determined to make the best of things.

When Morgan spoke again, it was to say, "There it is, straight ahead."

Oriel would never forget her first sight of the castle. On the crest of the hillside stood a majestic stone structure silhouetted against the purple-gray sky. It was so amazingly like every castle Oriel had ever imagined that she almost expected to see a moat and hear the creaking of chains as a drawbridge was let down for them to cross and armored knights rode out to greet them.

Nothing so dramatic happened, however. In another few minutes, they rumbled through scrolled iron gates and up the long, curving driveway.

As the carriage came to a stop, Morgan announced, "Well, here we are. Drummond Castle."

The massive carved front door opened and two men hurried down the stone steps. One opened the door while the other, a bald, dour-faced fellow wearing a dark coat, bowed formally. "Good evening, sir."

"Good evening, Finnegan. May I present Mrs. Drummond."

"Madam." Finnegan extended his hand to assist Oriel out of the carriage. As she stepped down, he spoke words Oriel could not understand, *"Cead mai failte."*

Morgan placed his hand under her elbow and they mounted the steps leading into the house. Curious, Oriel whispered, "What did he say?"

"It was a traditional Gaelic welcome. We are wished a long and happy life together here."

Oriel did not miss the hint of irony in his voice. Ironic, indeed. Their agreement was for only a year, and happiness? Happiness was not in the bargain she had made with Morgan Drummond.

Escorted by Finnegan, they walked through a massive carved door into the vast front hall. Tapestries hung from the vaulted ceiling and suits of armor stood in shadowed alcoves.

"May I introduce Mrs. Nesbitt," Finnegan said with obvious deference in his tone. Oriel knew the housekeeper was always next to the butler in the pecking order of household staff.

At Oriel's greeting, the woman inclined her head but did not extend her hand nor curtsey. Instead, she met Oriel's friendly smile with a chilling reserve.

The housekeeper's appearance was formidable. Her iron-gray hair was pulled back severely from a face with a prominent nose and narrow mouth. Her extreme pallor emphasized the brilliance of her small dark eyes, which regarded Oriel with suspicion. Perhaps it was only natural for someone who had been in charge to be wary, even suspicious, of a new mistress, Oriel decided. Then a second thought struck. Did Mrs. Nesbitt expect someone else—Edwina Parker, perhaps? There had probably been a picture of her in the society papers when the engagement was announced. Maybe the change of plans had not been made known to the staff.

Oriel thrust those questions aside and moved on to face the curious eyes of the stout, red-faced cook, Mrs. Mills, then the two rosy-cheeked maids, Molly and Carleen, and the two footmen, Conan and William.

These formalities over, Morgan said to Oriel, "Since it's been a long day, you must be weary from travel. I suggest we both make it an early night." He then said a few words to the housekeeper and turned again to Oriel. "Mrs. Nesbitt will show you to your room and have a supper tray brought up to you."

Before Oriel could respond, Morgan turned abruptly and walked away, leaving her standing in the great hall alone. Although she had not prepared herself for what to expect when they reached the castle, it was a shock to be left so completely on her own.

"Mrs. Drummond . . ." The housekeeper's use of her unfamiliar title brought Oriel sharply back to attention. "If you'll come this way." Mrs. Nesbitt gestured toward the shadowy staircase.

Oriel nodded. Conscious of being under the servants' surveillance, she followed the thin figure to the stairway. She wondered if the servants thought it unusual that the newlyweds were not sharing the master suite, then reminded herself that household staff in such manor houses as this one simply accepted the way of the gentry even if they did think them strange.

Oriel had to hurry to keep up with the housekeeper's swift pace up the winding steps. Reaching the top, she moved along a dark, drafty corridor to the end, where Mrs. Nesbitt opened a door.

Oriel stepped into a huge bedroom, dominated by a poster bed canopied in heavy damask. In a windowed alcove was a dressing table and a chaise lounge. Two wing chairs were placed on either side of the fireplace, where a fire had been laid but not yet lit. The room felt cold and had a damp, unused smell. Involuntarily, Oriel shivered.

"I'll send Molly up to get the fire started, ma'am," Mrs. Nesbitt said. "We weren't sure what time you'd get here. Didn't want to burn a fire for nothing." She moved to the door, saying, "I'll send up a tray for you, ma'am. If you need anything else, just ring." She pointed toward the tapestry bell pull by the massive stone fireplace.

As the door closed behind the housekeeper, Oriel stood in the middle of the room looking about her. Rubbing her arms to warm herself, she walked over to the windows. The wind moaned and she shivered again.

Edwina Parker's words as quoted by Morgan echoed in her mind: "What? Stay in a drafty old castle in an isolated village through a wretched Irish winter? You must be out of your mind!"

Just then, a gust of wind blew open one of the windows, crashing it against the outside wall. Startled, Oriel ran over to drag it shut. An icy blast of cold air swept over her.

Shuddering, Oriel wondered if Edwina had been right. Was it *she*, Oriel Banning, who had been out of her mind to agree to stay a year at Drummond Castle?

10

Although tired from all the traveling and tension, Oriel did not sleep well her first night at Drummond Castle. Her room was cavernous, filled with grotesque shadows cast onto the walls from the firelight. The storm that had threatened for the last few hours of their journey finally broke. The wind whistled down the chimney, sending sparks flying from the fireplace. Rain pounded on the slate roof with a staccato clattering sound. A clap of thunder rattled the windows. Oriel sat up in bed, clutching the covers. After that, it seemed hours before she could settle into a sound sleep. The last thing Oriel heard before drifting off was the pelting of rain against the windows.

What next woke her Oriel wasn't sure, nor was she sure how long she had been asleep. A murky, gray light filtered in between the folds of the draperies Oriel had drawn across the windows before she went to bed. The fire had gone out, and the room felt chilly and damp. As Oriel came fully awake, she heard a persistent clicking noise. One of the latches must have come loose. She threw aside the satin-covered quilt, got gingerly out of bed, and ran in her bare feet over to shut the casement.

Pushing aside the curtain, she reached out for the handle when she saw something. Just below, a hooded figure moved rapidly through the mist, a cape billowing behind it like a huge sail. The form seemed to glide across the grounds before disappearing at the stone wall. The morning fog hid what lay beyond the wall. Who or what was it? Could it be some kind of optical illusion of fog and gray dawn light? It had passed so swiftly Oriel wasn't even sure she'd actually seen it. She closed the window and fastened it. Hurrying back to bed, she dove under the quilt and burrowed her head in the pillows.

Some time later, she woke to the sound of crackling wood as a fire was being lit. Oriel sat up and saw Molly, the maid, sitting on her heels on the hearth, using a hand bellows to get the blaze going.

Hearing the movement behind her, Molly turned and gave Oriel a smile. "Good morning, ma'am. I brought up your tea. Will you have it in bed or would you like to sit in front of the fireplace?"

"I'll get up. Thank you."

Being waited on was such a novel experience, Oriel could only wonder what the maid would think if she knew what her situation had been only a few days ago.

As she took her first sip of the hearty tea and buttered a slice of soda bread, Oriel remembered what she had seen from her window earlier. In the light of day, with a snapping fire brightening the room and the solid presence of the cheerful maid, the eerie sight seemed unreal. Had it been simply her own sleepy state, a fragment of a dream? Last night she had been exhausted from her travels and the tension of her new role. She could have imagined it.

Finishing her breakfast, Oriel went to the window and looked out. The storm's wind that had blown rain against the windows and wakened her during the restless night had stopped. The sky showed signs of turning blue, and the soft green of the hills emerged in the distance. As Oriel stood there, she saw in the distance the outline of a building.

"Come here for a minute, Molly," Oriel called over her shoulder. "What is that building?"

"Which one, ma'am?" Molly came over to stand behind her.

"Over there." She pointed.

"Oh, that's just a pile of rubble, ma'am—what's left of an old monastery from many years ago."

"It looks interesting. Is there no one there anymore?"

"Oh, no, ma'am, for sure." There was a tiny pause before the girl said, "But some folks say . . ."

Whatever Molly was about to add was interrupted by a sharp rap on the bedroom door. It was Mrs. Nesbitt, the housekeeper. She gave Molly a pointed look, and the maid hurried out.

"Good morning, Mrs. Drummond."

Oriel cloaked her sense of surprise at being so addressed. "Good morning, Mrs. Nesbitt. Won't you sit down?"

"No, thank you, madam." Mrs. Nesbitt drew herself up coldly, as if Oriel had crossed some invisible threshold of proper decorum. "I just came to inquire if you want the cook to come up to discuss the menu or if you would prefer I do it?"

Feeling rebuffed by the housekeeper's condescending tone of voice, Oriel said quickly, "Oh, I think it best for you to carry on as usual, Mrs. Nesbitt—until I'm more settled."

The housekeeper gave a curt nod and departed, leaving Oriel feeling somewhat unnerved. It was almost as if Mrs. Nesbitt was trying to intimidate her. No, that was foolish, Oriel told herself. It would take time to establish herself with the staff. The housekeeper and Finnegan had been running the household without supervision for several years. The staff was probably apprehensive about how things were going to be with a new mistress.

In the meantime, Oriel had plenty to do. She spent most of the day unpacking, and with Molly's help, got her wardrobe sorted and hung in the huge armoire. She could tell the maid was impressed by her clothes, not knowing most of them were secondhand items.

Once during the afternoon, Oriel looked out her window and saw Morgan stride out across the stone terrace and push through the wrought-iron gate in the stone wall at the end of the wide lawn. "Where does that lead to?" Oriel asked Molly, pointing in the direction Morgan had disappeared.

Molly peered over her shoulder. "Oh, that's the path down to the beach, ma'am. It goes along the cliffs and down to the cove."

Oriel said nothing more, but made a mental note of it. She would like to explore all the surroundings of Drummond Castle in time. Before Molly left again, she told Oriel dinner would be at seven.

At five minutes to seven, Oriel went downstairs. She wore a dress Neecy had considered too plain, a simply cut blue velvet, with a deep neckline and long tapered sleeves. Morgan was just crossing the wide hall. He greeted Oriel rather absently, and they entered the dining room together. His expression was much the same as it had been last evening upon their arrival. Oriel was determined to ignore Morgan's moodiness and make the dinner hour as pleasant as possible.

The huge dining room was lighted by candles in wall sconces, a wrought-iron chandelier, and flickering tapers in a branched silver candelabra on the long table. Several dark tapestries depicting hunting scenes hung on the walls and over the huge fireplace at the far end of the room.

"Good evening, madam," Finnegan greeted her as he drew back a high-backed, richly carved chair for her. Morgan seated himself at the other end. It was only then Oriel noticed a third place was set.

Surprised, she remarked, "I didn't know we were expecting a dinner guest."

Morgan lifted his head and glanced at the other place setting. A fierce frown drew his heavy brows together. "We're not." Motioning to the footman standing at the sideboard, he ordered, "Take that away."

The footman looked startled. He turned beet red and glanced at Finnegan, who was overseeing the serving. Tension crackled in the air. Oriel felt it, but did not understand what had caused it. For a full minute, Finnegan did not move, nor did the footman.

Then Morgan banged his fist on the table and roared, "I said take that plate away. I don't want to see that done again, do you hear?"

The anger in his voice set Oriel's heart pounding.

Finnegan gave an imperceptible nod to Conan the footman, who moved forward quickly, swept up the setting, and left the room with it.

Soon the footman came back and began to serve the meal. After such an upsetting scene, Oriel found she had little appetite. She expected some sort of apology or explanation for the outburst, but none was forthcoming. Morgan made no effort to engage in conversation during the rest of dinner. Course after course was brought and removed, hardly touched.

Not wishing to offend the cook, Oriel took a few bites of the dessert pudding, then placed her spoon on the plate. She folded her hands in her lap, awaiting the signal from Morgan that he was finished and Oriel could excuse herself. Oriel longed to escape to the privacy of her room. Her first dinner at Drummond Castle had been completely ruined.

At length, Morgan drained his glass and stood. They left the dining room together. In the hall, he said a brief "Good night," turned on his heel, and walked down the hall to his own suite.

That was it. He was making it clear that as far as he was concerned, their marriage was an arrangement that needed neither courtesy nor accommodation to social amenities. Oriel mounted the broad stairway and went slowly down the shadowy corridor to her bedroom. The scene at dinner had been deeply disturbing.

Since their arrival in Ireland, Morgan Drummond had undergone a significant change. Gone was the sophisticated man Oriel had thought attractive, interesting, and intelligent. This moody, morose, rageful man who had taken his place was a frightening stranger. It was obvious he was desperately unhappy—not only about being in Ireland and at Drummond Castle—but also about being with the wrong woman.

When Molly came to turn down the bed, Oriel noticed the maid seemed more subdued than she had in the morning. Oriel presumed all the servants had heard about the uproar at the dinner table. Whatever was going on, the household servants knew. Oriel decided to ask Molly about the third place setting.

Given the opening, Molly was more than anxious to tell her the story behind the ruckus. It seemed, like many old houses, Drummond Castle had a legend.

"'Tis a story I've heard ever since I was a wee child," Molly began. "My own granny swears it's true and that once, as a little girl, she saw Shaleen herself!"

"Shaleen who?"

"Shaleen O'Connor, ma'am." Molly's eyes widened at her ignorance. "'Tis said she walks along the beach looking for lost ships and comes up to check the castle gates at night to see that they're not locked."

"I don't think I understand."

"Well, ma'am, if you like, I'll tell you about it." Molly warmed to her task of enlightening Oriel. "In the days of Queen Elizabeth when the English were fighting for lordship of the seas and battling the threat of the Spanish Armada, Shaleen O'Connor was a legendary pirate queen. The O'Connors were a powerful tribe, and Shaleen was the undisputed mistress of the many hundred islands and inlets about the bay. Her fame spread to London and to the court itself, where she was received by the queen. The queen welcomed her since Shaleen's band had destroyed many of the Spanish ships and plundered others shipwrecked on the treacherous Irish coast.

"However, on Shaleen's return trip to Ireland, her ship ran short of supplies and put into the harbor just below the land of Drummond Castle. In those days, this house and land were owned by Sir Tristam Lawrence. While Shaleen's men were stowing provisions on board, she knocked at the gates of the castle seeking hospitality.

"'Tis said the family was at dinner and she was refused admittance. This put Shaleen into a fury, and later she kidnapped the infant son and heir of the master and sailed off with him. Legend has it that part of the ransom paid for the child was the sworn agreement that the gates of the castle would always remain open and a place at the table always be set for the head of the O'Connor clan.

"And that was always done, ma'am, even up to the time the last of the Lawrence family left here, before Mr. Drummond's grandfather bought the castle," Molly said in a whispery voice. "Terrible things would happen if it wasn't done—at least, that's what people always said."

In spite of herself, Oriel shivered.

"Begging your pardon, ma'am, but if I was you and had any influence over the master, I'd persuade him to continue the practice of setting a place for Shaleen."

"Mr. Drummond must know about this legend, doesn't he?"

Molly pursed her mouth thoughtfully before answering. "Well, ma'am, Mr. Drummond's only been here twice before this. He stayed at the hotel in town the last time, come up here during the day to check out everything and make sure provisions were ordered, the wine cellar filled, and the beds made fresh."

Molly hesitated. "It's common talk in the village he don't care for Ireland nor living here at the castle." Molly gave her head a little toss. "Perhaps that's why he dislikes our traditions as well."

Something warned Oriel she had best drop the subject at this point. Did Molly know the only reason Morgan was here now was to insure his inheritance? While she had no intention of discussing the matter further, it bothered Oriel that she sensed a real resentment in Molly for Morgan. Did the rest of the staff feel the same way? If they believed what Molly had reported, that he had no love for the land or the country, it could mean nothing but trouble during this year.

Was accepting Morgan Drummond's bargain the worst mistake Oriel had ever made?

By the time Oriel had been at Drummond Castle a full week, she had reached the conclusion that her time here would be solitary indeed if she depended on Morgan for company. After a week of days left to her own devices, silent dinners, and long evenings alone, that had become clear. But then, what had she expected—for Morgan to see that she was constantly occupied and amused? Oriel had learned early in life to make the best of whatever circumstances in which she found herself. She would do the same here. What this year was like would be up to her.

This part of Ireland was beautiful, as she had already discovered. Although the spring weather had been stormy, signs of life and growth were everywhere. The terraced lawns were a rich velvety green, with trees and shrubs in various shades of emerald and jade. Giant rhododendron bushes lined the driveway with heavy blooms of rich pink, magenta, and purple.

So far, Oriel had only explored the castle grounds, but she had every intention of venturing farther. She had thought that would be something she and Morgan could enjoy together. After the strange incident at dinner her second night at Drummond Castle, however, she realized Morgan did not share her enthusiasm for the land.

One morning of her second week at Drummond Castle, Oriel went to her bedroom window to check the weather. For the first time, the heavy mist did not obscure her view. It would be a good day to take a walk to the cliffs, see the ocean. Just then something caught her attention—a small stone building with a pointed roof just beyond the terraced hedge of the gardens.

Oriel was eager to explore the sea, the cliffs, the lush green countryside, and the quaint little town of Kilmara. She would have to investigate the intriguing little building too.

She ate breakfast, then dressed in a tweed walking skirt and sturdy boots before going downstairs. Carleen, the other maid, was dusting, and Oriel stopped to ask, "How far is it to the village?"

"About three miles, ma'am."

"An easy walk, then?"

The girl's bright eyes widened in surprise. "Sure—that is if you're used to walking."

"Oh, I'm used to walking." Oriel smiled, remembering the miles of city streets she had walked in her job search in London.

Oriel was at the door when Carleen's voice halted her. "Shall I tell the cook you'll be back for luncheon?"

Oriel paused. Why should she hurry back to another meal eaten alone or opposite a glum Morgan. "No, Carleen, I won't be back until tea." She said good-bye and left the house.

Oriel walked down the drive, stopping here and there to examine a clump of white narcissus coming into bloom or touch the delicate petals of pink and lavender wood violets half-hidden under the trees. As she straightened up and began walking again, she noticed a ruddy-faced gardener, a short distance away. He had been observing her with some curiosity. "Good morning," she called, waving. "The flowers are lovely!"

He looked startled.

"I'm Mrs. Drummond," Oriel said, and the name sounded odd and unfamiliar even to her. "The new mistress here."

The man quickly took off his cap, mumbled, "Patrick's me name, ma'am," then head averted, he moved away.

Oriel stood there for a moment feeling rebuffed. Then, with a slight shrug, she walked on. The gardener was probably just shy or maybe just not used to American informality. It would take time for the people at Drummond Castle to warm up to her.

When she got to the wrought-iron gates, Oriel recalled the legend of Shaleen O'Connor, and as she pushed through the gates, she wondered if they were always kept unlocked—in spite of Morgan's violent objection. Was there someone at Drummond Castle who dared not risk the disaster promised if the gates were locked? They clanged behind her and she stood for a minute wondering which way to go. Then, spotting a path that looked well-worn at the edge of the road, she took that.

The path wound downward and crossed over a small curved stone bridge. Soon, Oriel found herself on the edge of the town of Kilmara. Kilmara looked picturesque and serene, a place far removed from the dense, crowded city of London with all its filth and noise. Of course, Oriel had no idea what lay beneath the placid surface of this little town. Proceeding slowly, she passed clusters of small houses with thatched roofs. Children at play stopped to stare at her, shyly returning her smile; women came to their doorways and watched her curiously. Some nodded, but a few turned their heads or frowned. Oriel had planned to stroll along the winding cobbled streets, perhaps stop at some cozy tearoom. However, she became aware of an indefinable tension.

Women holding shopping baskets and chatting on a corner turned away suddenly as she approached; others ducked quickly into a nearby store. Upon opening the door of the general store, Oriel saw something in the face of the man behind the counter that caused her to hesitate. She turned around and left the shop. Her sense of discomfort was strong, so Oriel quickened her pace and was soon out of the village, heading back to the castle.

Was Kilmara an unfriendly place, unwelcoming to strangers? Oriel remembered what Molly had told her, how the people were offended by Morgan's attitude. Knowing *she* was from the castle, were they including her in their resentment?

Oriel turned all this over in her mind as she walked. If something wasn't done, this kind of hostility would take all the pleasure out of her time at Drummond Castle. She didn't want to be a prisoner there. She must find her own place in Kilmara, show people she wasn't like Morgan. Realizing it was still quite early to return to the castle, Oriel slowed her steps. Then she remembered the ruins of the old monastery she had seen from her bedroom. Maybe this would be a good time to find it.

At the top of the hill, she saw a line of arching trees that led to the ruins, forming a cathedral-like ceiling. The wind moved through the trees above her, and her footsteps slowed as if she were approaching a sacred spot.

Oriel knew most of these ancient monasteries had been thriving hubs of activity in the past—housing busy monks who provided food and shelter for the poor, cared for the sick, and chanted prayers and praise to the glory of God. A pervasive, mysterious quality hovered over the ruined abbey. Almost overwhelmed by the sensation, Oriel turned to go, but something caught her attention.

A blurred figure came toward her through the broken arches. Instinctively, she drew back. Her heart jumped. Remembering the hooded figure she had seen from her window in the eerie dawn, her first thought was that she was observing a monastic ghost. Then, realizing that was silly, she stood still. Slowly, fear gave way to relief. She let out the breath she had been holding.

As the figure approached, she saw it was not the ghost of a monk, but a live man. His jacket, with its wide collar turned up, and his brown corduroy hiking outfit had given her the impression of a monk's garb.

A few feet away, the man stopped and raised a hand in a friendly wave. As he came closer, she saw he had a wide smile, very blue eyes in a sunburned face, and a thatch of brown windblown hair. "Ah, a kindred spirit!" he called. "You must love old haunted places too." He smiled. "I'm Bryan Moore."

"I'm Oriel Ban—" she started to say, then quickly corrected herself, "Oriel Drummond."

He looked at her with interest and amusement. "Ah, then I believe we must be neighbors. I rent a cottage just this side of Drummond Castle." He paused. "You've just arrived then? There was no one living at the castle when I first came and I haven't seen anyone about. I would have. I roam these hills and the cliffs above the ocean daily."

"We've been here a little over a week."

"We?"

"My husband, Morgan Drummond, and I."

He nodded. "Yes, I heard he was coming." He smiled again. "Village gossip. You'll find little goes on here that isn't discussed, mulled over, and given opinions about. I've been here before, you see. Every so often, I rent a cottage for a few months at a time. This time I'll be here for a year."

"I'll be here for a year too," Oriel said without thinking. Immediately she was sorry she'd blurted that out. What would Bryan Moore make of that? He hadn't *seemed* to mark it with any special significance. He was gazing about the ruins.

"What stories these rocks would tell if they could speak, right? I'm very keen on history—exploring and digging for the bits and pieces historians sometimes overlook, the human drama. Ireland is a wealth of such stories."

The late spring wind stirring the trees overhead became sharper, colder. Oriel began to feel somewhat awkward, standing in this lonely spot with a stranger. "Well, I must be on my way," she said and turned to retrace her steps.

"Wait, I'll go along with you. I'm headed for the village to lunch at the Shamrock. I go there at least twice a week to buy a *Times* and catch up on local news. You never know what you'll hear or learn. Otherwise I might find myself getting a bit daft living alone."

He lives alone, then, Oriel mused. *What is an attractive man in the prime of life doing in this isolated coastal Irish village, renting a cottage for a year?*

As they fell into step, Bryan answered her unspoken question. "Writing is a solitary business. A poet's life demands times of absolute aloneness, but the social part of my nature demands that I get out and about regularly."

They had reached the bottom of the path and were standing on the road again.

"Well, Mrs. Drummond, it's been delightful to meet you— one of those rare chances that gives life unexpected moments of pleasure." Bryan Moore gave her a little salute and started walking in the direction of the village.

A few steps farther, he turned. "Do give my regards to Mr. Drummond," he called with a slight smile. Then he continued down the road.

Oriel watched him for a minute longer, wondering if he knew Morgan. There was something in the way he had spoken that made her curious. She would have to mention meeting him to Morgan.

12

*B*efore she had the opportunity to bring up the subject of Bryan Moore that evening at dinner, Morgan announced that he was thinking of going up to Dublin for a few weeks. He would be looking at some horses, he told her.

Morgan glanced at Oriel to see her reaction to his statement, but her expression revealed nothing. He shifted uneasily in his chair, discomfited by her silence. "I thought I'd look for a good riding horse for you." He paused. "You do ride, don't you?"

He was rewarded by how her eyes brightened and by a smile that transformed her face.

"Yes, I do! And I'd very much enjoy having a horse to ride."

"Good! I'll see to it then," Morgan said, satisfied that his afterthought had given her such pleasure.

He'd not done much for Oriel since their arrival, and he'd been feeling somewhat guilty about her. Not that he should. After all, Oriel was a smart woman. She had accepted their arrangement when it was offered, must have considered what it meant.

However, to be truthful, neither of them had *really* known what this year would be like, nor what its outcome would be either.

At first, the thought of several weeks alone at the castle was daunting to Oriel. But then, what real difference would it make if Morgan were gone? So far he had kept to his own rooms and library, gone on solitary walks around the estate. In a way, it might be a relief to have him gone—better than having to force polite conversation as they did in the presence of the servants. The truth was their dinner hours were becoming more and more a strain.

The following morning, Oriel came downstairs and found Morgan standing at the front door, his suitcases piled in the hall. Oriel was not too disturbed at his departure. She wished him good-bye and good luck selecting the horses and went on into the dining room to have her breakfast.

Oriel considered that with Morgan gone this might be a good time to make her presence felt by the household staff. She felt sure the staff was puzzled by the relationship between her and Morgan. Still, since she was to be mistress here, if only for the year, it was important for her to assume the traditional role.

First, she would make a complete tour of the house, something she had been hesitant to do before. She felt awkward about opening the many doors that lined the great hall, thinking she should ask Morgan about them. Now it dawned on her, that as Morgan's *wife*, she could open any door she chose.

Oriel knew it was important to get to know the cook, to let Mrs. Mills know she was interested in how she ran her establishment. If meals were to be well cooked and presented with style, it was necessary to recognize that in the kitchen the cook reigned as queen. After finishing her breakfast, Oriel decided to begin her tour at the kitchen.

The kitchen at Drummond Castle was much more modern than Oriel had thought it might be. Morgan's grandfather, coming from his American mansion, must have made that a priority when he started restoring the place. There was a large cast-iron range, and its jet-black shine told Oriel the cook took great pride in her main working tool. In the center of the room was a rectangular wooden table, its surface scrubbed almost white. There was a sandstone sink with running water. Hanging from racks were copper pans, skillets, and pots of all sizes. Against one wall was a tall pine hutch with rows of pottery bowls, mugs, and platters. On one side off the kitchen was the scullery, where vegetables brought in from the garden were washed and prepared. A door on the other side led into the pantry, Finnegan's realm, where the fine china and silver were kept.

At first Mrs. Mills greeted Oriel warily, as though skeptical of why the lady of the house had come into *her* territory. Little by little, under Oriel's tactful questioning, the cook let down her reserve and recited her complaints.

"'Tis not much reward cookin' for them that don't enjoy their food. I never get so much as a word one way or t' other from t' master. I don't know what he likes or what he don't." She shrugged.

Oriel gave her a sympathetic smile. "That is hard, I'm sure, Mrs. Mills. I hope to change all that. I like simple food, but well cooked. You do a fine job with the local produce and the game and meat available here. There is a kitchen garden, isn't there?"

"Indeed there is, madam." Mrs. Mills launched into a description of some of the tasty dishes she liked to concoct with the vegetables grown on the property.

Warming to her subject, Mrs. Mills continued, "And there's no entertainin' whatsoever. I am a light hand with pastry, madam, and no one ever bested me on pudding or trifle."

"Perhaps we'll have occasion to put those skills to use," Oriel said warmly.

When Oriel left, the cook was all smiles, proof that a good rapport had been achieved.

Oriel mounted the broad staircase to the upper floor. So far she had not explored any of the other wings. Upstairs, a web of corridors fanned out from the broad stairway into wings consisting of six large bedroom suites. At the end of one wing was a room for the lady's maid to attend to the wardrobe of the mistress. It contained a pressing closet, an ironing board, and cabinets stocked with everything needed to keep the clothes cleaned, mended, and in order.

At the end of another corridor, the one to the right of the top of the steps, a door opened onto a balcony that overlooked the downstairs ballroom. Oriel knew from her historical reading that this was called the minstrels' gallery, the place where the musicians who played for the dancing that took place below were seated.

There was still another door within the minstrels' gallery, and Oriel cautiously opened it and peered in. Portraits heavily framed in gold lined the walls. Oriel stepped inside, looking about her. She circled the room slowly, stopping every so often to study individual pictures. There were soldiers in uniform, rows of medals on their chests, swords at their hips. The women were all quite elegant. Their gowns, painted with exquisite detail, were of lush velvet and shimmering satin. Standing in front of a particularly lovely lady's portrait, Oriel wondered if this might be the unfortunate young woman whose baby was kidnapped by Shaleen O'Connor.

Slowly an eerie shiver ran down Oriel's spine. All at once, she felt claustrophobic. The room felt cold, heavy with the weight of time and people who had lived in centuries past. Suddenly she was anxious to get out, to escape. She spun around and hurried to the door, pushing on the carved metal handle.

It wouldn't budge; the door wouldn't open. It was stuck— or locked. Oriel began to breathe hard. This was silly. Could it have latched behind her? Frantically, she pushed on it. After pressing hard on it, Oriel was finally able to push the door open and stumble through the minstrels' gallery out into the hall.

Just then, she saw the formidable figure of Mrs. Nesbitt approaching, her keys rattling at her waist. Upon seeing Oriel, the housekeeper stopped short. Looking both surprised and annoyed, she asked coldly, "May I help you, madam?" She regarded Oriel suspiciously, as if she were an unwelcome intruder, someone who had no business roaming around the house.

For a split second, Oriel felt intimidated. Did Mrs. Nesbitt suspect that her position here was temporary? In the mysterious way of servants, did she know the truth about her agreement with Morgan? Whatever the facts were, Oriel knew this was a critical moment, one that could go either way. Either she or the housekeeper would be the victor. It was important for the rest of her time at Drummond Castle that she be in control. The other servants' attitudes toward her depended on the housekeeper's. Oriel had learned in various situations to use tact. She decided to choose that now.

She smiled and said, "Good morning, Mrs. Nesbitt. I've just been acquainting myself with the house. It must be difficult to keep a large place in such fine order."

Mrs. Nesbitt ignored the obvious compliment. A muscle in her thin cheek moved slightly, but she did not respond.

Oriel rushed in to fill the awkward pause. Gesturing to the door, she said, "I have just discovered the minstrels' gallery."

"Viewing the family portraits, were you?"

Oriel stepped back inside. "Yes. I found them absolutely fascinating. I had no idea there were so many Drummond ancestors."

"They're *not* Drummonds," Mrs. Nesbitt said sharply, following Oriel into the portrait room. "They're of the Lawrence family. It was they who built this castle." Mrs. Nesbitt came in and stood behind Oriel. "They were a fine, honorable family, the Lawrences, with a proud heritage. They fought for their land, their faith, their honor." She moved along the line of paintings. "This has not always been Drummond Castle."

Mrs. Nesbitt stopped in front of the portrait Oriel had earlier admired. "Lady Lavinia Lawrence," she said softly, almost tenderly. "Now there was a *real* lady. In spite of all she had to endure, she put family first. It was her children who inherited this castle after her husband was betrayed and murdered." Mrs. Nesbitt spoke as if the eighteenth century event had happened only yesterday. "He had sent her away out of danger. But she came back and brought her children to live here in this castle—just as they were meant to do." Mrs. Nesbitt shook her head sadly. Oriel had not thought the housekeeper capable of such deep emotion. "She died of a broken heart . . ." The woman's stern expression relaxed. There was a noticeable softening of the straight-lipped mouth.

"This is certainly an interesting house with quite a history," Oriel said. She was about to broach the subject of the Shaleen O'Connor legend when Mrs. Nesbitt suddenly turned and walked swiftly away, seeming to disappear into the shadows of the far wing.

Oriel looked after her, bewildered by the abrupt end to their conversation. The woman was certainly caught up in the history of this place, as if it were her own. Oriel hoped by showing her interest, she had made a good impression on the housekeeper.

That night, for the first time since coming to Drummond Castle, Oriel slept through the night without once waking up. She knew her efforts had been worth it. She had taken a first step toward making a place for herself at Drummond Castle. The maids, the footmen, and even Finnegan now seemed willing to accept her as mistress. All the servants accepted her—except Mrs. Nesbitt. That lady would need a great deal more winning over.

13

With Morgan away, the castle felt larger and gloomier. Not that he provided much companionship, but there was some comfort in knowing he was there. For the past few weeks there had been rain, and Oriel had become restless, longing to get out to walk. She was happy to see that the morning looked clear. Possibly the sun would break through the mist and it would be a fair day—a good day to take the cliff path overlooking the ocean.

After breakfast, Oriel noted the clear weather and eagerly left the house. As she started out, she remembered the small stone building she'd been curious about and decided this would be a good time to find it and figure out what it was. She went out through the garden looking for it, turning into several paths that simply circled into an intricate bordered design. Had she mistaken its position?

She halted, looked up at the house to locate her bedroom window and the angle from which she had noticed the little structure. Following that line of direction, she passed through a twist of hedges. She came upon it suddenly, the stone structure almost obscured by a heavy growth of ivy vines. Coming closer, she saw it had narrow windows and an arched wooden door. Curious, she tried the latch, but it seemed to be bolted; at least it was too hard for her to open. She cupped her eyes with her hands and peered in through one of the windows. The glass was too murky for her to tell what it was like inside.

Instead of being a trysting place for lovers or a children's playhouse, it was probably used for storage or tools, or some other mundane purpose, not at all what her romantic fantasy imagined. From her reading, Oriel knew such structures were called "follies," a rather strange name for a building, evoking all sorts of mysterious connotations.

Her curiosity satisfied, Oriel went back the way she'd come. Outside the gates, she took the path opposite the one to the village. She had not gone far when she began to smell the tang of salt in the damp air. The climb was gradual, and she soon found herself near the top of the cliff. Stopping to catch her breath, she looked back and saw the castle. It looked like an illustration in a fairy-tale book, with its gray stones gilded by the morning sun, its diamond-paned windows shining like colored gems. Oriel felt a strange, soft warmth within her. It was a beautiful place, worthy to be cherished. Ireland was weaving its magic spell on her. She had come to love the hills, the sea, the rocky coast, the fields dotted with grazing sheep. Given a chance, Oriel felt she would also love the village of Kilmara with its whitewashed cottages and slanted thatch roofs—once she met its people and they got to know her. That might take time, but she had a year. It was time enough if she really tried. There was always time for the things you wanted, for love to grow if you cared enough.

Drawing a long breath, she continued walking. The climb was difficult but well worth it when she caught a glimpse of the sea, crashing against the jutting rocks, glistening with silver light from the sun breaking through the clouds. She halted, taking in the magnificent sight.

A few minutes later, she saw three people coming along the path from the other direction. It was Bryan Moore, accompanied by a man and woman whom she didn't recognize.

Bryan waved and shouted something she could not hear, his words carried away on the brisk wind. As they came closer, Bryan smiled and hailed her. "Another hardy soul! We should form a walking club. Mrs. Drummond, how nice to see you again. Let me introduce my friends, Mr. and Mrs. Wicklow. Michael and Suzanne are neighbors of yours at Bracken Hall, just over the hill from Drummond Castle."

The couple he introduced were both tall and fair-skinned, with aristocratic features. They were both bundled up warmly; Mrs. Wicklow in a bulky knit sweater. From under her woolly tam, tendrils of blond hair escaped, blowing in the sharp ocean wind. She had an engaging smile and bright blue eyes. The man's eyes were shaded by the beak of his deerstalker cap, and he was wearing a gray tweed Inverness cape.

The woman spoke first. "I'm delighted to meet you, Mrs. Drummond. We heard the castle was going to have occupants again. It's been empty so long."

"Indeed," Michael agreed. "For years it was crawling with workmen of every sort, renovating, restoring, rebuilding—whatever in the world Drummond was doing over there."

Oriel detected a sarcastic note in his tone and wondered why. His wife gave an embarrassed laugh. Putting her hand on his arm, she said in a playfully reproachful tone, "Darling, really!" She then turned to Oriel. "Don't mind Michael, Mrs. Drummond. He is one of those purists who thinks that an artifact, be it a Roman urn or a house built in the seventeenth century, should remain unaltered—nothing touched." She rolled her eyes in mocking amusement. "He'd still rather have maids trundling up with boiling water for his bath every morning than be able to turn the faucet and have it pour out nice and hot."

"I'm not *that* reactionary," Michael protested good-naturedly.

They all laughed.

"Mrs. Drummond is an American," Bryan told them.

"An American! How exciting! I'd love to visit the States, but Michael hates to travel and won't budge. Thinks Ireland's the world, don't you?" her voice was teasing.

"And it is, at least to *me*," he replied edgily.

Bryan stamped his feet. "It's getting cold standing here. You'll find Irish summers are unpredictable, Mrs. Drummond. Rarely the kind of summer days you find in the States. Misty mornings, short sunny afternoons, then the fog rolls in about five."

"The fog is tricky. Sneaks up on you sometimes before you know it," Suzanne commented.

"How far are you planning to walk, Mrs. Drummond?"

"I've heard there's a beautiful little cove around here somewhere. I thought I'd look for it."

Bryan frowned. "It's a treacherous climb down to it."

"But well worth it," Michael interjected.

"There is a ladder," Suzanne said. "It's makeshift, but usable."

"Just be careful going down. Watch that the tide doesn't surprise you," Bryan warned.

"We ought to be moving on." Michael put an arm protectively around his wife's shoulders. "Nice to have met you, Mrs. Drummond."

"You must come to tea some day soon, won't you?" Suzanne suggested. "You can't miss the house. It's very visible from the road."

"There's a shortcut through the woods from Drummond Castle," Michael told her. "It's a little dense, but there should still be a visible path winding through. I used to play there as a boy."

"Come along, Michael." Suzanne took his hand. "Good day, Mrs. Drummond. Remember, we'd love to have you for tea. When you come, I'd love to hear all about America. I'll send a note."

"Thank you, I'd like that very much," Oriel responded.

The couple hurried past, but Bryan lingered a moment. "So, do you always take solitary walks? Doesn't your husband enjoy tramping through our beautiful countryside?"

Oriel felt her cheeks flush. "He's away just now. Gone up to Dublin for the horse fair. He's planning to stock the stables." Why did she feel she had to explain Morgan's absence? How could she explain that whether he was here or not, he would not think of taking a walk with her?

"So he intends to stay, then?" Bryan's eyebrows lifted. "It was wagered in the village he wouldn't."

Oriel felt the heat in her face deepen. "Why, yes. His grandfather left him the castle."

"Well, then, so much for rumors, eh? I've never placed much credence in them anyway." He shrugged. "Have a nice walk and do be careful if you decide to check on the cove. Remember what I said about the tide."

They said good-bye and Bryan hurried to catch up with the Wicklows. Oriel resumed her walk along the path in the opposite direction. She felt happy for the first time in a long time. It had been a nice encounter. She had liked the Wicklows right away and she hoped Suzanne would follow up on her invitation to tea. Oriel had a feeling that Suzanne was someone with whom she could be friends.

Suddenly the year ahead at Drummond Castle did not seem so bleak. She loved the countryside, and she had just met some cordial people who might become friends. She had an intuitive feeling meeting the Wicklows would change her life in Ireland.

A week passed and Morgan still had not returned. Soon after meeting the Wicklows, Oriel found herself confined to the house as the weather had turned rainy once more. Oriel soon tired of reading, playing solitary card games, and eating meals alone in the large dining room. When a note was delivered from Suzanne Wicklow inviting her to tea at

Bracken Hall, she was inordinately pleased. She sent a note back accepting the invitation and saying she was very much looking forward to coming.

Happily, the next afternoon a sudden break came in the weather. The rain stopped and the fog evaporated, so Oriel decided to walk the short distance over to the Wicklows' home. Having been without exercise most of the week, she knew the fresh air and brisk walk would be good for her.

She kept to the road, not wanting to miss the way. However, she did see a path not far from the gates of the castle that was possibly the shortcut Michael Wicklow had mentioned. It was heavily overgrown with ferns and almost invisible. Oriel was afraid she might get lost if she tried that way.

At Bracken Hall, Suzanne opened the door herself. "Your cheeks are like roses!" she greeted Oriel. "Aren't we lucky to see some sunshine for a change? But don't get too happy, my dear, Irish summer being what it is." She laughed. "Some say it's like the Irish character—all smiles and laughter one moment, glower and gloom the next! I don't know if Mr. Drummond suits that description, but Michael certainly does. Come along, let's have our tea."

Suzanne led Oriel to the library, where the furnishings were unpretentious but in good taste. Draperies with overblown flowers and trailing vines were pulled across the windows, giving the room a more intimate feel. There was a large sofa piled with pillows. Several comfortable chairs were scattered around the room. In front of the fireplace was a table with a silver tray, on which a plate of sandwiches, two cups, and a silver teapot had been placed.

"I'm so delighted you could come." Suzanne gestured to one of the chairs. "Do sit down and I'll pour our tea. Michael's out on one of his rambles, so it will just be us."

Without the sweater she had worn on the day they'd met on the cliffs, Suzanne seemed thin, although attractive in a rather ethereal way. Her features were delicate, her skin like white marble. Her pale blonde hair was deeply waved and so thick it seemed almost too heavy for her slender neck. She was wearing a fitted coral dress, its severity softened by a fine Italian cameo.

When Suzanne poured the tea and handed Oriel a cup, Oriel noticed Suzanne wore a narrow gold wedding band much the same as her own. However, Oriel assumed Suzanne had received hers in a ceremony very different from the brief, impersonal one she had gone through in the London Registry Office.

Suzanne was animated and seemed happy to have company. Oriel herself had been starved for female companionship and found Suzanne charming and spontaneous. Suzanne was eager to learn about Oriel's American background. Her warmth and interest made it easy for Oriel to answer her questions. It was only when Suzanne asked about Morgan that Oriel decided she had better be more discreet. It would be unwise to reveal too much about their relationship. Suzanne would certainly never understand their strange bargain. When the conversation became too personal, Oriel changed the subject as subtly as she could by asking Suzanne about her delicate white china cups.

"It's an original design. Very rare because it's not made anymore, although the molds probably exist somewhere. It used to be made right here in Kilmara. It was a thriving village industry, exporting all over the world. The firing kilns and buildings are all boarded up now. It's very sad. It makes Michael livid." She broke off, as though she had said too much. "Of course, that was before—" she halted again as if uncertain whether to continue. "That was before everything got so bad. I'm sure you know of all that—the failure of the potato crop that caused such terrible famine. The factory was closed, and the men who worked in it had to emigrate or go to England to work."

"Have you lived here long?" Oriel asked.

"Only a few years. Michael's mother grew up here and he wanted to come back." A thoughtful expression came over Suzanne's face for a moment. "Houses have histories, you know. They say the past can influence the lives of later occupants of a house."

Oriel started to say she was sure Drummond Castle had a history. She might have gone on to ask Suzanne if she had ever heard of the legend of Shaleen O'Connor, but just then they heard the slam of the front door and footsteps in the hall. A moment later, the door opened and Michael stepped into the library.

Michael's entrance somehow shifted the mood between the two women, his presence subtly changing the intimate atmosphere. Suzanne darted several anxious looks in his direction, and Oriel got the impression that something was on Michael's mind he didn't feel free to discuss in front of company. He was, however, affable enough to Oriel, and both he and Suzanne walked her to the door.

"Not too far for you, is it?" Michael asked. "We can easily have one of the servants take you back in the trap."

"No, thanks. I love walking."

"Well, then, you'll enjoy it. It's still fair, so I suggest you take the cliff path. I just came that way and the ocean is really lovely—a sight to behold." He smiled ruefully. "That is, if you have the soul of an Irish poet."

Oriel laughed. "I guess I'll leave that to Bryan Moore, but I'm sure I'll enjoy the view." She thanked Suzanne for the tea and said good-bye.

"Do come again soon. I feel we're going to be great friends!"

"Thank you. I'd like that. You've been most kind."

Oriel set out from Bracken Hall with a lighter heart than she had had in weeks. The Wicklows were a friendly pair, and their home had a warmth that was sadly missing at Drummond Castle. Oriel suppressed a sigh. Taking Michael's advice, she took the road that led to the cliffs.

She walked briskly, and her breath was coming fast when she reached the path that overlooked the ocean. Mist had begun to rise quickly, and as she stopped to stand on the cliff's edge, she could hear the pounding of the surf against the rocks below. She swayed slightly in the strong wind blowing in from the sea.

Suddenly she felt frightened. A strange sensation of malevolence crept over her, as if someone or something was watching her, wishing her harm. She felt an urgency to get away from the cliffs. She turned and began to walk fast, then faster. Finally, she began to run. Ahead of her loomed the castle—stark, foreboding. Instead of reassuring her, the sight filled her with dread.

14

*T*hat evening, Oriel felt peculiarly restless. Suzanne's animated company had accentuated her aloneness at Drummond Castle. With Morgan still in Dublin, the castle seemed cavernous. After eating a solitary meal in the dining room, Oriel went up to her own rooms. She felt lonely and anxious. It was a different kind of anxiety than she had experienced those weeks in London. Then she had lived on the hope that her situation was only temporary; here the year stretched gloomily ahead. It was an odd paradox. Even though Ireland itself had captured her, life at Drummond Castle was far from what she had imagined it might be.

It struck her more than ever what a reckless thing she had done, agreeing to Morgan's bizarre proposition. If she had waited longer, possibly Mrs. McPhail would have come through. Even the day she left London there had still been that chance. That's why she had given her address to Nola. Perhaps something *had* come to her at the rooming house. Maybe she should write to Nola, remind her to forward any mail that might have come.

Oriel sat down at the desk in her sitting room and got out some stationery. It was engraved with the Drummond Castle crest. She hesitated. Would Nola think it too grand, be put off by the rich-looking heading? Oriel had told Nola she had a job as a companion. What would Nola think if she knew the truth of Oriel's situation at Drummond Castle? Oriel searched the desk drawer further and found some plain sheets to use instead.

Dipping her pen into the inkwell, Oriel began to write, "Dear Nola, I think of you often and of your kindness to me when I was in London looking for a job."

She paused. What to write next? Nola would not possibly comprehend Oriel's strange existence at Drummond Castle. There was no way to explain it. The important thing was to let Nola know she had arrived at her destination and was still hoping for a letter from her former employer.

Oriel started to write again when something—she was not sure quite what it was—halted her. She felt a quiver at the base of her neck, trailing like an icy finger down her spine.

She put the pen down and sat back in the chair, listening—for what? Then, drawn by some uncanny compulsion, she got up and moved over to the window. Her heart pulsing in her throat, she twisted the handle on the window and slowly pushed it open.

The night was clear. No mist or swirling fog obscured her view. There it was—moving, or rather *gliding* across the terrace toward the gates—an ethereal cloaked figure. As Oriel watched breathlessly, the figure seemed to float through the closed gates! Or had they been left *unlocked* for the spectral visit of Shaleen O'Connor?

Oriel slammed the window and fastened it. She was trembling. Was what she had seen real or imaginary? She moved over to the fireplace, hugging her arms and shivering. Was being alone in this ancient castle getting to her? Was she losing her good sense listening to old ghost stories? What she had seen was probably the movement of trees along the drive, she told herself firmly.

In a few minutes, Oriel went over to the window and made herself stare out into the night. There was nothing there. She drew the curtains shut and turned back into the warmth of the room. She refused to be trapped into believing the ghost of Shaleen O'Connor haunted Drummond Castle.

Sleep didn't come easily that night, and Oriel woke up the next morning feeling unrested. She decided that being alone and confined to the castle was unhealthy. She determined that whatever the weather, she would get out every day and walk.

Right after breakfast, she set out. Once outside, she felt her spirits rise. The sea breeze had blown away the fog and it looked as though it was going to be a clear summer day. As she turned up the path that led to the ocean cliffs, she heard the distant drum of the surf. Reaching the top, she saw the wide expanse of the sea. Moving along the edge, she looked down. The tide was out and the beach had been swept clean.

Oriel peered down at the cove. It looked inviting. Foamy ripples of blue water curled on the edge of the little beach. She very much wanted to go down there. However, when she tried the posts at the top, they felt unstable. The makeshift ladder was made of wooden boards, and it dropped steeply down the precipice. Oriel stood there for a few minutes debating. It would be a definite challenge. She recalled Bryan's caution, Michael's challenging glance. Both seemed to doubt her ability to climb down the steep hill. If only to be able to tell them both she had done it, she had to try.

Oriel hiked up her skirt, tucked it into her belt, and swung around backwards. Holding on to the two posts, she took the first step downward. The ladder shook with her weight, and she felt it sway. The last few rungs of the ladder were broken. Timidly, she turned her head and looked down. There was still quite a long way down to the beach. Oriel paused there for a minute, wondering how to proceed. Her feet fought for footholds. She held on to the side of the ladder with one hand, then gradually let go. Rocks rolled under her boots, causing her feet to slip. She clutched for something to break her downward slide. It was useless; she had to go with the shifting sand until she reached the bottom. She landed in a sitting position, scrambled to her feet, and looked around.

The sun sparkled on the deep blue of the ocean, flecked with dancing whitecaps. Above her, seagulls dove and screeched. The wind mingled with the roar of the surf. Oriel straightened her skirt and dusted off the sand. She found a smooth rock to sit on, hidden beneath the jutting cliffs. Michael had been right. It *had* been well worth the treacherous climb down. A wonderful, soothing peace came over her. This was surely a special place, a place that could be a refuge. Here she could find a private haven to escape from the oppressive atmosphere of Drummond Castle.

Nothing happened by chance. Oriel knew she had been given this opportunity, this year, as a learning experience. "Every good gift comes from above." Oriel had learned that Scripture as a child. A gift from God should be appreciated, used well. That's what she intended to do with the rest of her year in Ireland—despite Morgan's poor attitude and the myth-haunted castle. If she used this gift well, she might find something in it, something within herself, for which she'd been searching—a sense of God's purpose for her life.

After enjoying her surroundings for a while, Oriel was ready to leave. It was hard going scrambling back up the ladder. The unstable wooden structure swayed and shuddered with every foot placed on the rungs. Oriel was panting when she finally pulled herself up the last step and onto the top of the cliff.

"So, you did it!" a familiar voice exclaimed.

Surprised, Oriel turned to see Bryan Moore coming up the path. "Yes! And you were right—it was glorious!" she said breathlessly.

His blue eyes were amused. "Well, good for you! I wasn't sure you would make it. That shows you've got pluck, something I admire greatly in a woman, in anyone for that matter. Would you let me give you tea for a reward? My cottage is just down the beach a little."

Noting her hesitation, he said, "Oh, we'll be well chaperoned. Suzanne and Michael are coming too. They're on their way."

"Thank you, I'd like to," she responded. As a single woman it would have been improper for Oriel to go unaccompanied to a bachelor's home, but as a *married* woman, it was acceptable, and with the Wicklows also there it would be silly to turn down this generous offer of hospitality and friendship.

"Fine, come along." He held out his arm for her to take. "It's almost as treacherous a path to my place, but that keeps me snug and unbothered by visitors—*uninvited* ones, of course."

He laughed, and Oriel thought it was a good, hearty laugh. It had been a long time since she'd heard a man's laugh. Certainly she had not at Drummond Castle.

As he opened the door for her, he said, "We'll just have a country tea. Nothing fancy. I live very simply here, as a bachelor should." His blue eyes twinkled merrily.

Bryan's cottage, a whitewashed stucco with a thatched roof, was typical of those along the Irish coast. Inside it was small, but cozy. There was a fireplace, shelves of books, a desk in front of a window that looked out over an ocean view.

"What a charming cottage," Oriel remarked as she looked around, thinking it such a contrast to the large, gloomy castle. She almost added, "Just the sort of place I'd like myself." She caught herself in time, but not before Bryan gave her a glance as if he knew what she was thinking.

To cover her sudden discomfort, she went over to examine the painting over the mantel of a small stone church nestled among misty green hills. "You have everything anyone would need or want here. Didn't a poet write, 'May I a small house and a large garden have, and a few friends and many books both true, both wise, and both delightful too'?"

"Good heavens! You're not only a good climber but *literate* as well! As I live and breathe, quoting Abraham Cowley, one of my own favorites." Bryan looked at Oriel with admiration. "Do you like poetry, then?"

"I do. I'd love to borrow some of your books. I've not read much poetry lately."

"Isn't there a library at Drummond Castle?"

"Yes, but I haven't really explored the contents." She did not like to say that Morgan spent a great deal of time there and she did not like to intrude.

Bryan fixed her with his thoughtful gaze. "Why is it I have the feeling that you and Mr. Drummond do not share the same interests? If I had a beautiful bride, I would certainly not spend a day longer than I had to in Dublin."

Oriel could think of nothing to say. The gentle questioning in his eyes made her uncomfortable. Before she was forced to answer, there was a rousing knock at the cottage door.

"My other guests!" Bryan declared. "Another time you and I will have to discuss poetry."

Tea was enjoyable. Oriel could not remember when she had had such a good time. Bryan and Michael had a jovial yet adversarial friendship. There was a great deal of joking and mutual joshing. When Michael stood, saying it was time for them to leave, he offered to walk Oriel home.

"No need," Bryan said quickly. "I'll escort Mrs. Drummond home. It will soon be dark and you two will have to hurry to get home yourselves."

"Don't worry about us, Bryan. Michael knows a shortcut through the woods. He can see in the dark like some kind of woodland creature," Suzanne assured him.

After the Wicklows left, Bryan handed Oriel two slim volumes. "Here, take these. You can return them on your next visit, which I hope will be soon."

Bryan looked out one of the small windows. "The fog's already rolling in. We'd better be on our way."

It was fast growing dark. Large clouds moved overhead and wisps of fog were creeping in from the ocean. When they came in sight of Drummond Castle, Oriel saw lights blazing from most of the windows.

"Morgan must be back!" Oriel exclaimed. "You needn't come any farther. Thank you so much for a lovely afternoon, for tea and for these books! I know I shall enjoy them."

"You're sure you don't want me to see you to the door?"

"No, thanks. I'll be fine—really."

"You don't think your husband would approve of your being brought home by a stranger?"

"Oh, it's not that." Oriel felt flustered. The truth was she wasn't sure just *how* Morgan would react.

"Never mind," Bryan said amiably. "I enjoyed our time together. Good evening, Mrs. Drummond."

"Good evening," she said, pushing through the gate and hurrying up the driveway.

15

Oriel had hardly stepped inside the front hall when Morgan appeared at the door of the library and demanded, "Where have you been? No one—not Finnegan, Mrs. Nesbitt, or Molly—knew where you were. Don't you realize it's dangerous to go wandering past the grounds? The ocean cliffs quickly get masked in fog. It's easy for someone to get disoriented and fall. Those cliffs are—" He broke off, frowning. "It's a long way down to the beach."

Oriel stood there open-mouthed as he raved on. "See that you are more careful in the future," he finished. Then, just as abruptly, he spun around and stalked off to his suite. A part of Oriel was pleased at his obvious concern. On the other hand, to be reprimanded like some naughty child come home late for supper made her furious.

That evening at dinner, Oriel expected Morgan to apologize for the way he had behaved, but he never did. Acting as if the scene had never taken place, he asked her, "So what have you been doing to amuse yourself while I've been gone?"

Still miffed by his high-handed treatment earlier, but forced by the presence of Finnegan and Conan to carry on some kind of civil conversation, Oriel told him about the

Wicklows and Bryan Moore. "Well, I've met some very nice people. I think you'd like them, especially Bryan, who is a published poet and scholar. Michael knows a great deal about Irish history—Kilmara, in particular."

"I'm afraid neither interests me a great deal," Morgan said flatly.

"They have been most cordial. I should like to return their kindness by having them to tea some afternoon, unless you have some objection."

"I *do* object," Morgan said. "I don't want a lot of strangers coming in, asking a lot of questions, involving me in shallow conversation." He halted, realizing his reaction was too strong. "If you want to invite these new friends of yours on your own, that would be fine, I suppose."

"I wouldn't think of doing that. This is, after all, *your* home. Please, forget I said anything."

A strained silence followed. Morgan noted the tight line of Oriel's jaw and her flushed cheeks and was struck with the desire to smooth things over. After a minute or two, he said, "I've bought you a very fine saddle horse, a mare with a gentle nature and sensitive mouth. The dealer originally bought her for his daughter, but the young lady has gone in for jumping and this is strictly a riding horse."

Still smarting from the abrupt way he had dismissed her request, Oriel replied tightly, "Thank you, Morgan. That was very kind of you."

"Not kind at all," he said, smiling. "It will give you something else to do besides having tea with dreamy-eyed poets and amateur historians and wandering about in the mist."

Indignation flared up in her again. Was that remark Morgan's attempt at humor? If so, she did not appreciate it. Before she could utter a protest or defend her new friends, Morgan rose from the table. "They're bringing your horse down tomorrow or the next day. If you'll excuse me, I'm tired from my journey." After bowing slightly, he left the room.

110

Oriel sat there for a minute quietly fuming. Why did Morgan seem so intent on being difficult? Was there no common point of interest they could share? Was he truly satisfied with the isolated manner in which they were living? Oriel realized, somewhat to her surprise, how important it was to her that Morgan be happy, that they be friends.

"Your dessert, madam," Conan said, setting a dish of lemon custard before her. For Mrs. Mills's sake, Oriel ate every spoonful. Then she left the dining room. On her way upstairs past the library, she gave the closed door a furious look.

Two mornings later, Oriel woke to the sound of heavy rain. It was coming down in sheets. There was no chance of getting out today. More and more she looked forward to her walks and the chance of running into Bryan or the Wicklows. Morgan's reaction to her suggestion of inviting them to tea still rankled her, but she was hardly in a position to insist.

After breakfast, Oriel wandered into the empty library. She stood for a few moments at the long windows, watching the rain run in crooked rivulets down the diamond-paned glass.

The sound of male voices in the entrance hall and the clatter of heavy footsteps startled her. The library door was flung open and Morgan stood there. "The mare I bought for you has come," he said, his eyes beaming.

"In this weather?" she asked, surprised.

"Yes, yes, I know, it's one devil of a day for them to have arrived, but there it is. You can never tell about the Irish temperament or the weather. I was clever enough to give the man only half when I was in Dublin, to make sure he'd carry through his end of the bargain. Anyhow, would you like to take a look?"

"Of course!" Oriel said, pleased with the uncharacteristic eagerness Morgan displayed.

"Well, come along then. We'll go down to the stables together."

She hurried toward the door to the hall. "I won't be a minute."

She ran upstairs to get her jacket and then followed Morgan out to the stables.

The horse Morgan had bought for her use was a roan-colored mare, sleek and sweet-tempered. Mavourneen was her name. Oriel loved her the minute she saw her and stroked her velvety nose.

"Oh, I hope the weather clears soon so I can start riding," she said. Then, turning to Morgan, she smiled. "Thank you."

He was disconcerted by her obvious delight. He said an awkward "You're welcome," and quickly started talking to the groom.

Oriel realized Morgan wasn't the sort of man who wanted or needed excess gratitude. She should just accept Morgan's kind gesture and enjoy it. Perhaps, with a mount of his own, they might ride together and find a way to live in a more harmonious manner.

Over the next few weeks, Oriel began to ride daily. The horse was gentle and sensitive to her slightest touch on the reins, a real joy to ride. So began the happiest period in Oriel's life at Drummond Castle.

To Oriel's surprise and without her effort, as the summer progressed, Morgan's manner gradually changed. He was less gruff, more amiable. Sometimes at dinner, he initiated conversation and even seemed to enjoy talking as they lingered over their coffee.

Occasionally, after an unusually pleasant dinner hour, Oriel once again saw the man she had thought Morgan to be. She allowed herself to wonder what their relationship might be like if they were here under different circumstances. She imagined what might have happened if she and Morgan had met on the ocean liner as fellow passengers and been attracted to one another. They could have had one of those shipboard romances novelists are so fond of writing about. Sometimes her thoughts even went so far as to picture Morgan bringing her to Drummond Castle as his true bride.

At this point Oriel usually cut off her wild imaginings. Daydreams were one thing, but reality was something else entirely. When she tried to share her own growing love for Ireland with him, she found that line of conversation seemed to bore Morgan. She decided that his new congeniality was probably only because he had grown tired of his reclusiveness. Most likely, her company was tolerable because there was no alternative.

For Oriel, however, the days of that summer would have been long and lonely had it not been for Bryan. He seemed to genuinely enjoy her company. They shared many common interests—an appreciation of the beauty of this part of Ireland, a love of literature, especially poetry, and they both relished a good discussion, even if they did not agree on every topic.

"You're very American, you know, Bryan," Oriel teased him one day as they walked along the cliffs overlooking the ocean.

"And *you* are quite *Irish!*" he retorted mischievously. Then his voice softened. "Besides, you have the soul of a poet."

"I'll take that as a compliment." She smiled.

"That's what it was." He paused. "Alas, I have the feeling it is wasted at the castle."

For a moment something hovered between them, so seemingly natural, yet dangerous. The slightest word, gesture, movement would change their relationship. Oriel was starved for companionship. Bryan was warm, amusing, interesting, fun to be with, and she needed and longed for that.

However, both valued too much what they had found in each other to jeopardize it. Bryan was a gentleman of honor. Oriel had too much integrity even to hint at breaking the contract, bizarre as it was, she had made to Morgan.

She was not free to be anything more to Bryan than a friend. Neither would ever cross that line. That was understood, if never spoken.

*T*he summer months passed all too quickly. Fall seemed to come overnight. With it came a nagging feeling about the hospitality Bryan and the Wicklows had often extended to Oriel. Not to reciprocate seemed unspeakably bad manners. She felt she could not let their kindness be unreturned any longer. While she waited for the right opportunity to bring up the subject to Morgan, something happened that made it inevitable.

The local hunt season opened, and one afternoon, quite unexpectedly, Michael arrived with the gift of a brace of pheasant. As a result, Oriel impulsively invited him and Suzanne to dinner. When he accepted at once, she knew she must proceed to inform Morgan no matter the consequences.

That evening at dinner, Oriel knew she had to speak of her impromptu invitation. She waited until Conan had poured their coffee and removed their dessert plates. Then, taking a deep breath, she said, "Morgan, I know you may not like it, but I have invited the Wicklows to dinner next week and will include Bryan Moore too. It seems the only polite thing to do. I felt we must reciprocate. They have been so friendly and hospitable to me—especially when you were gone. Then, of course, with Michael bringing the pheasant—"

"Probably poached from Drummond land," Morgan sneered.

"You don't know that," Oriel said, her indignation rising. "Besides, doesn't it ever occur to you that I might long for more company?"

Morgan's expression underwent a change. His eyes softened and he looked at her intently. There was a flicker of uncertainty in his eyes, but when he spoke, his voice was firm.

"I thought you understood being here was temporary. I have no interest in establishing myself as a genial host among the local gentry."

Oriel stood up and flung her napkin down beside her plate. "Have it your own way, Morgan. Come or don't come—I don't care. I have issued an invitation to some very gracious people who have been kind to me, and I don't intend to cancel it."

With that, Oriel turned and walked out of the dining room. She was almost to the stairway when Morgan called, "Wait, Oriel." She turned to face him. He regarded her with something like respect.

"Look, I apologize," Morgan said. "You have every right to invite anyone you wish here, have a dinner party, whatever." He paused, biting his lower lip before going on. "I am an antisocial creature, as you may have noticed. I have a great deal on my mind. My grandfather laid many rather heavy and complicated responsibilities on me. I don't mean to make things unpleasant for you." He broke off, as if he didn't know what else to say.

There was something in his expression, a plea for understanding in his eyes that immediately struck a responsive chord in Oriel. Her natural inclination was to reach out, touch him, say something to comfort him. Knowing he might resent any such gesture, she restrained herself. She did nothing, allowing him his pride.

"Of course, Morgan. I understand," she said quietly. "I still think you would find the Wicklows and Mr. Moore interesting and enjoyable guests."

Morgan's conciliatory manner vanished. "Don't count on it," he said curtly. "Now, if you'll excuse me, I'll bid you good night."

With that, he turned on his heel and walked down the hall, leaving Oriel standing there, frustrated. She had more to say, things that Morgan should hear—like how unhealthy it was for him to let regret, remorse, or resentment eat at him, to turn inward, mourning a love he could not have.

Then, suddenly, Oriel felt drained. What was the use? Why did she even care? She turned and started up the stairs. A movement caught her attention, and she looked up just in time to see a shape leaning over the banister. Startled, she halted. As she glanced upward, it backed away, disappearing as quickly as a shadow, but not before she had caught a glimpse of the face and its smugly satisfied expression. It was Mrs. Nesbitt. Had the housekeeper been eavesdropping and found Oriel's argument with Morgan somehow satisfying?

In the days leading up to the dinner party with the Wicklows and Bryan Moore, Oriel was busy with preparations. She was anxious for her first entertaining at Drummond Castle to go well. Maybe that would impress Morgan. If he found it enjoyable, it might be the beginning of other such evenings. That, she knew, was a far-fetched hope, but it was still worth making the effort.

Oriel went over the menu in detail with Mrs. Mills, soliciting her suggestions, trying to include some of what she considered her specialties. The cook was excited about the chance to show her skills at this first social dinner. Oriel also consulted with Finnegan on which china, silverware, and table linens to use. She asked Morgan to select the wines, but he referred her to Finnegan, making his disinterest in their dinner party apparent. Oriel spent time with Patrick, the gardener, to see what flowers were available in the garden and greenhouse for the table centerpiece and for arrangements to be placed in vases in the drawing room.

To her surprise, Oriel enjoyed seeing to all these various details. Her natural talent and good taste made her suited to just such a role. Her only regret was Morgan's lack of interest and involvement.

Sometimes she imagined again how lovely it would be if this were real, if they were at Drummond Castle because they wanted to be here together. What if Morgan had remained the charming, considerate man she knew he could be—the kind of man it would be easy to fall in love with? Quickly, Oriel reminded herself that she was here in a business arrangement, playing a role. Still, there was no harm in enjoying what she could.

The evening of the dinner party, Oriel was nervous. Regardless of Morgan's attitude, she was determined to act the part of the charming hostess. By doing so, she might shame Morgan into doing his part. Certainly he would rise to the occasion, if only for pride's sake.

Molly helped Oriel dress and arrange her hair. "Oh, madam, you look ever so elegant!" Molly declared, carefully placing a high-backed comb into Oriel's chignon. Oriel's gown, a cinnamon satin, had been altered so skillfully even the original owner would not have recognized it. Daily rides and walks in the moist Irish sea air had enhanced Oriel's coloring, making the dress even more becoming.

When the Wicklows arrived, Oriel welcomed them and introduced them to Morgan. Bryan followed soon after. They gathered in the drawing room, where a selection of hors d'oeuvres had been laid out. To Oriel's increasing irritation, Morgan made no effort to engage anyone in conversation after the introductions. She tried to draw her guests out on various subjects. In an attempt to start a lively discussion, Bryan brought up the subject of how the pottery factory might be started again, reviving the economy of the village. This comment seemed to make Morgan belligerent.

"People seem to think all that's needed is money," Morgan snapped. "It takes more than that to revive an industry, to give people incentive."

"I agree," Bryan said quickly. "But someone with money *and* enthusiasm could give the community reason to get involved."

"That would take years," Morgan countered.

Bryan struggled valiantly on. "Perhaps, but . . ."

"I don't have years," Morgan said shortly.

A silence fell. After that and even before Finnegan announced dinner, glasses were emptied and the conversation languished.

Oriel led the way into the dining room, thinking the good food she and Mrs. Mills had planned would restore energy and brighten the talk at the dinner table.

Her hopes were quickly dashed. Instead of being the success she had hoped for, dinner was a disaster. She watched helplessly as the courses she had so carefully planned were presented in reverse order. The salad came before the fish course; the soup followed the meat and vegetables. Oriel felt herself grow more tense every minute. She could only imagine what must be going on in the kitchen. Desperately, she tried to keep up some conversation, avoiding the bewildered faces of Conan and the unflappable Finnegan as they stoically continued service.

At one point, Oriel thought Morgan might come to the rescue, but he seemed to be unaware of the awful drama of the ruined dinner. He failed to exercise the charming social skills she knew he possessed.

The dessert was brought in. The well-mannered guests, whatever they might have been thinking, tried several topics of conversation. Suzanne made a feeble comment on the weather and Michael asked Bryan if he had read a recently published book on the history of this part of Ireland. Morgan did not add anything to the discussion.

At last the final course had been taken away and they all went into the drawing room, where Finnegan served the coffee.

Oriel took this brief opportunity to dash into the kitchen, where she found a distraught Mrs. Mills weeping copiously.

"Oh, madam," she wailed, wiping her red eyes on her apron. "I don't know what happened. The dessert was near spoilt, so I had to make a soufflé instead, and Mrs. Nesbitt come into the kitchen slammin' the door and it fell! Then I forgot to ladle the soup out for Conan to carry in and—oh, madam, should I give notice?"

"No, no, Mrs. Mills, don't cry. It's all done now. I don't think anyone but I noticed. Just get a good night's sleep and we'll sort it all out tomorrow."

Oriel went back to her guests feeling like an early Christian going into the lions' den. What an evening it had been. *And no help from Morgan at all,* she thought furiously. By this time, Oriel wished the terrible evening was over. So must have the guests, for soon afterwards they declared they must be leaving. Bryan accompanied the Wicklows.

Too angry to trust herself to say anything to Morgan, Oriel bade him a cool good night and went immediately upstairs.

The next morning, Oriel awakened with a headache. Thinking that maybe a brisk canter in the crisp fall air would help, she put on her riding habit before going downstairs for breakfast.

She was still angry about Morgan's behavior the evening before. Why couldn't he have at least made an effort? Bryan had been a real help, bringing up every possible subject that might draw Morgan into friendly conversation. Finally, even he was exhausted. Michael had fallen into a resentful silence. Who could blame him with a host like Morgan? Even Suzanne and Oriel had run out of small talk. The evening had petered out to a dismal close. Oriel had to admit her first attempt at entertaining at Drummond Castle had been a miserable failure.

When she came into the dining room, she was surprised to find Morgan sitting at the table, reading the newspaper. With only a cool glance at him, Oriel helped herself to toast and eggs, then sat down at the other end of the table.

Realizing once again he had made Oriel unhappy, Morgan awkwardly apologized for being poor company the night before, mumbling something about having a great deal on his mind.

Carefully keeping her voice even and her expression composed, Oriel said, "It's more than that—something I think we should talk about, Morgan. Perhaps we should redefine my position here. Perhaps I misunderstood. Perhaps I am only a paid tenant at Drummond Castle. Perhaps I should not offer an opinion, speak only when spoken to, and not do anything to make life here more pleasant for either of us."

Not daring to linger, Oriel rose from the table and left the dining room. She walked toward the stables, trying vainly to control her disappointment. She had nearly reached the stables before she realized she was grasping her riding crop so tightly that there was a band of red across her palm.

Then she heard steps on the cobbled apron of the stable yard. Turning her head, she saw Morgan running toward her.

"Oriel, I apologize. I always seem to be doing that. If I seemed rude to your guests, I apologize, but, it's *you* I'm most sorry about." His voice softened. "I never meant to hurt you or offend you. Sometimes I think this whole thing's been a mistake. If you're not happy here, then—"

"Whether I'm happy or not is irrelevant," Oriel interrupted him. "A bargain is a bargain." She walked away, not wanting him to see the tears stinging her eyes. The pain of disappointment was keen, even though a part of her was touched by his concern. She had been optimistic about last evening, but had been horribly wrong. Why couldn't Morgan have behaved decently in the first place and spared her the apology later?

At least the weather was wonderful. The sun was shining, the sky a clear blue. Oriel prayed the ride in the brisk autumn air would clear her head and restore her spirits.

Tim, the groom, was waiting at the mounting block, holding Mavourneen's bridle. Oriel greeted him as cheerfully as she could manage. "What a glorious morning," she said.

"Now 'tis fine enough. But if I was you, madam, I'd not go far or stay out too long. Fog's going to roll in before too long."

"You're sure?" Oriel asked doubtfully. "There's certainly no sign of it now."

"It's in the air. I can smell it." He nodded his head.

Oriel had observed Irishmen came in two categories. Some were eternally optimistic; others, like the dour Tim, were given to dark predictions and warnings. Oriel had learned to enjoy the one and ignore the other. With a determinedly cheery good-bye, Oriel mounted and trotted out of the stable yard toward the hills.

Oriel should have listened to Tim's warning. Not twenty minutes later, she suddenly seemed to be immersed in fog. Turning Mavourneen around, she started back in the direction she had come. The horse seemed hesitant, and Oriel herself began to feel confused.

She was surrounded in a swirling mist, which was growing ever more dense. The horse would take a few steps and then stop. Oriel dared not urge her on, fearing she might be dangerously close to the cliffs. One false step and they would both go hurtling over, crashing onto the beach below. Holding tightly to the reins, Oriel dismounted. Perhaps it would be better to go on foot, leading the horse slowly, step by cautious step, back to Drummond Castle.

She squinted through the fog, hoping for some familiar sign to show her she was on the right path. Suddenly, Oriel thought she discerned the outline of the curved arch of the castle's wrought-iron gates. *Thank God,* she breathed a silent prayer of relief.

Almost there, she became aware of movement just ahead. A shadowy figure sprang out of the depths, coming toward her. A hooded figure, its cape was unfurled behind it like a huge fan. Oriel's heart began racing wildly; cold perspiration washed over her. Her hands became sweaty in her leather riding gloves. Her breath was caught in her throat, where a scream was trapped with fear. One terrified thought raced through her mind—*the ghost of Shaleen O'Connor!*

With a gasp, she turned, hiding her head against Mavourneen's neck, squeezing her eyes shut. She heard the horse whinny softly, shifting her feet to one side. She felt a swish of air, as if the figure had passed so close it left an icy breath on her cheek. Shuddering, Oriel clung to the horse's bridle.

She didn't know how long she stood there shivering, afraid to open her eyes. It could have been a minute or longer before she forced herself to pull away from the horse, to look forward. Thin swirls of gray obscured the house, but the gates were in plain sight. There was nothing else.

She moved her head, peering in each direction, but saw nothing. She felt faint. What had she *really* seen? She had certainly *felt* something. Someone—or some*thing*—had passed her as she stood rooted in place. But *who? What?* Her breath was still shallow and the urgency to get through the gates, back to the castle and safety, was strong. Dragging on her horse's reins, she started walking, stumbling at times because her legs were so shaky.

Finally, she left Mavourneen with a worried-looking Tim, who gave her a curious glance before taking the horse away. Unable to speak rationally, Oriel mumbled something and then hurried up to the house.

Breathlessly she struggled up the steps and was about to open the front door when it was yanked open by Morgan. His face was flushed and angry. "Where have you been? Tim was up here with all kinds of dire predictions about your getting lost and falling over the cliffs, or—"

"Morgan, I saw her!" Oriel gasped, shaken out of her gripping fear.

"Saw who? What are you talking about?"

"At the gates, just as I was coming in—she floated. It was Shaleen O'Connor."

"Are you crazy?" Morgan demanded. "Have you been thrown and hit your head?"

"No, listen! Morgan, I know I saw—"

Morgan's eyes flashed furiously. "Whatever you saw it *wasn't* that. I thought you had better sense than to be taken in by the superstitious tales of uneducated servants," he said furiously. "It's clear you've had a bad scare of some sort. Just don't ever mention Shaleen O'Connor, or any other silly Irish legend to me again." He turned around and stalked off toward his rooms. The slam of the door echoed in the hall.

Oriel stood there, stunned by his angry response to the incident. There was no use. He'd never believe that she had seen anything. He seemed unwilling to believe any Irish myth—especially one that concerned his castle. Wearily, she started toward the stairway. She needed a hot bath, a cup of tea.

As she reached the first step, she looked up and saw Molly standing on the landing, a strange, knowing expression on her round face. She knew Molly was curious about what she had overheard her tell Morgan, but she didn't feel free to bring up the subject again with the maid. It would just support the village contention that Drummond Castle was haunted and the wild rumors among the servants. No matter how much she wanted to discuss the apparition she'd seen, Oriel knew it was better to say nothing.

She did decide, however, to borrow some of Bryan's books about the old Irish castles and the families who had built them and lived in them. Maybe there'd be some factual information to give credence or disprove the Shaleen O'Connor story.

After that explosive scene with Morgan, Oriel made a decision. She could not change the situation nor Morgan. To expect anything more would only lead to disappointment. Still, a bargain was a bargain. It was October—six months more and this whole farce would be over. She would be free, independent, and richer than she could ever have imagined. And yet a part of her knew it would be difficult to leave the castle, to leave Morgan.

She knew her feelings for Morgan were dangerous. She had never dreamed she would feel anything but a kind of detached interest in the man with whom she had made such a perilous bargain. Realizing the impossibility of such feelings was one thing, but dreams and emotions had a life of their own. Sometimes she couldn't seem to control them, often drifting into thoughts of what might have been, if only . . .

More and more, the cove became Oriel's special place. One particular day after breakfast, she bundled up, put an apple and some biscuits in a small basket, and set out for the hidden beach. Morgan was nowhere in sight when she left. She knew he had taken to early morning rides by himself, sometimes not returning until late in the afternoon. In the current state of their relationship, what did it matter?

Oriel walked briskly up the cliff path, then went down the rickety ladder to the sheltered place hidden under the cliffs. The sea was slate gray and angry looking. As she stared out at the breaking waves, they seemed as turbulent as her own mood.

Sighing, she opened her book—*Wuthering Heights.* She had read it before, but its romantic plot about two star-crossed lovers appealed to her just now. She was soon lost in its compelling story, so much so that she was oblivious to the changing tide. All at once, the foamy edge of a wave washing up on the sand wet the hem of her dress. Startled, she looked up and saw she was surrounded by ripples of water. Remembering Bryan's earlier warning about the tide, she jumped to her feet, grabbed her basket, and hurried toward the ladder.

The quickly rising water was already lapping at her feet, the surf rapidly eating up the circles of remaining sand. Slipping the handle of her basket over one arm, Oriel grabbed hold of the side of the ladder with her free hand. As she did, she felt it sway back from the rock. She looked up and saw the top was leaning forward. Somehow it had come loose from where it was anchored at the top of the cliff. As unstable as it seemed, she would have to climb it, hoping she could manage to reach the top before it gave way entirely. She had to force herself to put her foot on the lowest rung. Since the bottom few rungs were missing, it was quite a way up to the first rung. She had done it before, but not with the top posts so unstable. There was no alternative. She had to try.

She started up. The flimsy ladder wobbled with her weight. Her fingers tightened on the rung above; moving slowly, she took the next step up. Two, then three steps. The ladder shuddered in the wind. She dared not look up, knowing how far she had to go to reach safety.

Suddenly, she heard a horrible snapping sound as the old wood cracked and splintered. The ladder swung precariously. Frozen with fear, Oriel looked up and saw that the upper part had been loosened entirely from the posts. Try as she might to hold on, her weight pulled the ladder away from the rocky cliff. Her hands lost their grasp, the basket fell, and she hurtled back toward the beach below.

*S*he fell backwards, landing on the wet sand with one leg twisted under her. Her breath was knocked out of her and the pain was intense. For a moment she lay there, stunned and immobilized from the shock of the fall. Slowly, the awareness of the danger she was in came back. Conscious of the oncoming tide swirling around her, she struggled painfully to a sitting position and dragged herself to her knees. Her skirt was soaked and her shoes were heavy with sand.

With tremendous effort, she got to her feet. An agonizing pain seared through her ankle, but there was no time to waste. The tide was coming in faster and faster. She had to get up the cliff or she would be trapped by the tide and drown. She slogged back toward the cliff, her sodden skirt and water-soaked boots impeding her progress. Ignoring the painful ankle, she hobbled to the side of the cliff. It seemed impossibly steep and high. Her legs felt weak. Behind her, the water level grew higher with each wave.

She started to climb. The jagged rocks scraped her bare hands as she searched for a hold. She pulled herself painfully up, then slipped back. A terrified sob caught in her throat. *Oh, dear God, help me,* she prayed. Desperately, she clawed her way up again, inch by inch. She must make it. She must! The fear of falling again down to the roaring water below kept her going, pulling herself with all her strength, panting and groaning with each movement.

Then, from far off, she heard shouts. *Oh, could it be— please God—maybe someone is coming,* Oriel thought.

"Hold on, Oriel, I'm here. Catch hold of this rope, and I'll pull you up." It was Bryan. He must have been out on one of his rambles and somehow seen her plight.

He gripped her upper arms and pulled her up over the edge of the cliff. His hands went around her waist, dragging her to her feet. As soon as she put weight on her foot, a wrenching pain stabbed her ankle and she collapsed against Bryan, crying out.

"What is it, Oriel? Are you hurt?"

"My foot," she gasped. "I think I twisted my ankle when I fell. I'm not sure I can walk."

Gingerly she tried, but the pain was too intense. Shaking her head, she said, "I can't. I'm sorry . . ."

"Don't," Bryan said firmly. "You'll injure it more if you try. Lean on me. Michael should be along in a few minutes. He was coming to my cottage, and I decided to walk up and meet him. As soon as he gets here, we'll carry you. Don't worry. It will be all right."

Oriel was feeling too shaky to object. It seemed like a miracle Bryan had happened by. If he hadn't, she didn't know how she would ever have made it back to the castle.

Within minutes, Michael Wicklow appeared walking jauntily from the woods. Michael looked startled when he saw Oriel clinging to Bryan.

"Michael, come here!" Bryan called. "Oriel's been hurt. That blasted ladder. Someone should have fixed it or taken it completely away. It's a death trap."

Oriel shuddered at his choice of words. It made her realize how horribly close her escape had been.

The two men crossed arms, making a seat. Then Oriel put an arm around each man's shoulder and was lifted up. As they approached Drummond Castle, Oriel whispered a prayer of thanksgiving that Bryan had happened along when he did. Another hour and she would have been clinging to the cliff alone, her strength waning and finally giving out. She would surely have fallen to her death.

A startled Finnegan opened the door. His expression rapidly changed to alarm.

"Your mistress has had an accident," Bryan said. "Best you inform your master at once and get someone to help her."

The two men carried Oriel into the great hall. By now her foot was throbbing fiercely and she was shuddering from the cold. All at once, the hall was filled with people hovering around her. Molly hurried to Oriel's side, murmuring expressions of distress and sympathy. Mrs. Nesbitt came down the stairway and glanced at the men, then asked Michael, "What's happened?"

"The ladder near the sea cove gave way and Mrs. Drummond fell," Michael replied.

Then Morgan came storming from his wing of the house, demanding explanation, barely listening to what Bryan tried to tell him.

Before Oriel could protest, Morgan swept her up in his arms. Barking orders for Molly to follow, he carried her up to her bedroom. Molly was right on his heels, all the while speaking words of comfort as he laid Oriel gently on her bed.

"See to your mistress," Morgan said before striding out of the room.

"Oh, ma'am, you're soaked! We must get these off before you catch your death," Molly proclaimed as she helped Oriel out of her wet clothes. "How ever did you get so drenched?"

Oriel's teeth were chattering too hard to answer.

"My, oh my!" Molly clucked her tongue as she wrapped blankets around Oriel's shivering body.

A few minutes later, after a brief knock at the door, Morgan returned. He handed Oriel a tumbler of brandy. "Here, drink this," he ordered. He turned to the maid. "Does she have a fever, Molly?"

"No, sir—not that I can tell. She will if we don't get her right into bed."

"Well, do it then," Morgan snapped. He turned to Oriel, anger belying the visible concern in his expression. "What were you doing down in that cove anyway? Didn't you know it was dangerous?"

Oriel was too upset to try to explain. Her head was aching and she couldn't seem to stop shivering. Morgan took the empty glass from her shaking hands and turned to leave.

"Wait, Morgan," Oriel said, and he halted. "Do thank Bryan and Michael. I don't know what would have happened if they hadn't come along."

He nodded curtly and left the room.

Molly wrapped Oriel's swollen ankle with strips of flannel, then helped her into her nightdress, which had been warmed by the fireplace. As she eased Oriel back into the bed piled high with comforters, Molly gave a puzzled frown. "I still don't see how it could have happened, madam—the beach ladder breaking apart like that. There should've been a sign or something, don't you think, ma'am? To warn people it wasn't safe. That is, unless—"

"Unless what, Molly?" There was something in the maid's voice that sent a nervous jolt through Oriel.

"Well, ma'am, it does seem like someone might have done it on purpose." She turned her head, busily tucking in the covers, avoiding Oriel's surprised gaze.

"Why should anyone do that?"

Molly turned back, her face flushed but determined. "To scare you off, maybe—you and the master both. It's no secret folks around here resent Mr. Drummond, hold grudges against him for all sorts of things, real and imagined. Now that he's come back with a wife, well, some people don't want him to stay."

Before Oriel could question Molly further, a sharp tap came on the bedroom door and Mrs. Nesbitt came in, carrying a small tray. She set it down on the table beside Oriel's bed. It held a pitcher of water, a glass, and a small envelope, which was propped against the glass on the lace doily. "I've brought you a sleeping powder, madam. I keep some in my supplies for emergencies and for when I cannot sleep myself. It will relax you and help you to rest after your frightening experience."

"That's very kind of you, Mrs. Nesbitt," Oriel said, but there was no kindness in the housekeeper's eyes nor compassion in her expression. The thought passed through Oriel's mind, *Why does Mrs. Nesbitt dislike me?* She quickly thrust it away. It was just the woman's stiff, reserved manner, she told herself.

Mrs. Nesbitt turned to the maid, who was still standing nearby. "Molly, I think you should leave Mrs. Drummond now. Don't tire her out with your talk."

"Yes, ma'am," Molly said hesitantly, darting a quick look at Oriel as if checking that she agreed.

"I'm fine, Molly," Oriel assured her. "Thank you for all your help."

"If you need anything in the night, just ring the bell," Mrs. Nesbitt said. She took a few steps toward the door, then stood waiting for Molly to obey her direction. With another anxious look at Oriel, Molly left. The housekeeper followed.

For some reason Oriel did not want to take the sleeping powder Mrs. Nesbitt had brought, even though the effect of the brandy had worn off. The one lamp left burning in the room cast strange shadows. Molly's scary explanation for what had happened kept Oriel wakeful. Could it possibly be true? Would anyone want them to leave Drummond Castle so badly as to risk endangering Oriel's life? Or was it all Molly's imagination?

The next morning, Oriel felt stiff and sore and her ankle was quite swollen. Her shallow sleep had been disturbed with nightmares of her ordeal.

"A day in bed is what's best, ma'am," Molly advised. "Don't even try to stand on that ankle. There's no need for you to stir yourself at all."

After Molly took her breakfast tray away, Oriel leaned back against the pillows. She was still mulling over what Molly had said the night before. Were there people in Kilmara who hated Morgan, resented the rich American who had come, flaunting his wealth? Were those vicious enough to use her to get to him? Whether it was true or not, Oriel felt she should talk to Morgan about it. Even Bryan had hinted at possible retribution. Did Morgan know his grandfather had been threatened? She should at least suggest the possibility to Morgan.

Molly returned to announce that Dr. O'Toole had arrived.

"But I don't need a doctor," Oriel protested.

Molly raised her eyebrows. "Well, the master thought you did, ma'am. He sent for him first thing this morning."

"Oh, well," Oriel shrugged resignedly.

The doctor, a ruddy-faced man with grizzled gray whiskers and merry eyes, examined her ankle. "It's a nasty sprain. You were lucky it wasn't broken. Stay off it until the swelling goes down. And stay away from those cliffs, young lady. They've been responsible for a few deaths, not all of them accidental."

Oriel hardly had time to absorb that statement when Molly was back. "The master asked if he could come up, ma'am." Molly helped Oriel into her pink quilted robe and assisted her over to the chaise lounge.

When Morgan came in, he rushed to Oriel's side. "You're sure you're all right? No serious injuries?"

"Yes, just fine. I'm a little sore, but the doctor says my ankle will be fine with some rest." Oriel looked around the room and lowered her voice. "There is something else we should talk about."

He frowned, a flicker of alarm in his eyes. "What is it? Is there something you need or want? Just name it." Morgan seemed anxious to please her, to make her happy.

Oriel saw something in Morgan's reaction she had never seen in him before. He really *had* been worried about her. Still, she knew she would have to tread carefully in laying out her theory about the accident. Slowly, she began, watching him closely as she spoke.

Disbelief, skepticism, and anger all flashed through his eyes. His jaw clenched several times and Oriel thought he might interrupt her, but he listened until she had finished.

He got up from the chair and began pacing, his hands clasped behind his back. He went over to the window and stood there for a long minute staring out. Then he whirled around and said angrily, "But why *you?* Why *now?* All that stuff happened centuries ago. It has nothing to do with now. We're in the late nineteenth century. And besides, Shaleen's vengeance was against the Lawrence family, *not* the Drummonds. We had nothing to do with it. Why would anyone want to harm you?"

"Memories are long in Ireland," she replied softly. "At least that's what Bryan Moore contends."

"What does *he* know about it?" Morgan demanded.

"He's a student of history—*Irish* history. You should talk to him sometime—especially since you are now a property owner here."

Morgan glowered, his handsome face a contradiction of emotions. "Sometimes I wish I'd never come here!" he said, pounding his clenched fist into his open palm. He gave Oriel a quick glance. "And I'm sure you do as well. I should never have brought you here, exposed you to this."

Impulsively, Oriel reached out her hand. "I don't feel that way, Morgan. Maybe I'm wrong. Maybe this is all wild speculation. I'm sorry."

"No, I'm the one who's sorry." He pressed her hand. Then slowly, as a smile broke across his face, Oriel realized once again how handsome he was.

"Well, I won't be scared off and I won't let you be either. They'll have to deal with me if they try anything else. I'll tell you what, as soon as you're up and about, we'll go up to Dublin—get away from this gloomy castle with all its old wives' tales and ghost stories. I just got a letter from my cousin, Paige. Her husband is Freddy Redmon. His family has a chain of stores in England and they're opening a new one in Dublin. They've rented a house there and have invited us to dine with them and go to the theater. A change of scenery might be the best thing for both of us. How does that sound?"

Oriel could hardly believe her ears or the change in Morgan toward her. "It sounds marvelous! I'd love it."

"Done! I'll write her immediately."

After Morgan left, Oriel smiled to herself. Maybe her accident had been worth it after all.

few weeks later, Oriel's ankle had fully healed. The date for departure on the promised trip to Dublin had been set and Morgan had made all the arrangements for their stay.

When Oriel came down to breakfast a few days before they were to leave, Morgan held up a note that had come in the morning post. "It's from my cousin, Paige, inviting us to stay at their townhouse. I've already written her back that we have reservations at a hotel. I thought that would avoid any awkward explanations about separate rooms." Although Morgan's tone was matter-of-fact, his face reddened slightly and he avoided looking directly at Oriel by glancing through the rest of the mail.

So, Oriel thought, Morgan had not shared the secret of their strange marriage with his relatives. That might make being with them difficult—to play the part of a newly married couple yet not act overtly affectionate toward one another. Oriel hoped Morgan didn't regret his impulsive suggestion that they take this trip. She was looking forward to it. The long days while her ankle was healing had been particularly tedious. She missed her daily horseback rides and brisk walks and felt very confined indeed. She was longing for some diversion.

Not that she could complain. Everything had been done to make her convalescence comfortable and pleasant. Bryan had sent over books for her to read; the Wicklows sent flowers and fruit. Morgan had been particularly considerate. He began having his dessert and coffee served upstairs in her sitting room each evening. Oriel felt that during this time, they had somehow gotten past the barriers of the first few months at Drummond Castle and become companionable friends.

The afternoon before their departure, Oriel was busy packing. She had sent Molly to the laundry room to get her freshly ironed clothes when a tap came on her bedroom door and Mrs. Nesbitt entered. She stood stiffly on the threshold, glancing disapprovingly around the cluttered room. An array of jackets, skirts, and blouses were spread out on the bed. Conscious of the disarray, Oriel laughingly apologized, "Don't worry, Mrs. Nesbitt, we'll soon make order out of chaos."

There was no answering smile. Mrs. Nesbitt clasped her hands together over her belt with the ever-present keys and said coldly, "A proper lady's maid would make short work of this. That is precisely why I wanted to speak to you before you left, Mrs. Drummond. I wondered if you intend, while you are in Dublin, to interview young women to hire for your personal maid? There is a very good domestic employment agency in Dublin. They require the best references and recommend only the most highly qualified people." She added disdainfully, "Most of the local girls are hopeless."

Puzzled, Oriel looked at her blankly for a minute. "No, Mrs. Nesbitt, I have no such intention. It never crossed my mind."

"You must realize, Mrs. Drummond, that Molly has not been trained as a lady's maid. She is a housemaid." Then, as if Oriel did not know the difference, she added, "The duties of each are totally different."

Oriel bit her lower lip to refrain from the indignant response that rushed to her mind. The nerve of the woman! For all her veneer of respect, it was obvious Mrs. Nesbitt was trying to embarrass her. Determined not to give the woman the satisfaction of upsetting her, Oriel replied calmly, "Molly suits me perfectly, Mrs. Nesbitt. I have no intention of replacing her."

This did not seem to deter the housekeeper, because Mrs. Nesbitt continued, "I just thought I should suggest it, madam. We were all rather surprised when you arrived unaccompanied by your own maid."

By this time, Oriel's temper was rising. Who did Mrs. Nesbitt think she was? "I understand that, Mrs. Nesbitt," Oriel replied with icy calm. "However, Molly is quick and smart and teachable. I'm entirely satisfied with her and do not intend to make a change."

Mrs. Nesbitt drew herself up with frigid dignity. "Very well, madam."

In a gesture of dismissal, Oriel turned her back and went over to the bed as if contemplating the choice of her dresses. She stood there waiting until she heard the rustle of the housekeeper's skirt and the click of the bedroom door as Mrs. Nesbitt went out. Then she let out a long sigh of relief.

Perhaps when she returned from Dublin she would have to deal more firmly with the housekeeper, establish herself in a more direct way as mistress at Drummond Castle. For now, however, she wasn't going to let this incident spoil her holiday.

Molly returned with a pile of starched clothes, remarking with a bit of a chuckle, "Mrs. Nesbitt just sailed by me looking like a thunderstorm."

Oriel knew better than to share Mrs. Nesbitt's comments with Molly. It would only serve to increase the friction that already existed between the two. Still, Mrs. Nesbitt's hostility bothered her. From the beginning, the woman had seemed to resent Oriel. Why? It was hard to figure. Had she known Edwina Parker? Perhaps the woman had expected Edwina to be her mistress and was disappointed when Morgan arrived with Oriel.

Oriel dismissed the worrisome problem. Tomorrow she would be away from both the castle and its resident "dragon," as she privately dubbed the housekeeper.

Dublin

November 1895

Upon their arrival in Dublin, Oriel knew Morgan had been right. A change of scene was just what she had needed. The busy streets, the bright store windows, and the well-dressed people were stimulating after her long time in the isolated country.

They checked in at the Shelbourne Hotel. Its red and white exterior led into an interior just as elegant. A uniformed bellhop showed Oriel to her room. Oriel looked around with delight. It was spacious yet very feminine, with cabbage roses on the wallpaper, a tall brass bed piled with pillows, a ruffle-skirted dressing table, and the luxury of an adjoining bath.

After freshening up, she was to meet Morgan back in the lobby, then do some shopping. Oriel felt excited. She hadn't realized how deprived of activity her life had been lately, especially when laid up with her sprained ankle. This trip was more than a welcome change, it was a lifesaver. She felt happier, more lighthearted than she had in months.

Oriel wasted no time washing up and fixing her hair. Soon she hurried back downstairs. Entering the lobby, she saw Morgan before he was aware of her coming. He was talking with a balding, red-whiskered man in a frock coat and striped trousers whom she guessed was the hotel manager.

At a discreet distance, she stood for a minute observing Morgan. In his belted tweed suit, he looked the epitome of a country squire. The role suited him—if only he would accept it. He was also extremely handsome, Oriel noted anew, with his black wavy hair, strongly molded features, and vivid blue eyes. She allowed herself to wonder what it might be like if the two of them were up from the country for a festive weekend holiday together, if things between them were different. Without realizing it, she sighed.

Just then, Morgan turned his head and saw her. He nodded to the manager, then strode across the lobby toward her.

"I thought you would enjoy doing the shops without a male tagging along." He smiled. "I know most women do. I want you to take all the time you need, then meet me back here in a few hours. There'll be plenty of time for you to rest before our evening out. Paige and Freddy will pick us up at seven. Paige said she has the theater tickets and we'll dine together beforehand." He paused, enjoying the pleasure in her eyes. "Does that suit you?"

"Oh, yes," she said, beaming.

"You have your letter of credit with you, don't you? I made a deposit with the manager here at the hotel in case you want to draw more."

Oriel blushed. "That isn't necessary. I have more than enough." As part of their marital agreement, Morgan's lawyer had opened an account for Oriel at a Dublin bank from which she could write checks.

"I know it isn't necessary," he said quietly. "I very much want you to enjoy yourself, Oriel. You deserve it. If you see something you want, I want you to get it. Understand?" His tone was decisive.

Feeling a little embarrassed by his making such a point of it, Oriel simply nodded. Did the fact she had had to scrimp and save for so many years show? It was certainly a glorious feeling to have money in her purse and be given license to spend it.

"See you later, then," Morgan said, smiling.

Oriel left the hotel and strolled along, gazing into the store windows. She stopped to look at a glittering display of cut glass. As she stared, the idea of buying a gift for Nola came to mind—something small, perhaps, as a gesture of gratitude for her friend's cheerful kindness.

Inside the store, all different patterns of beautiful china were presented in several table arrangements. As Oriel wandered up and down the aisles, she remembered the Wicklows talking about the factory in Kilmara that had once produced its own lovely dinnerware. She had seen examples of it in Suzanne's teacups. Now, however, Oriel saw nothing even similar. It was sad that the original designs had been lost when the factory shut down. If only Morgan were interested, if he wanted to stay in Kilmara and help bring the factory back to life . . . Well, it had nothing to do with her, not really. She was only going to be here a year, actually only another five months.

Oriel continued wandering through the store. She saw a gracefully shaped crystal vase and bought it at once. She knew Nola would be thrilled to receive it. She'd probably give it a place of honor in her keepsake-filled room.

After purchasing the vase, Oriel went down the street where there was a large women's clothing store. The minute she went through the etched glass doors of the fashionable store, Oriel felt she had stepped into the past. Its deep carpets and faintly perfumed air brought vague memories of accompanying her mother to similar exclusive Boston stores.

Slowly, Oriel walked around, surrounded by lavishly furred cloaks, hats adorned with exotic feathers, dresses gleaming with sequins, beaded handbags, silk scarves, and pearl-buttoned gloves. It was dizzying and seductive. Yet despite the letter of credit and Morgan's reminder that she was to buy whatever caught her fancy, Oriel felt hesitant.

"May I help you find something, madam?" a saleswoman asked.

"Oh, I'm not sure . . . perhaps—I'm going to the theater tonight."

"And what did madam have in mind? A gown, perhaps?"

"No, I have that." She had brought one of the most extravagant of Neecy's hand-me-downs, a jade taffeta with balloon sleeves and a pleated neckline. Oriel's wandering gaze stopped and she pointed to a flowing black panne velvet cape lined in pale green satin. "I think I'd like to try on that."

"The very thing, madam."

The next minute Oriel was standing before a full-length mirror in the dressing room while the saleswoman draped the cape over her shoulders. The ruffled collar framed her face like a fan.

"Ah, perfect!" the saleswoman declared. "It could have been made for you."

Oriel sighed. She could not possibly have walked out of the store without it. "I'll take it!"

Oriel was soon back out on the street with her packages, on her way back to the hotel. However, she could not resist pausing before a jeweler's shop window. As she halted there, she was startled by Morgan's voice just behind her. "Anything you like in there?"

She whirled around to meet his laughing eyes.

"Oh, indeed—half the window!"

"Anything particular?"

Still in a playful mode, she pointed to a jade and pearl pendant. "That for starters."

"Then you shall have it." Morgan took her arm and brought her along as he opened the store's door. They went inside together.

"Morgan," she whispered, trembling at his closeness, "I was only—"

He didn't let her finish. At the counter, Morgan spoke directly to the benignly smiling clerk, who came right up to wait on them. "We'd like to see the jade and pearl necklace in the window, if you please."

"Certainly, sir, at once. One minute while I get it."

"Morgan, no, please," she whispered. "I was only joking."

"Now, Oriel, don't fuss. You want it, and I want to give it to you. It will be a memento of a happy day in Dublin."

His voice was firm and she realized that to argue would be to cause an unnecessary scene. The clerk laid the necklace carefully on a cushion on the counter for them to view. The pale green jade stone was circled in tiny pearls. The pendant hung on a delicate gold chain.

"There are matching earrings," encouraged the clerk.

"We'll have them too," Morgan declared, and the transaction was quickly made.

The clerk handed the long, narrow box to Oriel, saying, "You have made an excellent choice. May you wear it with joy, madam."

Outside in the street again, Oriel said shyly, "Thank you, Morgan."

He smiled down at her. "I'm glad you've found something in Ireland that pleases you."

"Oh, but I've found much that pleases me! I thought you knew that."

He looked somewhat rueful. "I'm afraid I haven't noticed much that's been going on since we've been here." He drew her hand through his arm, saying, "But that's going to change."

20

efore she went down to the lobby, Oriel gave herself a critical appraisal, trying to imagine how she would be seen by Morgan's relatives. The cape *was* perfect and it went beautifully with the dress. The jade pendant was an added touch. Morgan should be pleased at the effect. Certainly he would not be ashamed to introduce his bride to his cousins.

Oriel felt very glamorous in the flowing cape with its flattering ruff as she swept down the hotel stairs. At the turn of the stairway overlooking the lobby, she paused. She saw Morgan chatting with a well-dressed couple; his cousins, she assumed. At that moment, Morgan turned and looked up and his expression caused her heart to give a little leap. It was a look of genuine admiration.

She halted, wanting to seem poised. Morgan said something to the couple and they both glanced at her as she came the rest of the way down the steps into the lobby. Meeting her at the bottom of the stairs, Morgan took her arm and introduced her. "Oriel, I'd like you to meet my cousins, Paige and Freddy Redmon."

Paige was a tall, handsome woman, bearing a strong family resemblance to Morgan, with her dark wavy hair and eyes the same deep blue. She wore a beautiful gown of dusty rose satin, a garnet and pearl necklace, and a short mink cape draped over her shoulders.

Paige extended both hands to Oriel. "This is too marvelous! We never dreamed we'd have a family reunion in Dublin! I'm so happy to meet Morgan's bride."

Oriel controlled the urge to look at Morgan. After this enthusiastic greeting, Oriel was certain he had not informed his cousin that their marriage was a business contract. She returned Paige's greeting cordially and turned to meet her husband.

Freddy was two or three inches shorter than his wife; he was balding, but had a rosy face and a cherubic expression. He wasn't at all what Oriel had expected as the scion of a prosperous family business, the successful chain of Redmon stores throughout Great Britain. His mild manner was in sharp contrast to his wife's ebullient one, but Oriel found his shyness rather endearing.

As Morgan escorted Oriel out of the lobby to the carriage waiting to take them to the restaurant, he glanced at her. She was glowing, her eyes shining with excitement. Suddenly Morgan realized Oriel was more than attractive, she was appealingly lovely. Impulsively, he leaned toward her and said, "You look absolutely stunning."

Surprised but pleased at his unexpected compliment, Oriel murmured, "Thank you, Morgan."

At the candlelit restaurant, the headwaiter seemed to know the Redmons, greeting them with friendly deference. They were seated at a round table covered with crisp Irish damask cloths, gleaming crystal, and fine china. Menus were brought immediately and the first few minutes were spent choosing their entrées.

When the waiter departed, Paige turned to Oriel and asked, "So how do you like Ireland thus far? And of course I want to know all about Drummond Castle." Not waiting for Oriel's answer, she went on, "I've heard about the castle all my life. Morgan's father and my father were brothers, you see, and they were both brought up hearing tales of Ireland—the village where Grandpa had been a barefoot boy, the whole family legend! I suppose Grandpa wanted to start his own dynasty here. He claimed we were all descendants from the kings of Ireland." She laughed. "I've never seen the castle, you know. I know Grandpa spent hundreds of thousands on restoring and modernizing it. I do hope to see it while we're here."

"Of course you must," Oriel said impulsively, then darted a quick look at Morgan.

His expression was unreadable, but he said, "Yes, of course. A weekend soon?"

"We'd love it, wouldn't we, Freddy?"

"We might have to bring Madame Tamsin along," Freddy said rather hesitantly. "We expect she will be arriving in Dublin within a week or so to be our guest."

Morgan frowned. "Who is Madame Tamsin?"

"Do tell them, Freddy," Paige urged. "It's totally fascinating."

"Madame Tamsin is a remarkable woman," Freddy explained. "She is a certified graphologist from Italy. My brothers, who head our stores in England, learned about her through a scientist friend of theirs. They actually met her later at a country weekend affair. It's not a fad or something totally on the fringe, such as the phrenology phase everyone was going through for a while. This is bona fide."

"Bona fide *what?*" Morgan asked.

"She analyzes people's handwriting," Freddy said.

"Now don't look like that, Morgan," Paige interjected. "Wait until you hear the rest."

"It's been proven to be quite authentic, Morgan," Freddy continued. "It seems character traits cannot be concealed in handwriting. It's very revealing as to traits of honesty, dishonesty, responsibility, dependability—just the sort of things you are looking for in managers. She has been hired to screen employees as well as potential customers, to determine whether they are good credit risks."

Morgan's raised eyebrows indicated skepticism.

"I admit it's a new profession, but it's being given credence by several eminent scientists," Freddy continued. "My brothers have found it to be a reliable way of hiring people for responsible positions. I've decided to try it as we set up our staff for the Dublin store."

"All this on hearsay?" Morgan said incredulously.

"It's more than that, Morgan. I've met the lady myself—both of us have."

Paige nodded vigorously. "We both found her very credible."

"Well, I have to hand it to you, Freddy. You're always willing to take a chance on something new." Morgan smiled. "And this is the lady you want to bring to Drummond Castle with you, is it?"

"If it's all right with you and Oriel."

Morgan laughed. "Indeed it is! It should make for a very interesting weekend."

The waiter arrived with their orders—delicate, tender filet of sole, saffron mushrooms, and fresh vegetables. As they began to enjoy their delicious food, conversation turned to other things. Paige was lively and amusing and kept the table talk interesting. As time was getting short—the theater curtain was scheduled for eight o'clock—they decided to pass on dessert and go somewhere after the performance.

The theater lobby was extravagantly decorated, hung with glistening crystal chandeliers. Women in gorgeous gowns and brilliant jewels and men in evening clothes added to the elegant scene. The Redmons had reserved box seats in the mezzanine with a great view of the stage. Oriel had not had many chances to attend the theater in this style. A few minutes after they settled into their places, the curtain parted and for the next hour Oriel became completely immersed in the play.

When Paige touched her arm at intermission, Oriel was still caught up in the drama. In the mezzanine, people began flowing toward the stairway to go downstairs in search of refreshment. Morgan and Freddy excused themselves, telling the ladies they would brave the crowd and return with a cool drink.

"Thank goodness!" sighed Paige, relieved. "It's always such a crush down there during intermission." She unfurled her fan. "You always bump into people you'd rather avoid, then are forced to carry on some inane conversation when all you actually want is to get some refreshment!" Her light laughter took the sting out of her remark.

As if on cue, a woman's high-pitched, imperious voice hailed, "Paige Redmon! My dear, I had no idea you were in Dublin."

Oriel and Paige turned to see a large, florid-faced woman, her silver hair magnificently coiffed, moving toward them. She wore a mauve lace gown.

Paige seemed a bit flustered at her approach. "Why, Lady Soames, how nice to see you. Freddy and I have only just arrived a few weeks ago. Freddy's opening a new store, and—"

"Yes, yes, I've heard that," the woman interrupted. "He's here with you, I presume?" Her gaze turned to Oriel, barely skimming her with a cursory glance.

"Yes," Paige said quickly. "We're here with our cousin and his bride." She turned to Oriel and introduced her, mumbling her name. She hastened on to explain, "We're still settling in—there's so much to be done. I haven't called on anyone yet—" Paige faltered.

Lady Soames nodded. "Of course, I assure you I quite understand. Life can be terribly trying and upsetting. Just let me tell you what I'm enduring. I'm just back from Italy, and what do you suppose? My niece is coming for a visit! Unexpected, to say the least. At the height of the season in

London, I could not understand it. Of course, my sister tells me the poor dear has had an emotional setback—a broken engagement, I think. Anyway, she suddenly decided she wants to come to Ireland. I shall have to find some way to entertain her, and I'm sure I haven't a clue. I don't have many young friends. That's why I'm delighted to see *you*, my dear."

Lady Soames went on, hardly stopping for breath. "I'm sure by the time she comes, you and Freddy will be entertaining within your Dublin circle and could see that she is invited to some of the more festive events . . ." Lady Soames seemed to have an endless source of topics to chat about. She did not slow down until a passing couple spoke to her and she suddenly sailed off to bend a new set of ears.

Paige seemed visibly relieved at Lady Soames's departure. Looking embarrassed, she said, "I hope it won't bother you to know that Lady Soames is Edwina Parker's aunt."

Edwina Parker. The name dropped like a leaden weight on Oriel's euphoric mood. She had been so happy all day, happier than she had been in months and months, then suddenly—that name.

Nothing more was said, and soon Morgan and Freddy were back, handing the women glasses of chilled Perrier to sip before the warning chimes sounded, announcing that the next act was about to begin. They went back to their box. Somehow Oriel couldn't get back her earlier interest in the unfolding drama.

During their after-theater dessert following the end of the play, Paige didn't mention the encounter with Lady Soames. Oriel was curious as to why she didn't. Did she think it would upset Morgan? Did Paige know how devastating the broken engagement had been for him? Whatever the reason, Oriel was grateful. Even so, the incident had left a bitter taste in an otherwise enjoyable evening.

Later, parting with the Redmons at their hotel entrance, Morgan and Oriel entered the lobby.

"Did you enjoy yourself, Oriel?" Morgan asked.

"Oh, very much. Your cousins are so nice."

"They liked you." Morgan smiled. "I could tell."

"I'm glad." Oriel felt her cheeks warm with pleasure. Afraid she might reveal too much, she thanked him and quickly said good night.

In her room as she took off the beautiful cape, Oriel thought that in spite of that one unfortunate moment, it had been a wonderful evening. Oriel wondered again why Paige had avoided mentioning that Edwina was coming to Ireland for a visit. Had she feared Morgan's reaction? Or had she tactfully not wanted to bring up the past and ruin what seemed, on the surface at least, to be a happy new marriage? If she knew the truth, would Paige still have refrained from mentioning Edwina Parker?

That name, Oriel thought, had been like a pebble dropped into a quiet pond, disturbing the surface, spreading ever-widening circles, ending who knew where.

It was late the following day when they arrived back at Drummond Castle. Although Morgan did not magically become a jovial fellow traveler, his attitude was decidedly changed. In comparison to their first trip to Kilmara, this journey home was most pleasant.

Finnegan came out to greet them. He opened the carriage door and assisted them out. As they started into the house, Morgan paused. "Wait a minute," he said. He walked over to the stone steps where a late-blooming rose bush boasted one lovely yellow flower. He snapped the stem, and with a smile, brought it over and presented it to Oriel. "Welcome back to Drummond Castle."

Touched by this unexpected gesture, Oriel felt a stirring within that was the whisper of hope. "Thank you, Morgan," she murmured, bringing it to the tip of her nose, inhaling its fragrance. As she did so, she happened to raise her eyes and see a shadowy figure at an upstairs window. Whoever it was stepped back from view, dropping the curtain quickly. With an involuntary shiver, Oriel felt the discomfort of having been observed. Instantly, she experienced a startling conviction. Whoever had witnessed the small scene between her and Morgan did not wish them well—did not want them to be happy at Drummond Castle.

21

$\mathcal{T}$he days following their return from Dublin were marked by a changed atmosphere at Drummond Castle. Most visible was the change in Morgan's attitude toward her. His new regard for her gave Oriel confidence to take a more active role as mistress of the castle. Her involvement in the household seemed to motivate the staff. The house took on a new shine. Fresh flowers from the greenhouse appeared in vases in the occupied rooms. Meals became more varied.

The only person who remained aloof, in spite of all Oriel's efforts, was Mrs. Nesbitt. She seemed to take Oriel's interest as interference. She resisted any changes Oriel suggested, either failing to inform the other servants or ignoring the suggestions altogether. It was obvious the woman resented Oriel. It seemed there was nothing Oriel could do to make a difference in the housekeeper's jaundiced manner toward her.

Two incidents that happened shortly after the Dublin trip made Oriel realize that trying to win over Mrs. Nesbitt was futile. The first one occurred the day after their return. Just as Oriel was about to leave for her daily ride on Mavourneen, Mrs. Nesbitt came into Oriel's sitting room.

"I believe this is for you, madam," she said disdainfully, holding between her thumb and index finger a pink envelope.

Puzzled, Oriel repeated, "For *me?*"

"I believe so, madam. It is addressed to *Miss* Oriel *Banning.*" The housekeeper's gaze was cold.

Oriel took it, and seeing the crooked, childish handwriting recognized at once that it was from Nola. Of course it would be addressed to her *real* name. Nola thought Oriel was single, at Drummond Castle as a companion. Oriel realized Mrs. Nesbitt was trying to fluster her. "Thank you, Mrs. Nesbitt," Oriel said coolly. She could have explained that it was from a friend who did not know of her marriage, but she refused to give the woman the satisfaction of an explanation.

The letter from Nola was short, and it carried the news that a letter for Oriel had come. Enclosed was a battered-looking envelope addressed to her in care of the Claridge Hotel. It was the long overdue check and letter of reference from Mrs. McPhail, with no explanation, no excuse as to why the delay. The reference stated simply that Oriel had been in her employ for two years and had been "most satisfactory." Nola also wrote that she and Will had nearly reached their financial goals and planned to be married within a few months. That reminded Oriel that the bud vase in which she had placed the rose from Morgan was actually meant as a gift for Nola. It had been the perfect repository for the exquisite flower, which Oriel had taken much pleasure in seeing on her dressing table. Now she must wrap it and mail it to Nola. It would make a lovely wedding present.

The second incident with Mrs. Nesbitt occurred when Oriel returned from riding later that same day. Her vase was nowhere in sight. She made a cursory search of the room, then rather absently opened the top drawer of her dressing table. Inside, to her dismay, she found the vase broken and the rose crumbled, its petals among the shattered pieces of glass. Impulsively, Oriel tugged the tapestry bell pull, summoning Molly. Instead, Mrs. Nesbitt appeared.

"Molly is polishing the silver, madam, one of her *regular* duties that she has neglected of late." Mrs. Nesbitt spoke with excessive emphasis. "Is there something I can do for you?"

Oriel was trembling. Instinctively, she felt Molly was not responsible for the broken vase. She tried to control her anger, asking as calmly as possible, "Has anyone been in my room while I've been out?"

Mrs. Nesbitt looked affronted. "Only Molly, I should think, madam. To bring down your tea tray and make your bed."

Oriel pointed to the broken vase, the crumpled rose. "How did this happen, then?"

Mrs. Nesbitt looked shocked, a look Oriel suspected was pretense. Then the housekeeper's face twisted scornfully. "I told you, madam, Molly is not used to being a lady's maid, to being around delicate objects such as your vase. It is a common thing with ignorant help. They break something valuable and then, in a panic, try to hide it." She paused significantly. "Why don't you question Molly, madam? Or would you rather I did? I could discipline her."

"No, thank you, Mrs. Nesbitt. I'll attend to this myself." Oriel knew she could not openly accuse the housekeeper, even though she felt instinctively that she had something to do with the broken vase. It looked like a deliberate act.

Oriel decided to say nothing to Molly about the vase. It would only upset the girl and cause dissension among the staff. She would simply get Nola something else. Peace at any price seemed the better choice. Oriel had no premonition her decision was wrong.

During the next few weeks, Oriel felt more and more comfortable at Drummond Castle. With her new confidence, Oriel embarked on an even more ambitious project. The idea came about quite casually on a day when she encountered Bryan Moore on the cliff path. Though the late autumn winds were sharp, she still enjoyed her daily walks.

"So, Oriel, you're looking blooming. Things must be going well at Drummond Castle. The trip to Dublin seems to have done you a world of good," Bryan commented.

"I think it did. I shopped and we saw a play. I met some of Morgan's relatives, a delightful couple who will be coming down for a weekend soon. I should like you and Suzanne and Michael to meet them when they come."

"Entertaining then? You should put on the kind of show they used to hold at Drummond Castle. From what I've read, those were fantastic times."

"How so?"

"I have a book all about the balls, parties, and festivities that used to be held at the castle. The whole village was invited to them."

"I'm not planning anything as grand as that," Oriel said, laughing, "but I'd like to read about the entertainment they had in the olden days."

"I'll lend you the book," Bryan said.

True to his word, he did, and Oriel found the reading fascinating. The book was lavish with illustrations and detail. Oriel read that every autumn, the manor house gave a huge party in celebration of a good harvest and to reward the farm workers and the villagers for their loyalty. Another was held at Christmas. It was then, while looking through the book of Irish lore, that the idea of a medieval ball came to her.

One evening after an especially pleasant dinner, Oriel outlined her plan for a costume ball. She watched Morgan's expression pass from astonishment, to doubt, to guarded caution.

"Good grief, Oriel. That would take an enormous amount of planning, preparation, and work. Are you sure you want to tackle something like that on such a grand scale?"

"Yes, I'd love it. It would be fun, and besides—" She halted before adding, "It would most certainly break the monotony of the days here."

A look of amusement crossed Morgan's face, almost as if he read her unspoken thought. "Well, then go ahead. If you're game to do it, I won't stand in your way."

Given Morgan's agreement, Oriel's imagination took off and the ball began to take on reality. As she began to make lists of things to do and ideas for entertainment, music, and games, Oriel's excitement rose. She knew Suzanne would help. Bryan would have suggestions, maybe Michael as well. Oriel wrote to Paige about her plans and received a letter by return post almost immediately.

"I love it!" Paige responded. "The weekend we come with Madame Tamsin, you and I can toss all sorts of ideas around. It will be the society affair of the season—what a brilliant idea."

Oriel researched the menu possibilities with Mrs. Mills. The cook was at her best, she told Oriel, with large dinner parties and feeding many guests. "Of course, we'd have to hire extra help, with all t' baking to be done beforehand. I know several of t' village women who would welcome t' work," she assured Oriel.

Suzanne entered into every phase of the planning. The two young women exchanged notes almost daily, listing new ideas about the party. Oriel became preoccupied with what kind of costume she would wear. She and Suzanne discussed sources to research authentic costumes. Oriel invited Suzanne over to look at the portraits in the castle gallery and study some of the ladies' outfits. Since Oriel was a skilled seamstress, she thought she might copy one of the gowns.

"Oh, I'm not that clever," Suzanne sighed. "I think I'll just order costumes for me and Michael from a Dublin firm that specializes in theatrical costumes."

Oriel lingered in front of a particularly splendid looking gentleman's portrait. She could just picture Morgan in a velvet tunic, a starched ruff, and a lined cape. He would make a fantastically handsome lord of the castle. She knew she could make one of those Elizabethan doublets for Morgan—that is, if he'd let her.

The date for the ball was finally set for the first week in December. Oriel got Bryan to help with the wording of the invitation, then sent the copy to a professional calligrapher to be penned onto parchment.

She had decided on her costume, ordered the velvet fabric, and begun tracing the pattern from the gown worn by Lady Lavinia Lawrence in the portrait gallery. Her coup was persuading Morgan to let her make his doublet.

At first he had adamantly refused.

"It will only take a few minutes," she argued. "I'll get your measurements then. One fitting should do it. I can make the ruff, and we can order tights and boots from the Dublin costume shop."

With her gentle urging, he finally gave in.

Molly was present in Oriel's sitting room the morning Morgan showed up for Oriel to take his measurements. The maid seemed highly amused at the sight of Morgan standing tall and stiff while Oriel, tape measure in hand, solemnly measured the breadth of his shoulders, chest, and waist and recorded the numbers in her small notebook.

"Taking my measure, are you?" Morgan said with gruff humor.

"Oh, I already have that, sir!" Oriel retorted.

"Indeed? And what, pray tell, is it?"

"All bark and no bite, perhaps. Or like a chestnut—hard shell and soft within." She put her head to one side and looked up at him with a mischievous smile.

They looked at each other as if for the first time. It was an electrifying moment, a moment of recognition. Oriel felt her breath taken away with its intensity. She lowered her eyes and made some meaningless scribbles on the paper. "That's all, Morgan," she said briskly. "That will do nicely. Thank you."

"You're sure?" His voice seemed to hold an underlying question.

"Quite," she replied, turning away so he wouldn't see the warm color flooding into her face.

Molly, observing the two, pressed her mouth tightly together so as not to break into the wide smile puckering the corners of her mouth.

On the weekend Paige, Freddy, and Madame Tamsin were expected, Oriel made one last round of their rooms and the rest of the house. She was determined this party would not be a repeat of her first attempt at entertaining. She wanted everything to go smoothly. If this visit went well, she knew the ball would also be a success.

She still wondered if Paige and Freddy knew of the bargain she and Morgan had made. In Dublin there had been no mention of what appeared to have been a whirlwind courtship and hasty marriage. Perhaps people like the Redmons were too well-mannered to bring up sensitive subjects or ones that might cause embarrassment. However, Paige obviously knew about Edwina Parker and had assumed that Oriel also knew of the broken engagement.

As she went through the entire house one last time, Oriel complimented herself, knowing everything was in perfect readiness. She was confident that she had anticipated every possibility. She couldn't have been more wrong. She was totally unprepared for the one possibility she had never imagined.

When she heard carriage wheels on the drive, she looked out from her bedroom window and saw not one, but two carriages coming toward the house. Hurrying downstairs, she stopped at the library door to alert Morgan their guests were arriving.

He followed her to meet the visitors at the front door just as the occupants of the second coach were emerging. To Oriel's stunned amazement they were Lady Soames and her niece, *Edwina Parker.*

22

*P*aige, looking embarrassed and flustered, skimmed up the steps and took Oriel's suddenly cold hands. She leaned forward to kiss her cheek and whispered, "I'm sorry, Oriel. I had no way out. We met them in the village. They are on their way to a house party at the Mosgraves of Linden Wood. When we told them where we were going, Edwina insisted on coming along!"

Oriel did not dare glance at Morgan for his reaction.

It was Edwina who broke the awful awkwardness of the moment. With infinite confidence and grace, she came up the steps. Under a short cape bordered with silver fox fur, she wore a scarlet traveling suit. Her feathered pancake hat was coquettishly tipped to one side. She seemed not the least conscious that her unexpected appearance might be upsetting. And if she knew, she did not seem to care.

Holding out both hands to Morgan, Edwina said, "I couldn't resist the temptation of seeing the king in his castle—or should I say the dragon in his lair!" She laughed.

Oriel thought it was the loveliest laugh she had ever heard—musical as crystal being tapped with a silver spoon—

but with as brittle an edge as cut glass. It stabbed like a jagged shard into her heart.

From some unknown, unplumbed source within, she gathered herself together. She welcomed Madame Tamsin and greeted Lady Soames, who at least had the grace to look somewhat uncomfortable.

"How nice to see you again. You will of course, stay to tea," Oriel said to Edwina's aunt, even while out of the corner of her eye she noted Edwina speaking to Morgan.

"Thank you very much, but the Mosgraves are expecting us. We should be there now." Lady Soames's voice was raised, Oriel was sure, to warn her niece. "Edwina just took it into her head to stop by here first." She shifted her mink collar and gave her gold-headed cane an impatient tap on the stone steps. "We really must be on our way."

"Well, perhaps another time?" Oriel heard herself suggest, then could have bitten her tongue for having put herself in such a position.

"That's very kind of you. But it is up to—well, we shall see." Lady Soames frowned, then raised her voice again, "Edwina, my dear!"

Edwina gave her aunt a quick glance. "Coming, Auntie!" She said something to Morgan, then came down the steps and flashed a smile at Oriel and Paige, saying, "I know I've displayed frightfully bad manners, but it was too good a chance to pass up as I'm *sure* you can both understand!" She turned to Madame Tamsin. "I am totally intrigued by your work, Madame. I would *so* like to know more about it. I do hope to see you again while we're here in Kilmara."

There seemed nothing polite to do but repeat the invitation Oriel had already issued to Lady Soames. "I've asked your aunt if you might join us for tea—"

"Oh, lovely! Of course, we'd adore it, but Morgan suggested dinner tonight." Edwina looked wide-eyed and innocent.

"Of course. Do join us then," Oriel replied evenly. If Morgan wanted her to come, who was she to argue?

"Well, good-bye for now," Edwina said with a flourishing gesture of one hand. She got gracefully into the carriage, leaving her aunt still standing outside.

Flushed and irritated, Lady Soames mumbled, "I do apologize." Then, assisted by Finnegan, she reentered the carriage. The door closed upon them, but not before Lady Soames was heard to say, "That was disgraceful of you, Edwina."

Paige gave a sympathetic look to Oriel, but Oriel did not need sympathy. She needed composure. She exerted all she had to give her other *expected* guests her full attention.

Madame Tamsin was a large woman with salt-and-pepper hair arranged in a most unusual way. Instead of a bonnet, she wore a long, multicolored chiffon scarf wound around her head in a sort of turban, the ends trailing, and she wore a long, velvet cape embroidered lavishly with colorful scrolls and flowers.

"I'll show you to your room, or would you like some tea first?" Oriel floundered, feeling distracted by what had happened. She looked around. Morgan was still standing at the top of the steps, staring down the drive in the direction the Soames carriage had disappeared. He looked white, tense.

"I find I am fatigued." Madame Tamsin spoke with a slight accent. "If I might have something in my room, perhaps, and a rest, I should be much better company this evening."

"Certainly, come this way." Oriel cast a searching look at Morgan, then took both Madame Tamsin and Paige upstairs. By the time she had shown both ladies to their rooms and Morgan had taken Freddy on a tour of the grounds, Oriel felt emotionally spent. She was stunned by this turn of events. What was Edwina trying to do—bait Morgan or beguile him back?

As if to suit her own depressing mood, the day darkened ominously. Heavy clouds moved across the sky, and late in the afternoon, rain began to fall. The guests were served tea in their rooms and Oriel took the opportunity to assess her situation. There was nothing she could do to prevent Edwina's coming or to offset whatever her purpose was. All Oriel could do was to meet her on her own terms, be as gracious a hostess as she could and, in so doing, contrast the rudeness Edwina had displayed in inviting herself for the evening.

After all, two could play at this game. Oriel had what Edwina had turned down—the role of mistress of this magnificent castle and, at least ostensibly, the master as well. She would take particular care with her appearance, look her best. She decided to wear the green taffeta she had worn in Dublin, the one Morgan had admired. With it, of course, she would wear the jade pendant and earrings. If anyone admired the set, she would mention that Morgan had given it to her.

She brushed her hair until it shone. Then she got her dress and hung it up on the door of the armoire. It was lovely, and she knew it was becoming. She went to bathe, pouring nearly half a jar of scented salts into the water before slipping into the fragrant warmth. Relaxed, her anxiety about the evening ahead seemed to float away.

At length, she got out, wrapped herself in her robe, and went back into the bedroom. A terrible sight met her shocked eyes. The casement windows were open and rain and wind were blowing in on her beautiful gown. The dress swung from the knob of the armoire as wildly as a ship's sail caught in a storm. The taffeta was wet and stained. With a cry of dismay, Oriel rushed over to the windows and slammed them shut. She turned with horror to examine her dress.

A low moan escaped her. Oriel knew enough about fabric to know the dress was ruined. There was nothing she could do to save it—at least to wear tonight. The taffeta had already begun to wrinkle and the material was soaked through.

How could this have happened? The storm was heavy, yes, but the windows had been securely fastened when she went in to take her bath. All at once, a sickening certainty washed over her. Someone had purposely unlocked the windows, knowing the gusty wind would send the driving rain onto her dress. Someone had deliberately done this mean-spirited thing. Someone wanted to ruin her gown. Oriel shuddered. Someone at Drummond Castle hated her.

23

*U*pset as she was, Oriel determined not to let the ruined dress become an omen. She refused to accept it as a premonition of a disastrous evening ahead. Later, she would deal with the full implication of it all. Right now there was no time to waste. She had guests, a dinner party to conduct.

Her first task was to find something else to wear. She made a quick survey of the possibilities, and within a few minutes, she had put together a charming outfit. With a white silk blouse trimmed lavishly in Irish lace, she wore a short black velvet jacket and a flaring skirt of green satin. Her jade and pearl jewelry provided the perfect accents. Pleased with her improvisation, she hurried downstairs and into the drawing room for a final check.

Draperies had been drawn against the dreary, rainy night. The pungent scent of purple asters and golden chrysanthemums mingled with the smell of logs burning in the fireplace. Everything was in perfect readiness. Except, Oriel thought ironically, for the hostess, who dreaded the arrival of guests she did not want to receive.

Oriel tried to tell herself it should not bother her if Morgan's feelings for Edwina had been rekindled. After all, they *had* been engaged. They must have been in love, and one doesn't get over love that easily. Even though they had quarreled, time had passed. Maybe Edwina's distorted image of the castle as an isolated, run-down building on the dreary coast had changed. Perhaps she felt she'd made a mistake letting Morgan go and wanted him back.

Whatever it was, there was nothing Oriel could do about it. Nor could she do anything about her own feelings except hide them. At least her friends, the Wicklows and Bryan, would be here this evening to support her. Madame Tamsin had agreed to give a demonstration of her craft, which would also make the evening interesting. All Oriel could hope for was to get through it.

Soon, Suzanne and Michael arrived with Bryan. Suzanne was excited, brimming with new ideas for the ball. Oriel introduced the Wicklows to Paige and Freddy. Madame Tamsin soon joined them, looking as eccentric as ever in a flowing gown that resembled an Arabian tent. Several colorful chiffon scarves were wound into a turban on her head.

Leaving her guests in a congenial conversation, Oriel went into the kitchen for a last-minute consultation with Mrs. Mills. She did not want a repetition of that first dinner party, which had been such a shambles.

Mrs. Mills seemed to have everything under control with Molly and Carleen helping her. Oriel was coming back from the kitchen when she saw Lady Soames and Edwina arrive at the front door. She slipped quietly into the drawing room to watch Edwina make her entrance.

Ushered by Finnegan, Edwina stood on the threshold for a moment, pausing dramatically. She looked stunning, tall and graceful, gowned in an elegant royal blue dress with a portrait neckline that revealed her gleaming white shoulders. Everyone turned to look at her. Her entrance had been brilliantly staged. Oriel glanced at Morgan, who was standing at the fireplace. When Edwina walked in, the only change in his expression was a visible clenching of his jaw. He set down the wine glass he was holding and took a step toward her. Edwina turned her back, however, sweeping into the center of the room.

Paige stepped up beside Oriel and whispered, "Everything is always a performance with Edwina." Her remark did nothing to reassure Oriel.

Edwina, smiling, glanced around the room, her gaze settling on Morgan, who remained standing, as though rooted to his spot in front of the fireplace. *Is he so stunned by Edwina's presence he can't function?* Oriel wondered. She realized it was up to her to do the honors as hostess and went forward to greet Edwina and her aunt.

Oriel gave Morgan a sharp glance. *Isn't he even going to introduce her to the rest of the guests?* she thought with dismay. He looked distracted, so Oriel was forced into doing it. Bryan seemed both amused and enchanted by this glorious, vibrant creature. Michael was a little more remote, but still fascinated. Suzanne was bedazzled by all the glamour.

Since Morgan continued to be distracted, Oriel saw to it that everyone had something to drink. She seated Lady Soames, resplendent in shimmering gray satin and rubies, beside Madame Tamsin. It was a relief when Finnegan came to announce dinner.

At dinner, Edwina shone. Oriel was sure she had never been more vivacious. She flirted with Freddy, surely aware of Morgan's glowering gaze on her. She tossed her golden head, laughed her lilting laughter, and gaily told anecdotes that showed off her wit and charm. In fact, Edwina took center stage, something she seemed to do naturally and easily, as if *she* belonged here at Drummond Castle.

While trying to carry on a sensible conversation with Freddy, who was seated at her right, Oriel watched Edwina with growing dismay. The excellent dinner she and Mrs. Mills had planned could have been cardboard for all she could taste of it. Course after course—clear mushroom soup, the saddle of lamb, baby carrots, onions in cream sauce, endive salad—came and went without Oriel's appreciation.

She felt her fork grow heavy in her right hand. She was aware of a new sensation, one she recognized as wounded pride, crushed hope. It hit her with its impact. Never in her wildest imagination had she imagined that she would one day feel any emotion—attraction, rage, certainly not jealousy or passion—for Morgan Drummond, worst of all, grief over the possibility of losing him.

It was ridiculous, her own fault. She should never have allowed herself to hope. But it was too late. She had let down her protective reserve, allowed herself to feel, to imagine, to dream. Oriel felt gradually diminished by Edwina, pushed into an ignominious shadow by the woman's electric brilliance.

Paige appeared miserable. Once in a while she attempted to catch Oriel's eye, with understanding and sympathy in her glance. Oriel knew Paige felt sorry about what she had inadvertently brought about.

Oriel would not have met Morgan's gaze even if he had been looking at her. All she wanted was for this dreadful evening to be over so she could escape to her room, where she could weep out her splintered dreams.

In one of those sudden lulls that occur sometimes even during the liveliest dinner parties, Freddy's comment addressed to Morgan was heard by all. "So, Morgan, have you gotten used to being an *Irish* country gentleman by now?"

Morgan replied, "Oh, I'm finding Ireland much to my liking in many unexpected ways."

"But what on earth do you find to do here?" Edwina asked.

Oriel felt herself stiffen. She glanced uneasily down the length of the table at Morgan. Edwina set her glass down and looked directly at Oriel. Her eyes glittered with malice, and there was something about the saccharine smile that lifted the corners of her perfectly shaped mouth that chilled Oriel.

To Oriel's immense relief, Finnegan and Conan entered just then with the chocolate mousse and cherry sorbet, and the moment passed as dessert was served. From the other end of the table, Oriel heard Edwina's crystalline laughter ring out again and she saw one of Morgan's rare smiles. In a reactive spasm of anger, Oriel crumpled her napkin in her lap.

After dinner, they all returned to the drawing room. Finnegan brought in trays bearing cups of coffee, which he solemnly passed among the seated guests. Oriel found herself sitting a little apart from the group. Voices faded into a background hum, underpinning the farce playing out in front of her. It was, after all, the stuff of high drama—the return of the intended bride to the scene where another holds her place.

Oriel looked at Morgan across the room and studied his expression as though he had been a portrait. It was animated in a way she had not seen it before. Was it because of Edwina's presence? she wondered. Was he trying to impress her by giving the role of perfect host a try? Oriel was sure the Wicklows must be surprised, especially after Morgan's morose, taciturn performance the night they had come to dinner before.

Eventually, the conversation turned to Madame Tamsin's reason for being in Dublin. Oriel's focus came back as Madame explained a little about graphology.

"It sounds like some sort of hocus-pocus to me," Lady Soames declared with a sniff. "If we all learned to write the same way, how can a few differences in loops and curlicues reveal a person's character?"

Madame Tamsin did not lose her temper, as Oriel thought she had every right to. Instead, she focused her direct gaze on Lady Soames and said, "Oh, but that's just it. It's in those very differences, those small insignificant twists an uninformed person might discount, that a trained eye can find meaning. The thief, the liar, the manipulator, the dishonest person—it all comes through. Handwriting comes directly from the heart, down the arm, into the hand gripping the pen, and out onto the paper. In a person's handwriting much can be revealed."

"It's true, Lady Soames. We've already used it most effectively in our London store and we are convinced it works." Freddy gestured to Madame Tamsin. "This lady is a genius at ferreting out a person's hidden character flaws, as well as revealing attributes. We have Madame Tamsin analyze the applications of our employees and she has been dead-on in all the choices we have made through her advice."

"It sounds logical to me," Bryan commented.

Michael chimed in. "A man's signature was extremely important in the days when only the aristocracy could write. Even an uneducated person felt it necessary to learn to sign his own name. The strength or weakness of his writing was there for all to see."

"What fun!" Edwina clapped her hands. "Why don't we all let Madame Tamsin analyze our handwriting?"

Madame Tamsin turned cool eyes on Edwina. "It is not a parlor game, Miss Parker," she said coldly. "I am not a fortune-teller or a soothsayer. I have studied for years to make this my profession."

Oriel felt the atmosphere fill with tension. Freddy and Paige exchanged a glance. Michael stared straight ahead, while Suzanne twisted her hands in her lap, looking embarrassed. Edwina seemed completely undaunted by Madame Tamsin's rejoinder.

"I'm sure Miss Parker meant no offense," Morgan said and was rewarded with one of Edwina's loveliest smiles.

Then Edwina, all eagerness, said, "Oh, do let's get on with it! What shall we write?"

Madame Tamsin turned to Oriel. "Could we have slips of paper for each one, please? And pencils or pens?"

Oriel, in turn, looked at Morgan. He waited a single second as if reluctant to take part in this. Then he got to his feet and left the room. He returned a moment later with paper and pencils, which he proceeded to pass out to the guests. Oriel looked down at hers, noticing the Drummond Castle crest at the top, embossed in gold lettering.

"It is very simple, actually," Madame Tamsin said. "Choose a sentence—it can be your own thought, a favorite quotation, a line from a poem, or whatever. The important thing for us tonight, in this small a group, is not to sign your name. You can give the source of your quote, if you like. What I need is enough letters of the alphabet used in ordinary writing. The main thing, and I emphasize this for those who think this is not scientific, is that what I do here tonight has very little similarity to the type of in-depth analysis I do with an employment application. Is that understood by everyone?" Madame Tamsin looked directly at Lady Soames, who seemed oblivious to her.

For the next five minutes, only the scratching of pencils on paper could be heard. Oriel hesitated. She couldn't think of anything to write down. Everything that came into her mind seemed too revealing in content. She lifted her head and looked across the room at Morgan. What would he choose to write? Her gaze passed to Edwina, who was tapping the end of her pencil on her perfect teeth as if she, too, was struggling to find something to write.

Just then, Oriel was aware of Morgan's gaze on her. She felt the warmth climbing up into her cheeks. For what seemed like a minute, their gaze held. Her heart twisted. *Oh, Morgan, if you only knew* . . . she thought desperately.

Oriel ducked her head and began to write.

A few minutes more went by, then Madame Tamsin spoke. "If everyone has finished, fold your piece of paper once. Will someone please collect them? Do we have some kind of bowl or dish to put them in so that I can pick one at random?"

Oriel gestured to a brass bowl. This time, not needing any prompting, Morgan went around the room for each guest to drop in the folded slip of paper.

One by one, Madame Tamsin took each slip of paper in her two hands. Her eyebrows met over closed eyes, as if she were meditating over it. Then, in her distinctive voice, she rapidly began the analyses. She explained how the slant of letters, the loop of an *l*, and the way a *t* was crossed all revealed something significant about the person writing.

Oriel only half-listened. Only one or two of the remarks struck a responsive chord in Oriel. "A tendency toward jealousy, vindictiveness," Madame Tamsin said. And about another sample, she declared, "It shows uncertainty, insecurity, indecisiveness." Her conscience pricked sharply. If she were truthful, tonight especially, either of those analytic statements could be about her. Was it *her* handwriting Madame Tamsin was analyzing? She glanced around the room. Was anyone else reacting like this, or was she the only one Madame's analysis fit?

With each slip, Madame's analysis was getting longer and more and more questions were asked. If she had not been so consumed with her own inner turmoil, Oriel was sure she would have found Madame Tamsin's talk interesting and informative.

As it was getting late, Oriel thought she should have some refreshment served. It had been a long evening. Quietly she excused herself, and went to find Finnegan. She told him the guests were playing a game that might go very late. She suggested that after bringing in a tray of biscuits, sparkling water, and teas, he needn't wait up.

On her way back to the drawing room, Oriel heard two voices from the cloakroom off the main hall, unmistakably Edwina's and her aunt's. "But just *who* is she?" Lady Soames asked.

"I'm sure I don't know." This was Edwina. "Except she's extremely attractive."

"You know what I mean—what is her background, her family? Where did Morgan meet her?" Lady Soames sounded impatient. "He certainly didn't pick her out of thin air!"

There was a laugh, a sharp one with a cutting edge, and Edwina replied, "On board ship coming from America! Isn't that ironic? On his way to marry *me*."

"Oh, one of those shipboard romances, then," her aunt remarked dismissingly.

Oriel started to hurry past, but not quickly enough. Edwina emerged into the hall. She had her fur cape over one arm. With a malicious smile, she stepped in front of Oriel, blocking her way.

The beautiful eyes were shooting sparks, and the lovely face was swiftly transformed into a hate-filled mask. "I hope you don't fantasize Morgan feels anything real for you. He only married you to spite me!"

Oriel attempted to pass by, but Edwina reached out and caught her arm, jerking her back. Her face was very close. "He acted out of anger because I refused to come to this drafty, godforsaken place for a year. But he's never stopped wanting me and he wants me still. Don't delude yourself into thinking you can prolong this ridiculous charade." She released Oriel's arm with a flinging motion. Tossing her fur cape over her shoulders, she swept off down the hall, the train of her dress sliding on the stone floor behind her.

Oriel stood staring after her, speechless. She heard voices coming from the drawing room. People were getting ready to leave. She had to pull herself enough together to go back to her guests. Everyone was talking and laughing as Oriel reentered the room. Edwina avoided eye contact and chatted amiably with Freddy as everyone moved toward the hall.

Oriel stood beside Morgan as they saw their guests out to the carriages. Busy accepting the enthusiastic thanks of Bryan and Suzanne, Oriel was still aware of Edwina. She noticed that Morgan took her and her aunt out to their carriage. Before getting in, Edwina put her graceful gloved hand on his arm and said a lingering good-bye.

While Oriel saw to her houseguests, she heard Morgan ask Freddy to join him for a nightcap in his study. After a worried glance at Oriel, Paige escorted Madame Tamsin upstairs. At the top of the stairs, Oriel bade them all good night, and without another word, went quickly to the haven of her own room. Of all the nights Oriel had been at Drummond Castle, this one seemed to her the worst of all.

24

*I*n her bedroom, Oriel undressed. She sat down at the dressing table and started to remove her jewelry. She unfastened the earrings and dropped them into the velvet case. As Oriel started to undo the clasp of her jade and pearl pendant, her fingers touched it lovingly. She recalled that afternoon in the Dublin shop when Morgan had declared that she should have it. He had halted her protests, saying, "You want it, and I want to give it to you. It will be a memento of a happy day in Dublin."

She stared at herself in the mirror, searching to see what she was really thinking and feeling. Did it show? The muscles around her mouth ached from smiling, but the drawn look in her eyes showed the strain of the evening. Had anyone guessed how unhappy she was?

She stretched out on the bed, knowing sleep would not come easily. The year was only half over, but now that Edwina had come and Morgan showed every inclination of succumbing to her charm, would he want to break their contract? Could he not see through that facade to a woman not only less than perfect, but deeply flawed, even spiteful?

Could a man like Morgan really be in love with Edwina, who seemed to have nothing to offer but her beauty?

Oriel knew her unexpressed feelings for Morgan made her vulnerable. She relived the humiliating encounter with Edwina, her cutting words. If they were true, maybe she should offer Morgan his freedom, break the contract. Finally, she fell into a sleep, disturbed by dreams.

She awoke with a start just as daylight was breaking. She was terribly thirsty. Her throat felt raw and dry. She decided to go downstairs, slip into the kitchen, and make some tea.

She drew on her robe and went down the steps in her bare feet. As she passed the drawing room, something compelled her to go in. She was drawn irresistibly to the brass bowl into which Madame Tamsin had tossed the slips of paper after she had done the analysis. Curious if she could find Morgan's and read what he had written, Oriel unfolded each one.

She recognized his bold, slanted handwriting at once. Morgan had written, "There is a tide in the affairs of men, which, taken at the flood, leads on to fortune; Omitted, all the voyage of their life is bound in shallows and miseries.—W. Shakespeare."

Were those Morgan's real sentiments—that he had not acted when he should have, missed the tide? That he now was spending his life "bound in shallows and miseries"? Oriel dropped the slip back into the bowl. She stayed another minute, looking for her own paper, but it wasn't there. She counted the slips. There had been nine people—the Wicklows, Freddy and Paige, Lady Soames, Edwina, Bryan, Morgan, and herself—but there were only *eight* slips left in the bowl. Hers was missing! How strange. Why would anyone take hers?

Still musing, she headed for the kitchen. After making a cup of tea, she returned to her room.

Later that morning at breakfast, Morgan suggested taking Freddy on a tour of the stables for a look at his new horses. Since Madame Tamsin had asked for a tray sent up to her room, this left Paige and Oriel alone at the table.

Immediately after the men left, Paige leaned forward to Oriel, saying, "I must apologize again, Oriel, for letting Edwina manipulate herself into the weekend. I don't know what she's up to, but I'm guessing it's not good. What she can't have, she wants. Goes after it." She raised her eyebrows. "I never thought she was right for Morgan from the first minute I met her, but she is clever. Before anyone knew it, she had him wound around her little finger. Last night she was up to her same old tricks—anyone could see that. It was outrageous. I felt terrible and so did Freddy. For her to do that right under your nose!"

"Hold on a minute, Paige," Oriel interrupted. "I have to tell you something. First, there's no need for you to apologize. I knew about Edwina before I was married. Morgan was very forthright, and—"

Conan came in with a silver pot of fresh coffee, and conversation was suspended while he refilled both of their cups. Oriel waited until he left before continuing. "You see, Paige, Morgan's and my marriage is not what you think it is."

Paige looked puzzled. "Well, I know it was rather sudden, coming soon after Edwina broke the engagement, but that's what makes it all the more romantic. You met on the ship coming over, didn't you?"

"Paige, that's what I'm trying to tell you. It's not romantic at all. It's—well, if it weren't for me, I'm sure Morgan and Edwina would patch things up, and—"

Paige rolled her eyes in mock horror. "Heaven forbid! She's all wrong for him—that's what I'm trying to tell you."

"No, Paige, what I'm trying to tell you is if I were not in the picture—"

"Good morning." Madame Tamsin's dramatic voice greeted them, and they both turned to see her standing in the doorway. She had on a caftan with chiffon scarves in blue, purple, and mauve floating in all directions. "What a glorious morning! I could no longer stay in bed on such a beautiful day."

Oriel rang for Conan to bring more coffee, and Madame Tamsin helped herself to a currant scone and joined them at the table. "What a curious session we had last night," she said. "It is always hard to analyze handwriting seriously when there are skeptics in the group. They rank this new science along with card reading or fortune-telling!" She shook her head disgustedly, causing her long, looped earrings to chime.

"I'm sorry you were put in such an awkward position, Madame," Oriel said apologetically.

"It's not you, my dear, I have a quarrel with. It's the other woman and her niece. They were so—so *unsimpatico*—criticizing things they do not understand. Not like you others." She looked at both of them approvingly. "The rest of you seemed eager to explore new ideas, most enthusiastic."

The men came back in from inspecting the stables and soon Paige, Freddy, and Madame Tamsin were ready to begin the return trip to Dublin.

Just before she got into the carriage, Paige came over to Oriel and kissed her cheek. "I am so sorry I inadvertently made this a difficult weekend for you, Oriel. I want you to know how much I admire your quiet courage, your graciousness in this most trying circumstance. You're the best thing that could possibly have happened to Morgan. I hope he's wise enough to realize—"

Whatever Paige hoped Morgan was wise enough to realize was cut off by Freddy's joining them to offer his thanks. "Jolly good time. Never saw Morgan in better form."

Oriel forced a smile. As the carriage pulled away from the house and went down the drive, Oriel realized she had never had the opportunity to explain to Paige the real circumstances of her relationship to Morgan.

Instead of going back inside, Oriel left Morgan standing on the steps and headed for the path to the cliffs. Though it was cold walking weather, she wasn't ready to be alone with him, to discuss the weekend and Edwina's surprise appearance. She needed time to deal with feelings she had only just admitted having. There were only five more months until the term of the contract would be fulfilled. She would be free to leave. The trouble was, she did not want to leave.

She had not counted on feeling this way. She assumed when the time came, she could walk away, forget Kilmara, forget Morgan. Now she knew that was no longer possible. Morgan still loved Edwina, wanted her back. Any thoughts Oriel had entertained of a future here with him were just fantasy.

But what could she do in the meantime? She bent her head against the wind, walking faster to the top of the hill. At length, the fuzziness of her thoughts cleared, like evaporating fog. She would go on with the medieval ball. Plans had gone too far to change them now. Invitations were being printed, musicians had been engaged, elaborate menus planned, extra help hired, decorations ordered. No, there was no way to cancel it. Besides, it would keep her busy.

Yes, if she *had* to leave Drummond Castle forever, she would leave in a blaze of glory.

25

The next afternoon, Oriel set out for Bracken Hall to see Suzanne. She longed for the comfort of being with her friend after the tension of the weekend.

She was in the front hall just ready to leave when Morgan came to the door of his study. "Oriel, would you come in here, please? I want to talk to you."

She hesitated. She was feeling very vulnerable and did not want to expose herself to Morgan's nearness. "Will it take long? I'm just off to see Suzanne."

"No, not long," he said, holding the door open for her to enter.

A small fluttering began in her stomach. Suddenly filled with dread, she wondered what he wanted to talk to her about. Nervously, she went into the room and took the chair he indicated. He stood by the fireplace, his hands behind his back.

"I wanted to commend you. You handled the unexpected company remarkably well. It must have been quite a strain."

"No, not really," she kept her voice crisp, light.

He waited, as if expecting her to say something else. When she didn't, he went on. "Oriel, I've been doing a great deal of thinking recently and more and more I've come to realize how unfair I have been to you. My lawyers tried to tell me that before I had them draw up the contract, but I insisted. I know now my motivation was—well, not of the highest. I was acting in anger—a state not conducive to rational action."

Oriel started to say something, but he held up a hand to halt her. "It was completely wrong to pressure you—knowing you were in desperate financial circumstances—into signing an agreement that must have been odious to a woman of your refinement, sensitivity, and high morals. In retrospect, it was a despicable thing to do."

"Oh, no, Morgan, I—"

He again raised his hand to ward off her protest. "Please, Oriel, let me finish." He went on. "If you are unhappy—and I wouldn't blame you if you are—I have been of little or no help in making your time here pleasant or enjoyable." He paused. "Anyway, if you are unhappy, I would be willing to release you from our agreement with no penalty. I'll send word to my lawyers, and you will receive what you've been promised." His voice roughened. "You've earned it—every penny."

Oriel felt the blood draining from her head and she was suddenly dizzy. She felt cold, as if someone had opened a window and let in a blast of icy air. She stared at Morgan. So! *He* wanted out of the contract—that must be it. Edwina's coming had made him realize his terrible mistake! In some moment, they must have had a chance to talk, to reconcile. If they could get rid of the impediment, they could get back together. *She* was the impediment. How easy for Morgan with his millions to pay off the obstacle in his way. How he would get around the rest of the requirements of the will, she couldn't guess. Maybe he didn't care anymore. He would let Drummond Castle go, let it deteriorate again, let all his grandfather's efforts come to nothing!

Something inside Oriel knotted with determination. Something in her said, *I won't let that happen.* Oriel realized how much she loved the castle, Kilmara, Ireland. Drawing herself up, she replied, "No, Morgan, a contract is a contract. I intend to keep my part of the bargain. But, let us be truthful to each other. Let's not pretend. Let us frankly admit what is at stake here. Edwina's coming upset you. However, we both signed our agreement in good faith. No matter what the motivation on each of our parts, it is a legal, binding contract."

Morgan regarded her somberly for a full minute. When he spoke, his voice softened and he seemed confused by her reaction. "I did not intend to hurt you by what I'm suggesting. I wanted to be fair in offering you a release from the contract. I didn't mean to offend you."

"You didn't," Oriel said evenly. *But neither did you deny you are still in love with Edwina,* she added silently.

"I just wanted to be fair, and—"

"You were. And I want to be fair too." Oriel stood up, took a few steps toward the door, and said, "Let us just go on as before."

"As you like," Morgan said formally.

Oriel, her back straight, walked to the door. Her hand ready to twist the knob, she turned back. Deliberately keeping her voice steady, she added, "Plans for the ball have progressed too far to cancel. Besides, it will create a more friendly feeling about Drummond Castle."

He looked startled, as though he had just remembered the ball. "Good," he said brusquely. Then, "I appreciate all you're doing, Oriel."

She nodded, opened the door, and went out. What had been building up in her over the last weeks suddenly came forth. She realized how deeply she cared for Morgan, had wanted him to care for her. It was insane, she knew. It was not part of the bargain. She could just be thankful that Morgan could not read her mind, look into her heart.

By the time Oriel got to Bracken Hall, her outer composure was shattered. All her vague hopes about a possible future were gone. Morgan could not wait to be free but was too honorable to break their contract. Somehow she would have to brave out the rest of her time at Drummond Castle.

Suzanne, her usual effervescent self, welcomed Oriel. For a few minutes she chattered happily about her ideas for the medieval ball. Then, noticing Oriel's lack of enthusiasm, she stopped mid-sentence. "Is something wrong? You look—what's the matter, Oriel?"

"Oh, forgive me, Suzanne. I guess I'm just not in the right mood."

Suzanne was instantly understanding. "Too much company over the weekend! I told Michael I thought you looked strained Saturday evening, not yourself at all."

Suzanne paused, then asked more tentatively, "Did you and Morgan quarrel? I know when Michael and I have an argument, it's usually when I'm worn out physically, or have a headache . . ."

Oriel gave a harsh little laugh. "Morgan and I *never* quarrel, Suzanne. He doesn't care enough to quarrel."

Suzanne looked shocked, then sympathetic. "Oh, I'm so sorry, Oriel."

"It doesn't matter. It's not like you and Michael—ours is not a love match." She shook her head, then shrugged. "Morgan's in love with someone else, someone he knew before he met me, before we were married."

Suzanne put her hand on Oriel's. "Oh, Oriel, I'm truly sorry."

Their conversation might have gone further, but just then the front door slammed and they heard male voices. A minute later, Michael and Bryan came into the room.

Upon seeing the open scrapbook in which they had been compiling ideas, pictures, and other material about the ball, Michael struck his forehead in dismay and exclaimed, "Not that ridiculous party again!" He turned to Bryan and said,

"These two ladies do nothing but eat, drink, and sleep that gaudy affair to be held at Drummond Castle."

"I think it's a capital idea myself." Bryan smiled encouragement. He sauntered over to the table where the scrapbook was spread out.

Oriel stood up. She didn't want to stay longer now; her emotions were too near the surface. "Oh, we've done enough for today." She glanced at Suzanne, knowing she would understand. "I'll come by tomorrow, perhaps, and we'll go over some of the ideas then."

Soon Oriel was on her way again. The fog had thickened considerably, wrapping itself around her as she walked, like a heavy, soggy blanket. Her mood was also heavy. She dreaded returning to Drummond Castle, having dinner with Morgan, pretending nothing had changed.

Morgan had never promised her anything. It was she who had let her feelings get out of hand, to imagine possibilities. *It's my own fault,* she told herself mercilessly as she hurried on.

At length, she saw the outline of the castle eerily shrouded in fog. Lights shone out like fuzzy slits through the gloom. It was only a little farther to the gates. That's when she saw it, floating toward her menacingly—the hooded figure. *Shaleen O'Connor.* Instinctively the name formed on her lips. She drew back in horror. The billowing cape and stealthy glide were familiar as it approached. A prayer for protection rose from her heart. She squeezed her eyes shut tight. When she opened them, the figure had disappeared.

Her heart was beating in her throat. She *had* seen it. This time there was no mistake. It wasn't a wisp of fog. Something *real* had passed by her in the swirling mist.

She ran toward the gates. They were closed. She jangled the handles and finally pushed through. She shoved them wider. If she had anything to do with it, Shaleen O'Connor would not find them closed again and bring disaster upon Drummond Castle.

She started running up the driveway toward the house, when all at once, she stopped short. What had come over her? She realized what a superstitious thing she had done. Was she silly enough to believe the story of the ghostly vengeance against the castle residents? Yet she had seen that same figure several times since she'd come here. A ghost? Her common sense told her there must be some other explanation. She slowed her steps as she neared the front entrance. She certainly didn't intend to tell Morgan about this, suffer his scorn. Still, Oriel knew she had seen something. If it wasn't a ghost, what was it?

Oriel plunged herself into weeks of meticulous planning and preparation for the ball. She had hoped such immersion would soothe her troubled emotions, her aching heart. It worked to some extent.

Her preoccupation in all this activity had proved enough of a distraction that she had not had much time to dwell on her relationship with Morgan. She had wondered, however, how long Edwina and her aunt had remained houseguests at Linden Wood. Had Morgan ridden over to visit his former fiancée there? Had he kept in contact with Edwina after she had returned with Lady Soames to Dublin? At her lowest times, Oriel could imagine they were counting the days until this farce of a marriage could be annulled and they could pick up their lives as if this year had never happened.

At last it was the night of the ball, and Oriel was getting dressed. Molly helped with the tiny hooks and eyes of the velvet bodice and the layers of crinoline that went underneath the bouffant taffeta skirt.

"Oh, ma'am, you look a fair picture!" the maid declared as she placed an ornamental comb in Oriel's hair. Oriel had gone countless times into the portrait gallery, studying the portrait of Lady Lavinia Lawrence. She had studied the painting so often—the details of the elaborate dress, her hairstyle—that she felt as if she knew her.

"It did turn out much better than I could have hoped," Oriel said with satisfaction, looking at the costume in the mirror. The color, a rich deep emerald, and the seventeenth-century style were surprisingly becoming. She could believe she looked just like a mistress of a manor might have in those olden days, about to welcome her guests to a gala ball.

Before she went downstairs, she picked up each of the two masks she had made, trying both in turn. Deciding upon the green satin one with beaded sequins along the edges, she put it on. It hid her eyes and the shape of her nose; a ruffle of gilt lace also covered her mouth. It was a perfect disguise. She wondered if she'd be able to guess which of her lady guests was Suzanne. Since they had decided to have the guests wear masks until midnight, Oriel and Suzanne thought it would be more fun not to divulge to each other what they would be wearing.

The great hall had been opened for the party, transformed into medieval splendor. Colorful banners hung from the rafters, along with red, gold, blue, and green streamers. Some of the banners bore appliquéd heraldic shields, copied from a book Bryan had lent Oriel. The music playing in the background might have been from ancient instruments. It all had the authentic look and feel of the kind of festive event that might have taken place in this very room long ago.

Carriage after carriage rolled through the gates and up the driveway, dispensing extravagantly costumed guests. Oriel had sent out over a hundred invitations. She had compiled lists with Suzanne of the landed gentry around Kilmara. She had also asked Paige for names of people in Dublin she would like to have invited. Morgan rather reluctantly had added a few of his own friends to be sent the calligraphy invitation.

As she received the dozens of guests flowing through the main entrance, Oriel decided she had been right. Costumes put partygoers in a certain mood, ready to have a special time. Everyone was in high spirits. As she moved about, Oriel heard such comments as, "There hasn't been a party like this in Kilmara for decades." "What a splendid idea this was." "Drummond Castle has become the center of social life here once again."

Oriel kept glancing at Morgan to see how he was responding to all of this. He looked handsome in his gentleman's black velvet doublet trimmed with gilt braid. The high starched ruff and a gold medallion swinging from a heavy chain perfectly set off his aristocratic good looks. He seemed to be enjoying himself.

After she had greeted and shaken hands with group after group of masked guests, Oriel looked around. Where were Suzanne and Michael? Had they come and she somehow missed them? Then, at last, she thought she spotted them. There was something about the tall couple who had just entered the hall arm in arm. Oriel was startled, however, when she saw the woman's costume. It was the dress worn in the portrait of Lady Lavinia Lawrence—exactly the same as the one Oriel had made for herself! What a coincidence—if that *was* Suzanne.

Oriel started toward them, ready to have a good laugh with them over the duplication, but just as she was near enough to speak, the couple turned away. Oriel felt a little taken aback. Had they not seen her, not recognized her? Surely Suzanne would have noticed they were wearing the same dress. But if it was not Suzanne, Oriel wanted to find out who else would have known about Lady Lavinia's portrait. She started to follow the couple, but they were swallowed up by the crowd and seemed to disappear. Bewildered, Oriel halted.

Someone touched her arm. "Oriel, what a success! Aren't you pleased?" It was Bryan. Even with the mask, she could tell. He was dressed as a medieval scholar in a dark robe and tasseled hat. "You've outdone yourself. I'm sure Morgan is very proud of you."

That remark brought her up short. As a matter of fact, Morgan had not said anything to show he was. She almost said as much, but bit her tongue. She was saved from having to reply when her attention was caught by the arrival of a group of four. She recognized Paige and Freddy's voices. Then she heard an unmistakable laugh—*Edwina!* On whose list had she been? The invitations had been addressed by a professional calligrapher, but Oriel had not seen Morgan's list. A chill went through her. Was her one moment of glory in her time at Drummond Castle going to be ruined by Edwina?

A mixture of feelings rushed up within Oriel at the sight of Edwina. Inexcusably rude though it was, she couldn't bring herself to greet the new arrivals. She would have to explain to Paige later. But it was impossible for her to welcome Edwina, especially after their unforgettable encounter when she had seen Edwina's malice toward her.

Edwina had come as Queen Elizabeth, bejeweled and bedecked in a gilt embroidered gown, a sparkling tiara set upon a curled auburn wig. She had not worn a mask but carried an ornate one on a small stick. She waved the mask flirtatiously as she chatted with Morgan.

Oriel's hands clenched. She suppressed a shudder and looked away. But not fast enough. She knew Bryan had witnessed her reaction. She tried to pick up their conversation but was too distracted. Her mind wandered hopelessly. When she chanced another look in their direction, it was just in time to see Morgan lead Edwina onto the dance floor.

Rigid with indignation, Oriel knew in order to face the rest of the evening she had to find a few minutes alone to compose herself. "Excuse me," she said to Bryan and moved, as in a trance, across the room in the opposite direction. She was stopped now and then by guests complimenting her on the party. Smiling, she murmured some appropriate response and went on. Minute by minute her need to escape became more desperate.

At length the chance came. She saw a path open up between the dancing couples and slipped out the door at the far side of the ballroom, into the hall, and up the stairs. The sound of music and voices, of dancing feet and laughter, all continued behind her. On the second floor, she moved along the darkened corridors to her room.

For some reason, she noticed the door leading to the minstrels' gallery was ajar. A faint light shone out. The musicians for the ball were in the great hall, so Oriel knew the room was not in use. She paused and heard voices—a man's and a woman's.

Although she could not make out the words, there was an intensity in their tone. Oriel felt a kind of furtive excitement tremble through her. Some dark instinct told her to stay where she was, to listen. Torn between what she knew was right and an urgency to hear what was being said, she hesitated. Then she heard her name. Morgan was the one who was using it.

Oriel stopped dead still.

She heard Edwina's voice, clearly wistful, pleading, seductive. "So, I was wrong. Are you never going to forgive me? What am I supposed to do? Be a penitent like in the medieval days? Wear sackcloth and ashes and come up the steps on my knees and beg you?"

Frozen, Oriel remained rooted to the spot, straining to hear Morgan's reply. Her heart was pounding. Part of her wanted to know, another part dreaded knowing it. There was a silence following Edwina's plaintive question. Were they embracing? Had Morgan *shown* her instead of *telling* her? Were they kissing?

Oriel felt stricken, knew it was ridiculous. She tiptoed away from the door, feeling weak and dizzy. She stopped, steadying herself by leaning against the wall. Gradually, the faintness passed.

She drew a long breath and started again on her way to her room. The hall was dark except for the dim glow of an old-fashioned globe lamp at the far end. She became aware of stealthy movement. Had someone followed her?

She twisted her head to look down the hall. It was empty, full of shadows. She saw no one. As she began walking again, she heard furtive footsteps moving swiftly, coming up behind her.

Before she could turn around to see who it was, she felt a hard thrusting shove on both shoulders that knocked her off balance. At the same time, she heard the sliding sound of something heavy being pushed aside. Before she could try to defend herself, there was a second shove, this time sending her stumbling on her knees into sudden darkness.

*H*er scream, strangled and incoherent, ended shrilly as the opening through which she'd been thrust slid shut again and impenetrable darkness closed around her. Her mind reeled. She felt shock, disbelief, fear. Where was she? Who had attacked her? Why?

At the hard shove, she had thrown out her hands to break her fall. The floor felt cold to her palms. It had uneven ridges. Stone? She fought the panic of being sealed away in some deep, dark place. The air was dank and moldy. She felt suffocated, and she fought for self-control. She tensed, listening for some sound. The stillness was unearthly. She could hear nothing—no voices, no music, no echoes of merriment from the party she had left only a short time ago. That meant she could not be heard either—no matter how long or loud she cried for help.

Oriel had heard a dying person sees their whole life flash before them—all the sins, errors, mistakes, regrets, remorse, the things done and undone. Something like that happened to her now. *I never should have signed that agreement*, she thought. *It was wrong to go through a false ceremony, to come here, live a lie. I am a liar, an impostor! This is my punish-*

ment! All kinds of terrible thoughts crowded in upon her, making Oriel cower against the wall and bury her face in her hands.

A choking fear gripped her. She battled it, telling herself not to lose control. There had to be a way out; she simply had to find it. She clasped her hands together in a desperate prayer. She tried to remember a fitting Scripture, perhaps David's cry to be saved from Saul's wicked plans. But all she could recall was part of something from the Old Testament, and not all of it. *Lord, show me thy way.* She fervently prayed it over and over. Gradually, she began to feel calmer. Assurance came. Surely God would show her a way out.

First, she had to try and figure out where she was. A secret room perhaps? A dungeon from the old days of the rack and other tortures? This was a nightmare, but she had to think her way out of it. She staggered up to a standing position, slowly reaching out with her arms to ascertain how wide a space she was in. She felt a wall to her right and moved over flat against it. She moved one foot, stretching her toe farther and farther. She felt an edge and moved cautiously forward. A step?

With her back against the wall, she took a step down. The wall seemed to curve. It must be a circular stair. Leading where? Her eyes were becoming somewhat used to the dark. She could just barely make out a slit farther down, one of those small alcoved windows she had noticed on the outside of the house. Why hadn't she investigated it, seen if there was a tower or a door?

Inching herself along, Oriel took another step and another, slowly, carefully, going down the steps. She became aware of the damp smell of old stones. The steps had to lead somewhere. If she kept going, she would come out somewhere. She counted the steps to herself in case she had to go up them again—in case there was nothing at the bottom of this stairway, or if what she found there was even more distressing.

Anxiety made her throat dry. Fear tightened her muscles. She couldn't be trapped in here! Would anyone even miss her, wonder where she was? But no, who would? Masks were not to be removed until midnight—hours from now. *Did someone want her to disappear, never be found? Did someone wish her dead? Who would benefit most from her disappearance?* she wondered. The name that immediately flashed into her mind horrified her. Could it be true? Edwina, of course. Then she would be free to have Morgan.

Suddenly there were no more steps. Oriel tested the space before her with her foot, then stretched out an arm. She seemed to be in a narrow corridor of some sort, a hallway. She drew a long, shaky breath. She couldn't stay here, and there was no use going back up the stairs. As she hesitated, she heard a scuttling noise along the passageway. Rats? Her stomach lurched. She had to get out of here, simply had to or she would go mad!

Like a blind person, she guided herself step by step by holding on to the slimy stone walls on either side. Then her toe hit a ridge. She ran her foot back and forth—another set of steps. This time they seemed to lead up. Still balancing herself with palms spread on each side, Oriel mounted the uneven steps.

These steps seemed to end at a blank wall. She reached out and felt the cold moisture of stone, the smell of mold prickling her nostrils. Was she still trapped? Was there no way out of this horrible tunnel through which she had just passed? Swallowing back a scream, she felt along the wall. Her hands met the roughness of wood—a makeshift ladder! It must lead somewhere. She lifted her arms and explored above her head. A door—leading up, out? She let out a small cry. Moving rapidly, her hands searched frantically. Splinters jagged her soft palms. Then she felt metal. It was some kind of handle, but there was a bar through it wedging it shut. She tugged at the bar, trying to loosen it. She pushed, wrenching it as hard as she could. Rusted with age, it didn't budge.

Despairingly, she began to claw at it, painfully breaking her fingernails in the attempt.

Tears of desperate frustration streamed down her face. Sobbing, she banged her fists against the unrelenting wood. *Oh, dear God, help me find a way out of here!*

I must not panic, she commanded herself. She took two deep breaths and then pulled at the bar with all her might. Finally, she felt it move. Again and again, using all her strength, she managed to slide it out. She pushed the latch back. Above her she felt the wood sag as it shifted.

Sobbing with relief, she pushed upward, heard the creaking of old wood. With a last great effort, she pushed hard with both hands and the door fell back with a crash onto a stone floor. A glimmer of light filtered into the darkness. With a groan that was also a prayer of thanksgiving, she realized she was free. Her breath coming in agonizing gasps, she managed to climb up the ladder and pull herself up through the door. She twisted into a sitting position, then staggered to her feet.

Her knees were so weak they were trembling. Dazed, she looked around her. She was in some sort of enclosure. Through mullioned windows, she could see the lights shining out from the castle. She took a few faltering steps. What had she come out of that awful place into? She was in some sort of circular structure.

All at once, Oriel realized it was the small stone folly. Still shivering, she glanced around. There was a wooden bench circling under the windows and some sort of round table in the center. She shuddered. Whatever its original use had been, she wanted to get out of it. There was a door. To her surprise, the knob turned easily and her hand came away feeling somewhat oily.

As she stepped out, she gulped the cold air gratefully. She looked at the house, saw the lighted windows, and felt an enormous sense of relief. She had escaped whatever danger lurked behind her. She became aware that snow was falling, and she quickened her step. She must get inside and up to her bedroom without anyone seeing her. Whoever had pushed her into that—whatever it was—was dangerous. But who could she tell? Who would believe her? Who was her enemy? Whoever it was wanted her out of the way—permanently. She had to get through the rest of the evening—somehow. There would be time enough later to sort through it all, to come to some conclusion and do whatever she must.

The party was going full force, so it was easy enough to slip unnoticed up the stairway. In her bedroom, Oriel quickly washed her face and hands and smoothed on some rose lotion to cool the stinging of her scratches. She filed the edges of her broken fingernails. Still, the condition of her hands would be noticeable. She yanked open a drawer and rummaged for a pair of suitable gloves. A pair of cream-colored ones would have to do. She winced a little as she worked them over her sore hands and buttoned them. Her dress had miraculously survived. Frantically, she brushed off dust and clinging cobwebs.

She had to do something with her hair, so she picked up her brush and tried to repair the damage. As she did, she realized she had lost the ornamental comb. It must have fallen out when she was pushed in that terrible cell. Well, if she needed it, it would be proof of her ordeal. Should she tell Morgan? No, that might not be best if—she dared not finish the thought. Her hand holding the hairbrush began to shake. "Later, later," she mumbled nervously to herself. When she could think rationally, she would figure everything out.

She knew she must still be in some kind of shock. She was unnaturally calm considering what she had just been through, yet she moved with energy, fueled by powerful twin emotions, fear and rage. Some evil force was afoot tonight in Drummond Castle.

Her mask, too, was gone. She must have dropped it somewhere in the passage when she was attacked. Involuntarily, she shuddered. It was all so horrible. But she mustn't think of it now. Luckily, she had made two masks, undecided as to which one to wear. She had another one she would be able to use. She had to get back downstairs and mingle among the guests. Perhaps she could attempt to discern who might be startled, even disappointed to see her alive and well. Then what? Should she confront her attacker or simply flee? She could pack her things tonight and escape Drummond Castle, with all its dark shadows and hovering danger.

She could decide that later. Right now she was going to make her appearance and watch for reactions. The culprit could, in surprise, tip his or her hand.

The party was still in full swing when Oriel descended the staircase. To her surprise, it was fifteen minutes before midnight—almost unmasking time. She had been gone longer than she thought. Oriel's gaze searched the room of dancing couples, looking for the dashing cavalier in a black velvet doublet. Ah, there he was, circling with a lady in an elaborate costume. Was it Edwina? She couldn't be sure. So many other couples were blocking her view. Could Edwina or Morgan have had time to follow her? Could either of them have been her attacker? No, there couldn't have been enough time for either of them to do it. Unless Oriel had been so stunned by what she had overheard in the minstrels' gallery that she had remained longer than she thought.

Oriel's glance swept the ballroom, looking for the lady wearing the same costume she wore. As long as that woman was still here, no one would have missed Oriel. She caught sight of the jade green dress. Ah, there she was. With whom was she dancing? A cavalier in a velvet cape and plumed hat. Michael? No one was to reveal his or her identity until the clock struck twelve. Oriel paused on the bottom of the steps.

"May I have this dance, m'lady?" A scholar bowed low and held out his hand to her. She recognized Bryan's voice. At least she felt safe with him. She inclined her head in acceptance, and putting her hand in his, allowed him to lead her onto the polished floor.

"You've done a magnificent job of recreating a medieval manor house party," he said admiringly. "It will go down in the annals of Kilmara society as the grandest ball given at the castle since the days of the ill-fated Lawrences."

Oriel's ears pricked up at his choice of descriptive words. "Why do you say ill-fated?"

"What else can you say about a family that over the years gradually lost everything—fortune, land, members of their family, those they had counted on to carry on their name and heritage."

"Yes, I suppose it is all very sad."

"It's almost like this castle was cursed. That is, until—"

"Until—?" Oriel prompted.

"I suppose some people—at least most in Kilmara—had hopes that the Drummonds would bring it all back to its former glory. And then—"

"Then what?" Oriel encouraged.

"It's common knowledge Morgan has no real interest in staying here, becoming part of this, building it into a thriving community with his grandfather's wealth."

Bryan had never spoken to her so frankly. Oriel started to ask him more when there was a roll of drums and the lead jester of the group of jugglers and performers leapt up on the platform. "Almost midnight, ladies and gentlemen. Time to find your favorite partners and unmask!"

"Excuse me," Oriel mumbled, disengaging herself from Bryan. Not waiting to explain, she moved quickly away, losing herself in the merry crowd. She wanted to find Suzanne. She would post herself where she could watch the unmasking. As soon as she saw Suzanne, she would go to her, seek her advice.

She found a place in one of the alcoved windows. Where was Morgan? Not that she would go to him—she wasn't sure she trusted him now. Everyone began removing their masks and there were shrieks of surprise as people made startling discoveries. Voices were raised and the whole place reverberated with laughter and fun. Where was Suzanne? Could she and Michael have left somehow without Oriel ever seeing them? She needed to get Suzanne alone. She must tell her what had happened and seek her help in getting away from Drummond Castle.

28

*N*ot long after the unmasking, the party began to wind up. It was agony for Oriel to stand beside Morgan as their departing guests expressed their thanks and compliments for the wonderful evening. Every time she glanced at him, she remembered his rendezvous with Edwina in the minstrels' gallery. What had been said? What had been planned between the two of them?

She shook hands and smiled without knowing to whom she was speaking or what she was saying. She kept looking for Suzanne and Michael to come through the line. She wanted to get some kind of message to her friend, maybe even make some excuse to go home with them or have Suzanne stay overnight.

Her nerves were tangled into agonizing knots. While she forced herself to smile, all she could think of was the moment she could escape. She found it hard to believe that Morgan would be involved in shoving her into that awful place, but she couldn't be sure. Enamored with Edwina again, perhaps he had been persuaded to try and frighten her into leaving. Aware of Morgan's nearness, Oriel felt threatened, vulnerable.

At last the final guest said good night and the last carriage drove away. Neither Suzanne, Michael, nor Bryan Moore had been among those last to depart. However, Oriel waited no longer. She was seized with a panic-driven need to get away. Without a word to Morgan, she turned and ran swiftly up the steps, down the corridor to her bedroom. She dismissed Molly, who was eager to discuss the party. Disappointed and miffed, the maid left and Oriel bolted the door behind her.

She felt weak and shaky. She took off her costume and cast it aside like her false hopes about this party bringing her and Morgan closer, allowing him to see her in a different light. It had all been for nothing. Or maybe not—maybe it had awakened her to the danger she had been in from the very beginning.

Oriel thought of all the things that had happened to her since coming to Drummond Castle—all the narrow escapes from injury, the accidents, the frightening episodes—and this one tonight! Were they all planned? And by whom?

Slowly, the fragments of her mind began to clear, like a lifting fog. Piece by piece, she tried to put the puzzle together. She knew for sure she had been shoved into that place by someone who meant her harm. How had they known about that room? It had to be someone familiar with Drummond Castle, or at least with a similar house.

With a gasp of sudden remembrance, she thought of the book Bryan had lent her about ancient homes and castles of Ireland. There had been floor plans and pictures of the rooms on page after page. Suddenly, Oriel remembered something she had read there. She found the book and read the passage.

In a time of severe religious persecution, many of the old families remained faithful to the Catholic religion. Although the practice of their religion was forbidden and punishable by death and the confiscation of their property, many broke the law. They built "priest's holes," secret rooms where they harbored fugitive priests and where they could hold mass and receive the sacrament according to their rite. This was a highly dangerous thing to do, and if caught, imprisonment or beheading was the fate of the master of such a household. That is why these hidden rooms do not show up in some of the floor plans.

Of course, that was it! It was a secret "priest's hole" into which she had been shoved. The steps down, the narrow hall, and the ladder led through the door into the folly, where the fugitive priests could escape in case the authorities came to search the house.

One thing was for certain, Oriel would not wait to be killed or injured. No, she would take matters into her own hands. Since sleep was out of the question, escape was her only choice. She would go to Bracken Hall, confide in Suzanne and Michael. They would help her.

Oriel packed a few things into her small valise, then waited for the first glimmer of dawn. She put on her coat with the shoulder cape, wrapped a light scarf over her head, and tiptoed out of her room into the upstairs hall. She did not take the Persian lamb, mink-collared cape Morgan had bought her as a wedding present nor the jade earrings and pendant. She wanted no reminders of times when there had been the hope of happiness here at Drummond Castle.

On the dressing table, she left a note for Molly to pack the rest of her belongings, telling her she would let her know later where to send them. Where would that be? In her distraught state of mind, Oriel had no idea. At least the check from Mrs. McPhail had finally come, giving her enough money to buy a steamship ticket to America. Perhaps one day she would be far enough away to forget all that had happened to her.

She crept quietly down the darkened staircase, carefully opened the front door, and slipped outside. Early morning fog blurred everything in sight. However, she knew her way and would have no trouble getting to the Wicklows' home, the place where she'd known warmth and friendship.

She hurried through the gardens. As she passed the stone folly, she shuddered. Down the driveway, almost to the gates, she began to have the feeling she was being followed. *It's my nerves*, she thought, quickening her step. *It's gotten to the point where I don't know reality from illusion.*

When she reached the gates, she put down her valise to free both hands to pull back the bolt, undo the chain. However, to her amazement the gates were unlocked and opened easily.

Just at that moment, she heard footsteps on the gravel. It *wasn't* her imagination. Whirling around, she saw a hooded figure approaching. A strangled cry rose in her throat. Not waiting to grab her valise, she spun back around, picked up her skirt, and started to run. Fear gave strength to her legs, and she ran as she had never done before, not stopping to look back, not taking even a moment to check to see if the harrowing figure was gaining on her.

It isn't my imagination. The words kept drumming into her. *I don't care what anyone says. It's real! I'm not going crazy—I'm not!* Someone *was* following her. Phantom or human—it wished her harm.

She was out of breath and panic-stricken, when she at last saw the fence surrounding Bracken Hall and knew safety was only a few yards away.

She stumbled up the driveway and onto the porch. There didn't seem to be any sign that anyone was up this early, but Oriel didn't care if she had to disturb them. Suzanne would understand—Michael too. Once she told them the danger she was in, her friends would give her protection.

She knocked furiously on the door even as she kept glancing fearfully over her shoulder. Surely Shaleen O'Connor would not pursue her here. *Please, please, answer,* Oriel thought frantically. *Somebody come to the door. Let me in!* Surely the servants would hear her and come to investigate.

She was panting painfully from running so hard and fast. At last, through the etched-glass panel of the front door, she saw the outline of a figure approaching. The door opened, and Oriel looked into the startled face of Nell, Suzanne's maid.

"Why, Mrs. Drummond," she sputtered. "It's ever so early—"

"I know, I know," Oriel said, ignoring the inference that it was a highly improper time to be calling. She brushed by the maid standing in the doorway, saying, "Please, Nell, I had to come. Something's happened. I must see Suzanne."

"Miss Suzanne's still asleep, ma'am. I haven't yet taken up her tea. It was a late night, you know," Nell said reproachfully.

"Yes, I know. That's why I must see her." Oriel was agitatedly rubbing her cold hands, glancing up the stairs to the upper floor. "It's important. Can't you wake her?"

"Well, ma'am, I dunno." Nell seemed very hesitant.

It was then Oriel noticed the dress hanging over the maid's arm. It was jade green velvet. It was exactly the same as *her* costume for the ball. She reached out and tentatively fingered the material, then looked at Nell in astonishment. "Is this Miss Suzanne's costume, the one she wore to the ball?"

"Yes, and 'tis a real pity. It's stained something terrible. The hem's ruined—looks as though it was dragged through the mud. Don't know if I can do anything about it." The maid looked worried.

Oriel frowned. Nothing made sense. "Well, she probably won't be wearing it again," she said vaguely. She had more urgent things on her mind. "Please, Nell, do take Miss Suzanne her tea and tell her I'm here. It's very important."

"If you say so, ma'am," Nell agreed reluctantly. "You can wait in the parlor."

Preoccupied, Oriel followed her. Nell opened the door for her and Oriel went in. There was no fire lit, and the room felt cold. Since Oriel was already so chilled, it hardly made any difference.

Nell, however, noticed it at once. She looked at Oriel anxiously. "This room is rarely used, ma'am," she said in explanation. "I'll send in someone to get a fire going."

"No, don't bother." Oriel's voice was tense. "Please, just get Suzanne's tea and tell her I'm here."

Oriel was so distracted by her own thoughts, it was a few minutes before she became aware of two things. First, she had never been in this room before. She and Suzanne had always met in her upstairs sitting room or in the library. This was a more formally furnished room. The second thing she noticed was the portrait hanging over the mantel. It took another second or two to make the connection. Oriel took a step closer. It was—yes, she was almost sure—Lady Lavinia Lawrence!

The portrait was smaller than the one at Drummond Castle, but the features, the hairstyle, and the dress were all the same! She was wearing a jade green velvet dress, the same costume Oriel *and* Suzanne had worn.

As these realizations came into Oriel's mind, a compelling question begged an answer. Why was a portrait of Lavinia Lawrence hanging in the Wicklows' parlor. *Why?* Unless . . . *unless* . . . Oriel's heart began thudding.

A door slammed hard in the hall and Oriel jumped. She whirled around. Swiftly, she moved across the room and to the closed parlor door. Listening to the voices, she felt relieved. It was Michael and Nell.

"I'm just taking up Miss Suzanne's tea, sir. Mrs. Drummond is here to see her and is waiting in the parlor."

"The *parlor?*" he repeated, sounding annoyed. "Why not the library?"

"I dunno, sir. I didn't think. She was so upset—"

"Never mind," he said curtly. "Bring us some coffee in the library. I'll take care of Mrs. Drummond. Just hurry."

Oriel quickly took a seat away from the fireplace, not facing the portrait. She tried to quiet her tingling nerves and appear calm when Michael opened the parlor door.

"Well, well, Oriel. Good morning!" he greeted her jovially. "What brings you out and about so early?" He glanced past her over to the empty fireplace. "It's colder than the arctic in here. Let's go into the library. I'll get the fire started. It will be much cozier in there." He motioned with his arm. "Come along."

Oriel felt prickles along her scalp. Michael's cheeks were ruddy, as if he had been out in the morning air. All through her body, warning signals coursed. She didn't want to have to explain to Michael why she was here, what she suspected about Edwina and Morgan. Michael had always struck her as being cynical and somewhat unfeeling. But there was no rational reason for her to feel such hesitancy about going into the other room with him. He had always been polite and cordial. Maybe there was even a simple explanation about Lady Lavinia's portrait being in the Wicklows' possession. Michael was an avid collector of Celtic artifacts and Irish antiques. He might well have seen it at an estate auction, liked it, and bought it. All she had to do was remark on it and ask him. Why did she feel that would be a mistake?

"Come along, Oriel. I'll have a fire going in a minute," he called over his shoulder as he went out the door.

Oriel got up from the chair and stiffly walked to the doorway. Then she turned again and looked at the painting of Lady Lavinia Lawrence, who had once been mistress at Drummond Castle. Why was it hung in a place of honor at Bracken Hall? A chill shuddered through her, a cold feeling of apprehension. She could hear Michael moving about in the library, the sound of brass hearth tools, the crackling of kindling as he coaxed the fire into a blaze.

The kitchen door swung open and Nell came down the hall carrying a tray with a coffeepot and cups. She went into the library and set down the tray on a low table before the fireplace. Nell passed Oriel again, gave her a curious glance, then proceeded up the stairs.

Oriel took a few steps into the hall and stopped. Through the open door, she saw Michael emptying the contents of a small envelope into one of the cups. She watched as if viewing a scene in a play. She was unable to move. Then she felt a surge of fear sweep over her entire body.

"Oriel!" The sound of her name being called in a hoarse whisper jolted her. Oriel spun around and saw Suzanne in her nightgown, hair streaming loosely over her shoulders, standing at the top of the stairs. Suzanne leaned over the banister, her eyes wide and frightened. "Oriel, don't—" Her words were cut off when suddenly a woman in a dark dress came up behind her and clapped a hand over her mouth.

Startled, Oriel recognized who it was—*Mrs. Nesbitt!* What was *she* doing at Bracken Hall? And at this time of day? As Oriel stared in shocked astonishment, the housekeeper pulled Suzanne back out of sight.

Fear swept through Oriel, and all her senses alerted her to her peril. The fact she was in danger moved her to action. She took a few steps backward, stumbling into a massive coatrack. Putting out her hand to steady herself, she grabbed onto the rough fabric of a garment already hanging there.

Turning her head, she saw a gray tweed cape hanging by its hood. Her hand slipped down the length of the garment. It was damp. Little beads of moisture clung to the rough, coarsely woven material. Little bits of twigs and fern were caught in the fabric. It had just been worn. Oriel stifled a gasp.

She recognized it. It was Michael's cape. She'd seen it on him many times. Suddenly she envisioned the frightening gray hooded figure she'd mistaken for some kind of apparition . . . in the fog . . . slipping through the gates of Drummond Castle. If this was *his* then . . . Fear gripped her. She sensed she was in terrible danger.

She shuddered. Her hands dropped away from the cape and she spun around. All the experiences since coming to Ireland began to fall into a pattern. It all came together—a sadistic plan to terrorize her. She knew she must get out of Bracken Hall. *Now.*

She dashed to the front door and tried to open it. Just as she reached it, she heard Mrs. Nesbitt's harsh voice calling out angrily, "Michael! Michael! She's getting away! Quick!"

Oriel's heart pounded. She twisted the door handle, desperately aware that behind her Michael had come out of the library. "What are you doing? Where are you going?" he yelled.

Oriel looked over her shoulder and saw he was standing at the library door, his face flushed, twisted. Fear gave her strength, and with one hard pull, she yanked the door open and ran out onto the porch, down the steps, and along the driveway.

She ran blindly, wildly, caring for nothing but escape. Now, she knew her pursuer, her tormentor, the one who meant her harm—and she had to get away from him.

29

Outside, the wind cut Oriel like a cold knife. The sky was now a mottled gray, with heavy clouds moving quickly across it. Not looking behind her, she started for the road then decided to take the way through the woods, the shortcut to Drummond Castle. She ran on, stumbling over twigs and stones on the woodland path. Clutching her skirt above her ankles, she kept running.

A sharp pain in her side slowed her and she staggered, brought to a stop by her agonized breathing. She leaned against a tree, gasping. Frantically, she glanced about, looking for a place she could hide. Where could she go—to Drummond Castle? She had just run away from there. Had she been wrong? Was it Michael who wanted to drive her away? But why? She had no time to dwell on reasons. She had seen the villainous look in Michael's face. She had seen hatred, something she had never expected to see in the eyes of a friend. But he was *not* her friend. Then neither was Suzanne! But Suzanne had tried to warn her. It was all so confusing.

Tears rushed into her eyes, her throat thickened, and she gasped for breath. To be betrayed by friends was hard to bear. Why had she ever thought coming to Ireland would be the solution to her problems? It had brought her not only heartache, but danger.

The fog was quite thick now, and it seemed to be encircling her. Suddenly she stiffened, alert. Did she hear footsteps on the path? They *were* footsteps—even though muffled by the heavy fog. Had Michael come after her? He was strong, athletic. He could outrun her, catch her. She had to find someplace she could hide so that he couldn't get her.

She started running again. Her foot struck a rock and she tripped, but immediately hurried on. Her heart was racing. She couldn't run much longer. The footsteps were real, and they were close behind her. She determined she wouldn't die like some cowering, terrified woodland animal. She would defend herself. She looked around her. Seeing a fallen branch, she staggered forward, picked it up, and whirled around, bracing herself to confront her pursuer.

The figure was approaching her fast. She lifted the branch with aching arms and swung it wildly with all her might. She felt the wood hit something solid. The figure ducked, but she landed another blow on the side of his head that momentarily stunned him.

She flung the stick, then whirled around. Tears streaming down her cheeks, she started to run again. But her strength was gone—it was no use. She gave a gulping sob. Staggering forward, she limped to a halt.

Suddenly, she felt a hard punch in the middle of her back, sending her pitching forward. She flung out her hands, but there was nothing to hold on to, and she fell face down onto the rough path. Someone tossed her cape over her head, then with a strong hand pressed her cheek in a grinding motion into the gritty damp sand. A gulping scream caused her to inhale a mouthful of sand. She choked.

Terrified, she tensed her body, not knowing what to expect. Then, in the distance, she heard horses' hooves and men's voices coming through the fog. Raising her head tentatively, she pulled back the cape over her head and listened. It wasn't some hopeful wish for rescue. It was real.

Through the lifting fog, she saw the two horsemen. One swung a lantern in his hand. Then she recognized the voices. One had a strong brogue—Tim, the groom! The other voice was Morgan's.

Oriel pushed herself up onto her hands and knees and struggled to her feet, her skirt and cape damp and gritty. With great effort, feeling the muscles in her throat stretch, she managed to call out, "Morgan! I'm here! Over here!"

There was a shout back. "I'm coming, Oriel!"

Standing now, she leaned weakly against a tree. Her legs were trembling, and she felt bruised and shaken from the brutal attack.

The next thing she knew, Morgan was beside her. She felt his strength as he towered over her, saying, "What is going on, Oriel? Where were you going? What happened?"

She shook her head. It was all too impossible to explain.

"Never mind, now," Morgan said soothingly. "First, we'll get you home and take care of you."

"Thank you," she whispered, and let him put his arm around her waist and lead her to his horse. It seemed strange that she had fled in fear of this man and was now depending on him—this man, who was treating her with such gentle concern.

"Hold my horse, Tim," Morgan ordered. "I'm going to lift Mrs. Drummond into my saddle, then mount. We have to get back to Drummond Castle as soon as possible. She's had a bad scare of some kind and she looks hurt."

A worried Molly met them at the door, helped Oriel out of her coat, and gently placed a warm shawl around her shoulders.

"Bring her in here, Molly." Morgan gestured toward his study, where a fire was roaring in the fireplace.

Seated in a deep wing chair, sipping on a bracing hot toddy Morgan had made, Oriel stammered out her story. She thought she might as well get the whole thing out. There was no longer any use concealing that she had eavesdropped on

Morgan's private conversation with Edwina just before being attacked. Now she knew there had to be some other explanation. She had to be wrong.

She drew a long breath and began. "Last night during the party, I came upstairs. As I was passing the minstrels' gallery, I overheard you and Edwina—" Embarrassed under Morgan's unmoving gaze, she paused. "I know you want to be free to marry her, and so when I—"

"I don't know what you think you heard," Morgan interrupted. "I told her it was all over between us, that I—"

"But—"

"Afterwards, I went looking for you, but you were always with someone, dancing, talking, mingling with the guests. Then, suddenly, you were gone."

"Of course I was gone!" Oriel exclaimed. "A few minutes later someone pushed me into a hidden room and I was trapped. I thought that once you realized you had a chance to get Edwina back, the two of you were trying to get rid of me!"

Morgan looked offended. "I'm humbled you think so little of me. I may be many things, but I'm not an attacker of women."

"I know that now. I'm so sorry, Morgan. But at the time—"

"How could I have seen you at the ball if you were trapped in a hidden room?"

"That's what I've just figured out, Morgan. I think the Wicklows are behind it all. I don't know why. Suzanne was in exactly the same costume as the one I copied from the portrait in the gallery here." Oriel paused, frowning. "I don't know how she knew what I was wearing, unless—" Her frown deepened. "Mrs. Nesbitt saw me making it." She stopped. "I saw Mrs. Nesbitt at Bracken Hall this morning. I don't know what she has to do with all this."

Morgan looked fierce. "I don't either. She was the first person I sent for when Molly told me about the note you'd left. However, the woman was not in her room. She had left not a trace. At least now we know where she disappeared to, though not exactly why." His mouth pressed into a grim line. "I intend to find out."

"Anyway," Oriel continued, "when you looked for me, it was Suzanne you saw. I suppose they didn't want me to be missed—at least not right away." She gave a little shudder. "Maybe I never would have been found. Maybe I would have died in there. That is, if I hadn't been able to find my way out. Thank God."

"Yes, indeed. Thank God," Morgan agreed sincerely. He looked very serious. "I didn't even know there was such a thing as a hidden room here." He shook his head. "You'll have to show me."

When she shrank back into the chair as if his suggestion appalled her, he quickly said, "When you feel better, I mean." He paused. "When I couldn't find you during the ball, I planned to talk to you afterwards, to tell you about Edwina and me. But you disappeared as soon as our last guests left and I didn't have a chance. Then, this morning, I found this on my desk." He produced an envelope. "Your note."

He handed it to her. Opening the envelope, she read, "Morgan, I'm leaving. Don't try to find me. I'll let you know through Suzanne where you can send my things. Oriel." She shook her head, handed it back. "I never wrote that. I *did* leave a note, but it was for *Molly*."

A stricken look passed briefly over Morgan's face. "You weren't going to leave any word for me?" Then as if he had spoken too openly, he did not give her a chance to explain, but went on. "After I found this, going to the Wicklows seemed the only thing I could do. Thank goodness I did, or I'd never have found you." His eyes were troubled. "If not you, then who wrote this?" He handed the note back to her.

She examined it closely. "It's a pretty good imitation of my handwriting, but this is not it. Someone has tried to copy it, but how?" Then she remembered the missing slip from the brass bowl the night Madame Tamsin had done the handwriting analysis. "Someone must have taken the slip I wrote on for Madame Tamsin and copied it."

"No, I took that," Morgan said, looking embarrassed.

"*You?* But why?"

He reached into his vest pocket and brought out the folded slip of paper. "Listen to what it says, then maybe you'll understand. 'Never tell your love, the love that never told should be. P.S. I don't know what this is from.'" Morgan smiled. "How honest this writer is and, according to Madame Tamsin's reading of it, also sensitive, loyal, loving, and generous. It could not have been anyone else in that room that night but *you!*"

Oriel's mind was whirling with so many questions that she missed the significance of Morgan's words. She reread the note and asked, "So why did you come looking for me?"

"I couldn't let you go—not like that, not with so much misunderstanding between us. I had to explain about Edwina and me."

"Well, thank goodness you came. Hearing you and Tim coming must have scared my attacker away." Slowly, more and more of the plot against her and Morgan took shape in Oriel's mind. She thought of what she had seen and learned that morning at the Wicklows.

"Suzanne's costume was copied from Lady Lavinia Lawrence's portrait—a separate one from the one here at Drummond Castle. I saw it this morning, hanging over the fireplace in their parlor. I'd never seen it there before. Why didn't they want me to see it or know about the costume?"

Oriel paused, then said very slowly, "Morgan, what do you make of that? It was Suzanne you saw after leaving the minstrels' gallery, not me. I was already locked in the hidden room off the corridor. Someone didn't want me to be missed until it was too late. Even *you* would think I'd gone. Don't you see, it was all a plot to drive you away, to break your contract to inherit Drummond Castle?"

They were both silent a minute, then Oriel asked, "So who pushed me into the secret room? Could it be the same person who just attacked me in the woods?" Her eyes widened in realization. "The same one who sabotaged the ladder the day I was trapped down at the cove!"

She understood now. It all came together through a fog of fear and disbelief. "Michael!" Oriel gasped. She thought of the scene she had viewed from the hallway at Bracken Hall. What were the mysterious contents he had been putting in the cup he planned to give her to drink? The envelope resembled the small packets of sleeping powders Mrs. Nesbitt said she kept on hand. How was Mrs. Nesbitt involved in all this? Now convinced, Oriel nodded her head and repeated the name. "Michael. I see it all now—he was the one all along . . ."

"Michael," Morgan said furiously. "It looks like it, and he'll pay dearly for it!"

"Michael." Her lips were numb as she said his name again. "I should have seen it before. The night of the ball was supposed to be the final thing. To leave me there to die and then the note would lead you to believe I'd left."

Morgan, his fists clenched, got up and started pacing, mumbling under his breath furiously. "But how did he know? Where is that room? I've been all over this house, I never knew there was some kind of secret room."

"It might be in the book Bryan lent me. It has the original floor plans of some of the old Irish castles. It's still in my sitting room. We can check."

The books Bryan had lent Oriel were placed ready to return along with the belongings Molly had been instructed to pack. Morgan went up to Oriel's sitting room and brought the books back. Together they started looking through the one on coastal Ireland. Almost right away, they found the answer in the genealogy tables of county families. They discovered a link between the Lawrence family who had once owned Drummond Castle and the Wicklows. Michael's mother had been a Lawrence, so Lady Lavinia Lawrence was his ancestor. This explained but did not excuse his bitterness and envy toward those he considered interlopers in his heritage home.

"So you see, Morgan, Michael would do anything to drive you out. When Brendan Drummond died and the house stood empty for so long, perhaps he had hoped to buy it back. Then, when you came bringing a bride, he must have decided to resort to more drastic measures."

"He's committed unspeakable crimes—attempted murder among them. He could spend a great deal of time in jail for this."

"But we have no evidence—only my word."

Oriel told Morgan what she had learned about secret rooms being used to harbor fugitive priests. They continued to leaf through the book to see if they could find the hidden room in any of the floor plans. The Lawrence house plans showed only a long corridor running the length of the upstairs hall with rooms off of it. There was no sign of a passageway.

"Do you think you could find it and show me?" Morgan asked.

Oriel tossed aside the blanket. "Of course."

Morgan took her arm and helped her stand. Her legs still felt a little shaky, but she was eager to confirm her nightmarish ordeal.

Morgan took an oil lamp and they went upstairs. Each taking a side of the hall a few yards from the minstrels' gallery, they walked slowly along, pressing their hands up and down the wall, searching for anything out of the ordinary.

"Ah, here's something!" Morgan exclaimed. He pointed to a small button, which he then pushed. A creaking sound followed. They both watched in amazement as a partition of the wall swung back, revealing a small cubicle. Instinctively, Oriel drew back, reliving the horror of being closed up within that dark space.

"Wait until I light this." Morgan quickly struck a match and put it to the wick of a small lamp. When it flamed, he replaced the glass chimney and held out his hand to Oriel. "Are you ready? Or shall I go alone?"

"No. I'll come," she said, and stepped forward. He took hold of her wrist tightly.

With the arc of light thrown by the lamp he was holding, they stepped into what appeared to be an entry into a somewhat smaller room. This had a cot, table, and chair. Morgan slowly circled so they got a good look. "This is probably where the priest stayed until it was safe for him to leave."

"And the way he escaped was down the stairs and out through that tunnel that comes up inside the folly!" Oriel finished.

"Come, we'll go down the steps. Don't worry, I've got you," Morgan said reassuringly.

After a few steps Oriel's foot touched something hard. "Wait, Morgan, shine the light over here," she said.

What her toe had nearly crushed was the ornamental comb she had worn in her hair the night of the ball. This was the proof she needed that her terrifying experience had been real.

"Here, I'll put it in my pocket," Morgan said. "Are you all right? It's so stuffy in here. You sure you don't want to go back, wait for me?"

"No, I'm coming," Oriel said firmly.

"I must say, you've no lack of courage." Morgan's voice held admiration.

With her hand in Morgan's, the retreading of the stone steps down to the narrow passage did not seem half as terrible as when she had been alone, despairing of escape.

Within a few more minutes, they were making their way through the last part of the tunnel. When they stepped up into the interior of the folly, it was daylight, and they could see everything clearly. Morgan found a can of oil underneath the bench near the door. How often had Michael hidden in here, then donned the hooded cape to play the part of Shaleen O'Connor?

"What a devilish scheme," Morgan said between clenched teeth.

"And it almost worked." Then Oriel had another thought. "But he must have had help—someone to let him in the house, investigate, find the secret room, and devise the plan. There was plenty of time. The house was empty. Except for the servants—"

In unison they said, *"Mrs. Nesbitt."*

"Why would she want to help Michael? She worked for you." Oriel shook her head in bewilderment.

"It's a mystery, all right. But we'll solve it. And whoever's involved will pay dearly."

Oriel shivered.

At once Morgan was concerned. "You're cold. Here, put this on." He took off his jacket and put it around her shoulders. "Let's go back inside before you get chilled."

Oriel shook her head vigorously and pointed to the way they had just come. "Not back through there, please."

"Of course not," Morgan said, opening the folly door. They hurried over the soggy grass and reentered the house.

Back in his study, with Oriel again wrapped in a warm shawl, Morgan yanked the tapestry pull. When Finnegan appeared, Morgan ordered tea.

"Now we must bring this madman to justice." Morgan paced back and forth. "I will go over there and confront him—maybe take a magistrate with me—"

"I'll go with you. I have so many questions," Oriel said, "especially about Suzanne. Do you think she knew? I can't believe she would go along with such a plan. She was my friend." Oriel's voice trailed off as she remembered what she'd seen on the stairs at Bracken Hall that morning. "Morgan, I think Suzanne tried to warn me. Mrs. Nesbitt pulled her away from the balcony, and . . ."

Morgan looked at her with compassion. "Poor Oriel, you've really had a bad time here, haven't you? False friends, narrow escapes, frightening experiences. We shall try to make up for it." His gaze rested on her sympathetically.

She started to rise from the chair, but Morgan stopped her. "Not now. What you need is a good rest. You'll feel stronger tomorrow—we'll go first thing. That will be soon enough."

It wasn't. When they arrived at Bracken Hall early the next morning, they found the Wicklows gone. When Nell, looking flushed and harried, opened the door, they saw the other servants busily putting dustcloths over the furniture.

"They left early this morning, went up to Dublin." Oriel could see Nell was miffed. "From there to England, and maybe the Continent. I don't know for sure." She lifted her chin, obviously injured about something. "Mr. Wicklow wouldn't even let me accompany Miss Suzanne. Took Mrs. Nesbitt, they did."

At this information, Oriel and Morgan exchanged a baffled look.

"I'm to close the house and wait for word," Nell continued.

"When did they say they'd return?" Oriel asked.

"They didn't say. Miss Suzanne was very upset." Nell sniffed, then added somewhat grudgingly, "They did give me two weeks' wages and a reference letter." Then Nell took an envelope out of her apron pocket and held it out to Oriel. "She left this for you, Mrs. Drummond."

Oriel glanced at Morgan, then opened the letter.

My dear Oriel,

You must believe that I never meant to hurt you. Michael said it was just to scare you a little—dressing in the hooded cape to make you think it was the ghost of Shaleen O'Connor. He oiled the lock on the folly so he could wait there and watch. When the light went on in your bedroom or he saw you going out, he'd follow you. He used the shortcut through the woods known from his childhood.

To understand, you have to know the truth about us. I have another confession to make. Michael and I are brother and

223

sister, not a married couple. He thought that was a better "front," more respectable! You see, I am totally dependent on him for everything. He is older, and our parents left him what little they had left. So no matter what, in the end I had to do what he told me.

Mrs. Nesbitt used to be our mother's maid, and when we were little, she became our nanny. She adored Michael, and filled him with stories of what it was like when Mama was a little girl and lived at Drummond Castle (it used to be called Lawrence Manor). As he grew up, Michael was obsessed with getting the castle back. He felt it was his heritage. Of course, Mrs. Nesbitt knew about the "priest's hole," so she showed it to him.

The plan was to get Morgan to leave by frightening you. They made me copy your handwriting and leave the note for Morgan. I did protest. The night of the ball, I tried to warn you. I ran across the grass to get in the folly and open the door for you, but Michael caught me and dragged me back.

You are so strong, Oriel, and have so much courage. You must think me weak and spineless to have gone along with this wicked scheme. I feel most dreadfully about lying to you. I *did* come to love and treasure you as a friend. I begged Michael not to go on with it, but he assured me all he wanted was to make you leave, and so make Morgan give up the house. Please try to forgive me.

Suzanne

Without a word, Oriel passed the letter to Morgan. When he finished reading it, she asked, "Well?"

He simply shrugged.

They drove back to Drummond Castle silently.

When they arrived, Morgan asked her, "Are you still determined to leave? I wouldn't blame you after all you've been through."

"No, Morgan, I'm not going to leave." She smiled wanly. "A contract is a contract. There's no need to leave before the year is up."

Drummond Castle

April 1896

*O*riel awakened from a strange dream. She got out of bed, tossed her robe around her shoulders, and went over to open the windows. She leaned on the sill and looked out. The first pink streaks of dawn and the fragrance of flowers from the garden below gave the promise of a fine spring day.

Breathing deeply of the soft, scented air, she felt a wrenching sadness. The heaviness she had felt all week welled up painfully. Tomorrow was the last morning she would gaze out at this scene—the acres spreading out from the castle in beautiful shades of green, the narrow line of blue of the ocean beyond.

One year ago she had come to Drummond Castle. She remembered the first time she looked out these windows, the excitement she had felt as the curtain of mist parted. Ireland had promised so much. It had almost been love at first sight.

It was ironic, Oriel thought. Love had nothing to do with her coming but had everything to do with her leaving. And it was a good thing she was leaving. Another week—another day, even—and she might have betrayed herself, revealed the things she was finding it harder and harder to hide. Sighing, she closed the window and turned back into the room.

She had many things to do before she left for Dublin tomorrow. Her trunk stood open, waiting for her to pack the last of her clothing and personal belongings. She stood uncertainly in the middle of the room, not knowing where to start. When she came here, a year had seemed a long time. Now it seemed incredibly short. The last four months, especially, seemed to have flown by.

Morgan had followed up on his intention to bring Michael Wicklow to justice, but so far it had been impossible. Even though Morgan had hired a private detective, evidently Michael had parted ways with Suzanne and Mrs. Nesbitt upon reaching London. No trace of a couple or an older woman fitting the description of the Wicklows and Mrs. Nesbitt was found. As the detective reported, it would have been easy for them to change their appearance with wigs, hair color, spectacles, and other disguises. Then, if they escaped to the Continent, the trail would become even more difficult.

Bracken Hall had remained boarded up, and no one seemed to have any information as to when the Wicklows might return.

Morgan had been very disturbed that nothing could be done about Michael's vicious attempts. He told Oriel he decided to keep the detective on a retainer for a while longer. Perhaps eventually Michael would slip up and some charges could be filed.

After the Wicklows' conspiracy against them had been uncovered, Oriel and Morgan's relationship had changed subtly. No longer two people trapped in an untenable situation, they had become even closer friends. They spent many companionable times together, riding, walking, talking. Their dinner hours had become pleasurable exchanges of ideas and opinions. They had spent many quiet evenings in front of the fire, sharing excerpts from books they were each reading. Oriel had even felt the freedom to play the piano sometimes, as Morgan seemed to enjoy listening. They had discussed some of Morgan's grandfather's ideas of bringing new employment to the area—reactivating the pottery plant, encouraging cottage crafts. Oriel tried not to let herself dream that it could be anything more than a rich, interesting friendship. They could talk about almost anything—except Edwina Parker. Morgan was too much of a gentleman to say much. All he had said was that he had been blind to their incompatibility and that it was over. Oriel had to believe him.

Now it was time for her to go. She looked around. There were still decisions to be made. She had not meant to accumulate so much—clothes, books, and especially so many memories.

Stop being so sentimental, she ordered herself. *You knew this day would come.* She should be as businesslike and impersonal about ending this job as she had been taking it, signing the agreement. It was all a matter of control.

There were many good-byes to be said. She had already been to the village to bid farewell to the shopkeepers, all of whom she had made an effort to become friendly with, hoping they would lose their animosity toward Drummond Castle. She thought she had accomplished that.

For the staff here, she had small individual gifts for each of the servants, with a special one for Molly, who had been so caring and faithful. Before saying good-bye to the servants, Oriel thought she would go out to the stables and say farewell to her darling Mavourneen. How she would miss her and her daily rides.

It was a heartbreaking moment. The mare seemed to sense her sadness when Oriel rested her head against her neck and stroked her mane. Blinking back tears, Oriel gave the horse a final pat and two lumps of sugar, then left the stable. Head bowed, she started back toward the house through the garden. That was why she didn't see Morgan approaching until she was within a few feet of him.

"Morgan!" she exclaimed in surprise.

He was in riding clothes—a tweed jacket and buff breeches. "What are you doing?" he asked, his voice snapping like the slap of the riding crop he flicked against the top of his polished boots.

"Saying good-byes." She was so startled by running into him that she forgot to guard the wistfulness in her voice.

Morgan frowned. "I was just going for a ride, hoping you would come along."

Oriel was tempted. During the last several months, she and Morgan had fallen into the habit of riding together several times a week. Those had been some of the happiest days she had spent at Drummond Castle. She would cherish them. But it would be too much for her to handle today. "Sorry," she said regretfully.

She felt his presence strongly, her own keen awareness that this would be the last such day, the last chance to ride along the ocean cliffs or the rolling hillside with him. The ache of a rising lump in her throat made her anxious, so she said quickly, "Thanks, but I really can't. I have things to do that I can't put off." She moved to go past him on the path, but he caught her arm.

"Can't they wait?" he asked softly.

Not daring to look at him, she shook her head. "No. I'm afraid not."

He held her arm a second longer. "Sure?"

Their gaze met, and his eyes seemed troubled. Then he released her. "I'll see you at dinner then," he said. Making a stiff bow, he walked slowly off in the direction of the stables.

Oriel returned to the castle. She found saying good-bye to the staff very difficult. She understood the accepted code between employers and servants was strictly defined so that she did not have to explain her leave-taking. No explanation was necessary—indeed, no explanation was possible.

She was touched when Mrs. Mills said, "We all shall miss you, ma'am. This year's been such a welcome change." She wiped her eyes on her flour-dusted apron, sighing. "Oh, ma'am, don't know what I'll be doin' cookin' for just t' master by himself. He don't know what he's eatin' half t' time. Takes all t' pleasure out of my work."

Molly, of course, was the most verbal of all. "I wish you'd say you was coming back, ma'am. I know a lot of bad things happened to you, but now that the Wicklows are gone . . ." She let her question hang hopefully. Oriel knew Molly wanted her to offer to take her with her as her personal maid.

Although Oriel did not know what her future held, she was sure it wouldn't include the need for a lady's maid. Knowing she couldn't fulfill that hope, she said, "Thank you, Molly. You've been wonderful." Then she gave her a small silver pin in the shape of a spray of shamrocks. Molly dissolved into tears and had to leave the room.

Later that afternoon, Oriel walked down to Bryan's cottage. He would also be leaving Ireland soon. Bryan had been as shocked and angered by Michael Wicklow's despicable scheme as she had been. He blamed himself for not picking up on what now seemed obvious.

"You were a good friend, Bryan," Oriel told him as they said good-bye. "I don't know what I would have done sometimes without your friendship." Oriel turned to go.

"Wait, Oriel, I'd like you to have something to remember me and this year in Ireland." He handed her a book of his own poetry.

"Thank you," Oriel said, knowing this year in Ireland would be impossible for her to forget.

That evening, while Oriel sat at her dressing table fixing her hair, her glance fell on the box containing the jade and pearl jewelry Morgan had bought for her. She hesitated. Should she wear them tonight for her last dinner at Drummond Castle? Or would it be too obvious a gesture? She had loved the set, more for their meaning than their value. She had lived on the memory of that happy day in Dublin. A happiness that had been as ephemeral as the Irish mist. Determinedly, Oriel closed the lid of the jewelry box. She would not wear them, not tonight, maybe not ever. She also took off her wedding ring. No point in wearing it any longer. After she left for Dublin, Morgan would contact his lawyers and make all the necessary arrangements for the legal annulment. Their bargain would be finished; their contract fulfilled. All obligations would end.

As Oriel came down the steps, she saw that the door to Morgan's study was open, a welcoming blaze in the fireplace. Morgan was standing in front of it, one arm resting on the mantel, his face thoughtful. Seeing Oriel, he smiled.

"Come in," he invited. His eyes swept over her as if searching for something. "Did you get everything done you had to do?" Without waiting for her reply, he went on. "You should have come riding with me. It was wonderful up along the cliffs today."

On the side table, she saw an ice bucket with a champagne bottle in it. Following her glance, Morgan said, "I thought since this is an anniversary of sorts, maybe we should have some champagne?"

"Yes, that would be lovely." She took the glass he handed her, and their fingers brushed briefly.

"One year." Morgan raised his glass in a toasting gesture. "But, then, maybe it has seemed longer than that to you."

Oriel could not tell if he was being sarcastic. She looked up into his dark, restless face—the smile that came and went so quickly she was never sure what was meant by it; the eyes that could be mocking or soft as music by candlelight; the mouth that could say things that hurt or soothed with their gentleness; and the charm, the maddening, Gaelic charm that had been her undoing.

Oriel looked down into the bubbles in her glass and said nothing. *After tomorrow none of it can touch me,* she thought, *not his careless words, that smile that rocks my heart, or the charm. I shall be far away, and eventually I will forget—I shall make myself forget.*

"Have you any plans?" Morgan asked. "I mean, after you leave?"

"I plan to visit Paris. After that I suppose I shall get passage back to the States," she replied evenly.

His expression was suddenly morose. She longed to ask him what *he* intended to do. Would he carry through on any of the plans they had discussed to revitalize Kilmara? Would he stay in Ireland or at least live part of the year at Drummond Castle? What before would have been natural for her to ask now seemed impossible.

The room became very quiet. A log broke, shifting in the fireplace, sending up a sudden spiral of sparks.

Oriel's heart pounded in her ears. What did she want Morgan to say? "Oriel, I love you. You're beautiful. I want you, need you." Yes, all those things and more. "I can't live without you. Stay here in Ireland and be my love." But nothing was said.

Finnegan came to the door to announce dinner, and they went in together. Mrs. Mills had outdone herself for this final dinner, cooking all Oriel's favorite foods. Oriel could only take a few bites; she wasn't able to swallow any more than that. She had to get away from Morgan. She couldn't trust herself, this last night, to keep from speaking what was in her heart.

As they left the dining room, she turned to Morgan. Her throat was so dry, it was almost impossible for her to speak. "I think I'll make it an early night, Morgan. I'm tired and I'm leaving early in the morning."

"Of course," Morgan replied stiffly.

Oriel walked to the staircase, and Morgan strode toward his study. At the bottom of the steps, Oriel's hand circled the carved post. Almost as if to herself, she remarked, "I shall hate to leave."

Morgan spun around. "What did you say?"

"Just that I shall be sorry to leave here." Oriel made a sweeping gesture with one hand. She was surprised to realize she had spoken her thoughts out loud. But it was the truth. Why pretend? "I've been happy here, happier than I've been for a very long time."

"Even after all that's happened?" Morgan asked, his voice soft.

"Yes, even after that," she said, then quickly turned and ran up the stairs.

London

April 1896

*O*riel had made the boat in Dublin with plenty of time. She stood at the railing and watched the coast of Ireland slip away as the steamer put to sea. This was really good-bye.

She had avoided a long farewell with Morgan earlier. She'd had Molly bring a tray of tea and toast to her room, finished her last-minute packing, then sent Molly to have the carriage brought around.

Oriel had moved in a kind of trance, not allowing herself to think or feel. When Molly came to tell her the carriage was out front, she bid the tearful maid an affectionate good-bye, then hurried downstairs. Morgan stood at the door to see her into the carriage.

"You have everything? Your ticket, your passport, enough money?" he asked.

"Yes, everything," she had said, getting into the carriage.

Morgan thrust his head in the window. "Good-bye then, and God bless."

"Good-bye," she said through tight lips.

She had stared straight ahead as the carriage started down the drive, not looking back once as it went through the gates and on the road to Dublin.

It was best that way, Oriel told herself—not to look back for a last glimpse at the castle she'd come to love, or the man she had also come to love. Both were now in her past. She had to look forward to the rest of her life, whatever that held.

Oriel had decided she would go to France. She had never been there, so there would be nothing to remind her of Morgan. In Paris, she would visit the great art galleries, the cathedrals, and all the historical places. There'd be no memories there to haunt her. Then she'd return to America.

On her arrival in London, Oriel went to the Claridge Hotel. This time, there was no question of not being able to afford it. She was a very rich woman now. However, she was not prepared for the nostalgia she felt as she entered the luxurious lobby, remembering the day of her fateful encounter with Morgan, going to tea with him in the plush dining room. She made her reservations for the boat train, then had supper brought to her room. After a good cry, she went to bed.

She spent the next two days shopping the grand London stores. She did not have to worry about price tags, but she found little she wanted to buy for herself.

She thought of going to see Nola, but there was too much to explain and her own heart was too heavy. She would not have been good company. She did, however, find a lovely porcelain tea set that she knew Nola would love. She bought it and had it wrapped to be delivered to Nola and Will's new home. With the package, she put a note: "Wishing you great happiness. You deserve it." She signed it, after a second's hesitation, with the name she had not used for a year, "Oriel Banning."

Three days later, as she stood on the platform of the railroad station waiting to board the train that would take her to the boat to France, Oriel was filled with melancholy. She had not realized how much she had changed in the past year. She had been alone for years, ever since her parents died, yet now she felt lonelier than ever before. Why? Just because one person was no longer in her life?

Then, as if in a dream, she heard her name being called. She must be imagining it. Over the noise of the busy terminal, how could she hear a voice she thought she knew?

"Oriel!" It came again, and this time there was no mistake—that *had* to be Morgan's voice.

She turned around and saw Morgan hurrying toward her, quickly covering the space with his long strides. "Oriel! Wait."

She stood there in amazement. As he reached her, she said, "I *am* waiting."

"I'm so glad. I thought I might have missed you, that I was too late—but you're here."

"Yes, Morgan, I'm here."

"Thank goodness. I was so afraid—" He halted. "Afraid I'd missed you."

"Well, you almost did. My train will be leaving any minute."

"I must talk to you. Let's go somewhere we can talk."

"I can't, Morgan, I'll miss my train."

"Miss it then. There'll be another boat train soon. Please, Oriel, it's important."

She glanced around, bewildered. She spotted the porter who was standing beside her luggage, ready to put it on the train. Morgan followed her glance, signaled the man, gave him some money, and directed him, "Keep those in a safe place until we decide which train the lady is taking."

"But, Morgan—" Oriel's protest died on her lips as the porter pocketed the money, nodded, and trundled off with her bags.

Morgan took her firmly by the arm and led her down the platform to the station tea shop. After the waitress had been given their order for two cups of tea, Morgan crossed his arms and leaned forward on the table. "Oriel, I followed you here because I couldn't bear to let you go, let you walk out of my life, without telling you."

"Telling me what, Morgan?" Oriel's heart was beating wildly.

"What you have come to mean to me." He paused. "It's hard to explain, but ever since your accident at the cove, ever since we went to Dublin, I have realized—"

The waitress came with their tea, set down the cups, and left.

Morgan picked up again where he had halted. "Realized that I cared for you. More than I knew, more than I had ever intended. I began to see in you all the qualities I'd always wanted in the woman I loved. Maybe it wasn't really until Edwina came and I saw you two together that I realized how wrong I had been about *her*." He shook his head a little. "You handled everything that weekend so well, with such grace. I was filled with admiration. I guess I knew then I loved you."

Oriel's hands felt icy. She put them around the cup of steaming tea to warm them. Through stiff lips she mumbled, "But you never let on. You never gave me the slightest reason to think—"

"I know. I thought it was the honorable thing to do. I had no idea what your feelings toward me were. I had certainly given you no reason to care for me. I was a boor most of the time. Can you forgive me for that? I was in a dilemma. I thought it would be unfair to speak to you, put pressure on you. After all, as you mentioned many times, a bargain is a bargain, a contract, a contract. Ours was a business arrangement—nothing else."

Oriel was too moved to speak.

"It wasn't until you actually were gone that I realized I'd been a fool not to let you know and beg you to stay." He reached across the table and put his hands over hers. "Is it too late, Oriel? I love you. Will you . . . would you possibly consider marrying me?"

The clatter all around them in the noisy tea shop was deafening. Oriel could scarcely believe her ears, what Morgan was asking over the banging of teacups, the shriek of train whistles, and the noise from arriving and departing travelers.

Morgan's eyes anxiously searched her face, waiting for some answer.

"*Marry* you, Morgan?" she repeated, still unbelieving.

"Yes, my darling, will you?"

Tears came and laughter too as Oriel said, "But Morgan, we *are* married."

For a second he looked blank, then threw back his head and laughed heartily. "Of course we are! I'd forgotten. Can you put up with such a man?"

Just then Oriel's porter appeared at the door of the tea shop. Spotting them, he came over to the table.

"Beg pardon, miss, the next train is about to board passengers."

Morgan looked at Oriel. "Well, what is it to be, Oriel? Shall we honeymoon in Paris, since you already have your ticket?" He paused. "But then you haven't answered my question."

"Yes, Morgan. I will." She smiled. "Stay married, that is!"

Smiling broadly, Morgan said to the porter, "Take those things on board. I'll buy my ticket on the way from the conductor."

He turned back to her. "Does that suit you, Oriel?"

"Oh, yes, Morgan. It suits me just fine."

"Come along, my dear." He got up from the table and held out his hand to her. They walked out onto the station platform together.

The next thing Oriel knew, she was caught up in his strong arms, her cheek pressed against the rough tweed of his coat. Then, very gently, he released her and framed her face in both hands so she had to look up at him.

Oblivious to the curious glances of people pushing past, the shouts of the porters, the rattle of baggage carts, and the noise and bustle all about them, Morgan kissed her. A kiss that was intense, but tender.

When it came to a slow end, Morgan said softly, "When we get to France, we'll have a real wedding—maybe in a country church in Provence. How does that sound? Romantic enough?"

Surely this was a dream come true—the words Oriel had said in the Registry Office she would repeat with her heart—fully this time, completely aware of what those vows really meant. Happily she looked up at the man she loved. "Indeed it does, Morgan."

"Splendid! Then after Paris, shall we go home to Drummond Castle?"

Oriel couldn't seem to stop smiling, "Yes! Yes, Morgan! How many American girls can go *home* to a *castle?*"

Morgan drew her close, holding her in his arms. They looked into each other's eyes, searching for something, an answer. They found what they had been looking for. They kissed again. It was not a long kiss, but one of discovery, full of sweetness and the promise of enduring love.

Jane Peart is a prolific author of romantic fiction who lives in Fortuna, California. She is the author of the Orphan Train West series and the International Romance series.